HRM

Colorado
WEDDINGS

Colorado
WEDDINGS

The Grooms Take Charge
in Three Surprising Romances

JOYCE
LIVINGSTON

BARBOUR
PUBLISHING

ISBN 978-1-59789-304-6

Cover photography by Peter Rodger and Karen Beard; Getty Images

Published by Barbour Publishing, Inc., P.O. Box 719, Uhrichsville, Ohio 44683, www.barbourbooks.com

Our mission is to publish and distribute inspirational products offering exceptional value and biblical encouragement to the masses.

Member of the
Evangelical Christian
Publishers Association

Printed in the United States of America.
5 4 3 2 1

Dear Reader,

Thank you for choosing to read *Colorado Weddings*. It is my hope that you will enjoy the stories of Shelley and Bart, Stormi and Mark, and Tula and Clint, as they make their way from courtship, to engagement, to the altar. Through the writing of this book, I've come to love each of these characters. Life is not always easy. *Things* happen to each of us, but despite disappointment, adversity, and conflict, we must go on, just as these six wonderful people went on with their lives. The rocky, yet exciting, ride to romance is like a roller-coaster ride, with many highs and lows, ups and downs. But, in the end, when you find that one person who is right for you, the one God called to be your soul mate, you know that ride has been worthwhile.

Writing Christian romance fiction is a dream come true for me. If I've counted right, *Colorado Weddings* is my twenty-ninth published fiction book, with many more to come, my first one being published in 1999. What a joy it is to sit in front of my computer and, with God's leading, come up with stories that touch hearts. Writing is fun, but it is also hard work. There are days I want to bang my head against the keyboard and give up. But then an idea, a theme, even a single word arrives, and I'm off and flying again. Inspiration, sometimes, comes from amazing, unusual places. Much of what I write is taken from my own life and background as a former television broadcaster of eighteen years and from my eleven years of experience as a tour escort to some of the world's most interesting and romantic places. Some of what I write is taken from my various roles in life—as the wife of Don Livingston (whom the Lord recently took to be with Him), as the mother of four grown sons and two daughters, and as a grandmother to more grandchildren than I can keep track of.

I hope, after reading this book, you will look for my other books. I feel writing inspirational fiction is my ministry, my high calling from God. I want to be an encourager of women of all ages. It is my prayer and my desire that something in these stories, which I have written, will touch your heart and fill a need in your life. I'd love to hear from you. E-mail me: joyce@joycelivingston.com, or write to me through my publisher.

Happy reading!
Joyce Livingston

A Winning Match

Dedication

To my precious husband, Don Livingston,
who went to be with the Lord in 2004.
He was my number one fan, my encourager,
my lover, my friend, and my protector;
he is the hero of every book I write.
A love like ours comes along once in a lifetime.
Without him, my life will never be the same.
Love is fragile. Life is even more fragile.
We must handle both with care
and never forget to say,
"I love you."

Chapter 1

No, Kip, you are not going out with your friends. Not tonight, not tomorrow, not next week, or next month." Shelley Morris glared at her son, her fists clenched, her anger nearly to the boiling point. "Until you get your grades up, you—are—grounded, and this time I mean it!"

His eyes narrowed, his jaw firmly set, Kip glared back. "What are you gonna do? Lock me in my room?"

The rage she saw in his eyes broke her heart. Kip was a big kid for his age, tall and gangly. Though she never feared he'd strike her, this wasn't the first battle she'd had with her son. Confrontation had become a daily routine in their home ever since Kip had turned fourteen. There was something about turning fourteen that brought out the worst in him, and she didn't like it one bit.

"If you lock me in my room, I'll crawl out the window."

In total frustration, Shelley grabbed her son's hand and pulled him toward her. "I love you, Kip. I'm trying to help you. Why can't you see that?"

He huffed, then yanked his hand away. "It sure doesn't sound that way to me."

"I'm not your enemy, Kip. I'm your mother."

Kip stared at her for a moment, then, grabbing up his jacket, headed for the door. "I'm outta here."

Shelley raced after him, barely catching hold of his sleeve as he pulled the door open and stepped out onto the porch. "You come right back in here! You can't leave. I said you were grounded."

He yanked his arm away, sending her slightly off balance, then took off in a sprint across the yard, leaving her alone on the porch, rubbing at her shoulder. "Kip, come back this minute. I mean it!"

But Kip didn't come back. Not for supper. Not to pick up the video game he constantly kept with him. Not even at bedtime. And though Shelley called the homes of all his closest friends, no one had seen him. She wanted so much to call the police, ask them to help find him but, remembering the last time he'd pulled this same trick—when she'd called the police and he'd returned home before the police arrived—she didn't. Instead, she sat staring at the clock, praying over and over God would bring him safely home.

Ten o'clock. Midnight. One o'clock, then two, and still Kip didn't come home.

Chilled by the coolness of the night, at three, she fixed herself a cup of hot tea, then headed for her room to pull on her robe. But as she passed Kip's closed door, she heard a sound. Her heart thundering, she paused to listen. There it was again, and it sounded very much like snoring.

It sounded again, and this time, there was no doubt in her mind it was a snore. Moving cautiously forward, she took hold of the doorknob, gave it a slight twist, and pushed the door open a crack. A narrow wedge of light from the hallway fell across the bed, revealing Kip's familiar figure hunched up beneath the covers. *Obviously,* she thought, *he came home and crawled in through his window rather than face me.* Though a wave of relief flooded over her, her first reaction was to rush to him, jerk the covers off, and give him a piece of her mind for worrying her. But that would only lead to another confrontation, and they were each too tired for that. They'd both say things they didn't mean. Instead, she moved stealthily across the room, bent, and kissed his cheek. No matter what he did, or how little he seemed to care for her, he was still her baby, and she loved him more than life itself.

Bart Steel closed the lid on his laptop, leaned back in his chair, and propped his feet on his desk. "Not bad," he said with a grin of satisfaction toward his mom as he gazed at the figures he'd entered on the spreadsheet. "If business stays this good the second half of my fiscal year, it'll be my best year yet."

Maggie Steel returned his grin. "It should be. You give every waking moment to that Genesis business of yours."

"Don't say it."

"Don't say what?"

"That having a successful business is nice, but it's not enough—that I need to find me a wife. Have a bunch of kids."

Her smile disappeared. "I know you get tired of hearing me say it, Bart, but I *am* concerned about you. Life is passing you by, sweetie. You're thirty-four years old. I can think of at least a dozen gorgeous women, who come here to The Genesis Hut and take that Whole New You exercise class of yours, who would jump at the chance to marry you."

"I'm not only not ready to marry, Mom, I doubt many of those women share my faith."

"I understand that, and though that's the way you should feel about it, isn't it about time you put old hurts aside and move forward with your life? I know you love what you do, but is it enough?"

Bart locked his hands behind his head and stared at the ceiling. "Maybe I'm happy being a bachelor."

"Happy, maybe, but how about content? Can you honestly tell me you wouldn't like to have a wife with whom to share your life? Someone to come home to at the end of a long day? To cuddle with at night? To share your dreams, your hopes? Your ambitions? Attend church with you? Pray with you?"

Bart searched his heart. The questions his mother was asking were the same questions he'd asked himself every day for the past eight years, ever since Julie had broken their engagement to accept the regional manager position for the large pharmaceutical company she'd worked for since graduating college. He'd begged her to reconsider—told her how much he loved her—but it hadn't made any difference. The inordinate amount of salary, the extensive travel, and the many perks the promotion had included had easily wooed her away from him. She'd walked out on him and never looked back. And from the little newsletters she tucked into the Christmas card he received from her each December, she was still single and as ambitious as ever.

"You can't let Julie's rejection ruin your life, son. Not every woman is like her. At least she didn't leave you for another man."

Slowly lowering his feet, he sat up straight, his gaze going back to the face of the only woman he'd ever felt had truly loved him. "I know, Mom. I can't tell you how many times I've told myself that same thing, but when a woman begins to get that look in her eye, the look that says she's getting serious, I get cold feet. I refuse to let myself go through that kind of trauma again. It was too painful. I'd rather spend the rest of my life alone." A slight grin played at his lips. "Unless I can find a woman like you. Dad was the lucky one."

His mother swatted at his arm. "Thanks for the compliment, but there was no luck involved in your father and me finding each other. To this day, I believe God intended for the two of us to be together. Can you honestly say that about you and Julie?"

Bart turned the question over in his mind several times before answering. He'd never told his mother about the misgivings he'd had right from the beginning about his and Julie's relationship. "I'd like to say yes, but I'd be lying. I hate to admit it, but at times, I had my doubts about Julie; I guess her beauty made me overlook them. From the moment we started dating, her career always took first place. Everything in our lives centered around it. I can't tell you how many dates she canceled at the last minute because of a phone call from an important client or a business associate, or an idea she had to take action on immediately. How I felt about playing second fiddle to her career never really seemed to matter to her. And if I complained about it, she ended up making me feel guilty for trying to hold her back. Of course, the fact that I was in awe of her and her success didn't help."

His mom reached across and cupped her hand over his wrist. "What you're saying is no surprise, son. Mothers have a sixth sense about those things. I liked Julie, I really did, but I, too, had concerns about the two of you marrying. I rarely voiced them for fear you'd think I was meddling, but I did voice them to your father and to God. Many times."

Bart huffed. "I wish you'd told me."

"You say that now, but I'm not sure you would have then. You had stars in your eyes where that girl was concerned."

He let loose a long sigh. "I guess I should be glad she broke things off, since we seemed to disagree on practically everything. I can't imagine what it would have been like if we'd actually gotten married. But even considering all of that, it still hurt when she broke our engagement."

His mother lovingly shifted her hand to his shoulder. "I know it did, son. My heart ached for you. But I have to admit, I've often wondered if her breaking up with you was God's way of answering my prayers."

"It may have been, but, take it from me, the downtown streets of Denver will be cloaked in two feet of snow on a ninety-degree day in July before I give my heart to another woman."

"Don't say that, Bart. Somewhere out there"—she paused, her arm making a wide sweep—"God may have just the right woman for you. . . . One who will love you with her whole heart."

Bart inclined his head thoughtfully. "Look, Mom, I know you want the very best for me, but I'm just not sure the very best is a wife. My business is growing each year. I like what I'm doing. I love our church and attending the singles' group. I'm happy; honest I am. Why rock the boat?"

Bending, she kissed his forehead. "But wouldn't you be happier if you shared that life with someone? Someone you could love and who would love you in return?"

Bart thoughtfully rubbed at his chin. "Maybe. But I'm afraid to find out. What if I made the wrong choice again?"

"You said you had misgivings about Julie. If you would have paid attention to those misgivings, you could have saved yourself that big heartache. From what you've told me, the signs were all there."

He nodded. "Talk about naïveté. I just wasn't smart enough to recognize those warning signs and take action until it was too late. That or maybe I deluded myself by purposely ignoring them."

"More than likely, those misgivings were God's way of telling you she wasn't the right girl for you. I think you'll know the right one when she comes along."

He rose, moved around the desk, slipped an arm about his mother's shoulders, then smiled at her. "Did Dad know you were the right girl for him?"

"I sure did." Both Bart and his mother turned quickly as his father came into the room. "I knew she was the one for me as surely as if God had spelled out her name in the sky."

"But how did you know, Dad?"

After planting a loud smacking kiss on his wife's cheek, his father grinned. "It's hard to explain to someone who has never felt it, but it's a feeling of security, a desire, a hollow place in your heart only one woman can fill; once you have felt it, you know she's the one God has for you. I didn't mean to eavesdrop, but I heard you say you'd had misgivings about Julie. I never had those feelings with your mother. Oh, everyone has last-minute wedding jitters, but it's not the same thing. I would have walked barefoot over live coals to get to that altar to marry this sweet little girl and make her mine."

Bart shrugged. Though he'd had feelings for Julie, they had been nothing like the ones his father described. "I should be so lucky."

"No, Bart. Like your mother said, it doesn't take luck to find the right girl. All it takes is God's leading. If your heart is right with Him and you're seeking His will, you'll recognize her when she comes along."

"*If* she comes along. What if God wants me to remain single?"

"Only God knows the answer to that question, son. Just keep your options open and look for His leading."

"But I don't want to take an exercise class." Shelley backed away as Marsha, her best friend, pushed open the big glass door. "I don't know why I ever let you talk me into this."

"Relax. Today is only a demonstration. The actual Whole New You class doesn't start until Wednesday. You don't have to sign up unless you want to. Nobody is gonna twist your arm or yank your credit card from your purse." Marsha waited until Shelley stepped inside, then gestured toward a good-looking man standing a few feet away, talking with several women who looked to be hanging on his every word. "That's him. The owner. His picture was in the flyer."

Shelley turned to stare at the man. She'd seen the picture, too, but it hadn't done him justice. The man was gorgeous and so-o-o physically fit.

Marsha let out a low whistle. "If he's the one who teaches the women's fitness class, I don't even have to see the demonstration. I'm ready to sign up now. How about you?"

Shelley frowned. "Me? No way. I only came along so you wouldn't have to come alone."

The room grew silent as the microphone crackled and the handsome man's strong masculine voice boomed out, "Good morning, ladies. My name is Bart Steel. I want to welcome you to The Genesis Hut. I know some of you already because you, your husbands, or your children are in our classes. The rest of you, I hope to get to know as new class members."

Marsha gave Shelley's arm a pinch. "I'm going to make sure he gets to know me!"

Shelley rolled her eyes. "You're impossible."

"As the name of the class implies," he continued, "our goal is a whole new you. Being physically fit is a goal we should all strive to attain, but even more important than that is a good mental attitude and a terrific feeling about ourselves. This class will give you that and more." His eyes twinkled as he added, "It will add sparkle and zest to your life."

"Um, sparkle and zest," Shelley said sarcastically, adding a flip of her hand. "Sounds like a description of household cleaners."

Bart Steel leaned forward, his blue-eyed gaze zeroing in on her. "You, the pretty woman in the red jacket, did you have a question?"

Shelley felt herself blush. Had he heard what she said? "No—ah—I was just making a comment to my friend."

He gave her a smile that sent a shiver down her spine. "Well, anytime anyone has a question, just ask it. Now, let me explain more about the class. How long it will last. What you should wear; when it will start. And the question I'm sure most of you have on your mind—what it will cost. If you would like to sign up for the class after we have covered all of those things and you've seen the demonstration by some of the ladies in my advanced fitness class, several of my associates will be waiting at that table over there to answer any questions you may have and get you enrolled."

"Are you going to be the one to teach the women's fitness class?" a pretty brunette standing on the sidelines yelled out with an impish grin.

Bart's mouth widened into a full-fledged smile, revealing a set of perfectly shaped, sparkling white teeth. "You bet I am, and I have some great things in store for those of you who sign up."

Marsha's eyes widened. "Forget the demonstration. I'm ready now."

"Have you forgotten you already have a man in your life? A husband who adores you?"

Marsha gave Shelley an ornery wink. "I haven't forgotten, but it doesn't hurt to look, does it?"

Shelley's brows rose. "Doesn't hurt to look? Ask David. Wasn't he only *looking* when he got entangled with Bathsheba?"

Their conversation ended as Bart continued his spiel.

"Wow, I hope his class can make me look like that redhead," Marsha quipped as his speech ended and the six women who were to be part of the demonstration walked to the center of the room and began doing warm-up stretches.

Shelley jabbed at her friend's arm. "I doubt that man's class will take you from four-foot-eleven to five-foot-nine, but I have to admit she does look good. Wonder what she looked like before she started. They sure make all those moves look easy."

"As you'll note," Bart explained, gesturing toward the six women going through their paces, "even though we mostly use traditional exercise techniques in this class, we also use various karate-type movements. Many of the movements you'll learn could prove beneficial should you ever find yourself in a situation where it becomes necessary to defend yourself."

Marsha gave Shelley's arm a nudge. "See? Being able to defend yourself. That's another reason you need to sign up for this class with me."

"In your dreams. I've no interest in taking a class, nor the time to do it. Besides, I can't afford it."

"Then I'll just have to do it alone, but don't say I didn't invite you."

The blinking red light on the answering machine caught Shelley's attention when she entered her house through the garage door for a quick bite of lunch. After tossing her purse onto the sofa and pulling off her jacket, she punched the PLAY button and listened.

"Mrs. Morris, this is Principal Taylor. Kip and two of his friends were caught smoking. I'm concerned about him. I think we need to have a talk. If you get this message and are able to come to the school by one o'clock, I'll have time to see you then. If not, call and we'll set up an appointment."

Shelley stared at the machine. She'd found cigarettes in Kip's pants pocket when she'd sorted the laundry and had confronted him, but as usual, he'd said he was only carrying them for a friend, the same story he'd told her when she'd found a pocketknife that didn't belong to him. Though she'd been afraid he'd stolen it, she'd chosen to accept his story rather than believe he could be a thief. Now this.

After a quick glance at the clock, she grabbed her jacket and headed for the car. If she hurried, she could make it to the school by one. This certainly wasn't the way she had intended to spend her day off, but her son always took priority over anything else going on in her life.

"Principal Taylor is with someone right now, but he should be through shortly. Have a seat, Mrs. Morris," the secretary told

Shelley when she raced into the office at five minutes of one.

No more than two minutes later, the inner door opened and Principal Taylor stepped out, accompanied by someone Shelley recognized immediately. *Bart? The man from The Genesis Hut?*

Principal Taylor reached out his hand. "Mrs. Morris, good, you got my message. Please step into my office."

But as she moved past the Genesis man, he took hold of her arm. "I remember you. You were at the demonstration today."

She gave him a sheepish grin, remembering the silly comment she'd made about his sparkle-and-zest line. "Yes, I was."

He gave her that toothy smile. "I hope you signed up for the class."

"No, I didn't. I—I don't have time to take your class. I only came so my friend wouldn't have to come alone."

Principal Taylor latched onto Bart's arm. "Maybe you should stay for my meeting with Mrs. Morris. With her permission, of course. I think you could be of great help with her son."

Shelley's gaze flitted from the principal to The Genesis Hut man and back again. "I don't understand. Why should he be in on our meeting?"

"Come in, and I'll explain."

Reluctantly, Shelley moved through the door. To her, it seemed the presence of Bart What's-His-Name was an intrusion on her privacy, and she didn't like it one bit.

The principal gestured toward the two chairs opposite his desk, then seated himself. "As I'm sure you've already discovered, Mrs. Morris, most boys your son's age are going through a difficult time in their lives. They're old enough to know better, but too young, often too weak, and sometimes too afraid to resist the temptations and peer pressure that confront them every day. They'll do anything to fit in, even if it goes against their parents' wishes and all they've learned at home. As their principal, I try to do everything in my power to help them, but in their eyes, I represent the establishment." He nodded toward the man seated next to her. "A few years ago, I met Bart Steel, and he became the best tool, if you will, that I've found to help these boys."

"I—still don't understand."

"With very few exceptions, all boys want to be macho, Mrs. Morris. Some come by it naturally. They're either big for their age and automatically dominate those smaller in stature, or perhaps they're small for their age and compensate by being mouthy and intimidating. Often, whatever their size, they become bullies. These boys always have a following, thus the gangs we have nowadays. In many communities, to survive, you either join them and they become your protectors—your family, so to speak—or you try to make it on your own and take the consequences. As much as I and other administrators try to combat this ridiculous element of our society, it exists, and unfortunately, we find ourselves in a quandary, with very little help at our disposal. Things that used to begin happening at the high school level we now find rampant in junior high, sometimes even the grade school level."

The beat of Shelley's heart quickened. "Are you saying my son is part of a gang?"

"No, I'm not saying that, Mrs. Morris, nor am I implying

it. At this point, I have no evidence of such a thing. I'm only telling you all of this so you will understand the pressures that go on in our schools every day. I know you're a single mom and have to work, so even though you do your best, it is not possible for you to keep track of Kip 24-7."

She lifted her hands in frustration, an ache settling in the pit of her stomach. "Contrary to what you may believe, I *am* a good mother. I've done everything I can to make up for the loss of my son's father."

Principal Taylor gave her a placating smile. "I'm sure you are a good mother, Mrs. Morris. You came immediately when I called you. You'd be surprised how many parents ignore my calls and take very little interest in their children's education. Some respond by simply making a few threats to their children, like taking away their allowance, their electronic games, that sort of thing, but they rarely follow through. To be effective, a parent should never make a threat without carrying it through."

Bart, who had remained silent and hadn't contributed to the conversation, nodded in agreement.

The principal continued. "But having a father in the home isn't always the answer. Sometimes, it's part of the problem. I almost think life is better for the boys who are fatherless than for those who have a father who doesn't care about them, ignores them, or abuses them mentally or physically."

Shelley lowered her gaze and fidgeted with the clasp on her purse. "You said he and two other boys were caught smoking?"

"Yes."

"Is—is this the first time he's been in trouble?"

Principal Taylor cleared his throat loudly. "The first time he has been caught smoking on school grounds, but not the first time he has been in trouble. Your son has developed a propensity for trouble, Mrs. Taylor. His teacher, Mrs. Grainger, says that once Kip realized he could get the attention of the other students by acting up, he became the class clown. Most of his antics, thus far, have been mostly harmless. At first, his teacher was pleased to see him coming out of his shell and let him get away with things without disciplining him, but it's gotten way out of hand. His actions have become disruptive, many times disrespectful, and always disturbing to the class. The Kip who is with us now is belligerent and mouthy, not at all like the good student we knew a year ago. Mrs. Grainger and I agree this has to stop."

Shelley's gut felt as if she'd been sucker punched. "I—I had no idea. Kip likes Mrs. Grainger. And smoking? Are you sure he was the one smoking? I've never smelled smoke on his breath or even on his clothes."

"Yes, he was definitely smoking. All three boys were. I'm the one who caught them. I doubt this was the first time they've smoked in the restroom, just the first time they were caught." The principal's lips turned up into a faint smile. "I did the same thing when I was his age, and I got caught by my principal."

"Me, too," the Genesis man interjected. "Though, looking back now, I realize that was the stupid beginning of a bad habit it took me years to break."

Her boy in trouble? Shelley fought back tears. She didn't want to cry. At home, in the sanctity of her room, maybe, but not in front of these men. "So what can I do?"

Principal Taylor gestured toward the man seated next to her. "That's where Bart comes in. I can't tell you how grateful I am to this man. He's taken several of my students under his wing, boys about Kip's age who had just begun to show signs of rebellion and disrespect for authority, and performed near miracles in their lives."

Smiling, Bart gave his head a shake. "Principal Taylor gives me way too much credit. If there is any miracle performed in their lives through what I do, the credit goes to God. I'm just the vessel He uses."

Shelley frowned. "Maybe I'm a little dense, but I still don't understand how you can do what the school officials and parents can't do."

"Sorry, I guess neither of us has made ourselves clear. I don't have any magic potion or mystic answers. All I do is take a personal interest in a boy, bring him into one of my Genesis classes as a student, and help him develop some self-worth. Nearly all boys are interested in karate and other types of martial arts. Karate, or *Genesis*, as I call it, involves not only art forms for the body but a disciplining of the mind, as well. Being involved in martial arts helps students gain not only self-control but respect for themselves and others."

"You'd be surprised what Bart has done for a number of our male students," Principal Taylor added.

Bart's expression turned serious. "I know it sounds arrogant, Mrs. Morris, but I want these boys to look to me as their role model. I'm certainly a long way from perfect—but I like to think I've learned some things along the way, and I enjoy sharing with them."

Shelley nervously fingered her handbag. "As you know, I'm a single mom. Paying for expensive martial arts lessons isn't in my budget."

The principal's face took on a broad smile. "Ah, but that's the best part. It won't cost you a penny. Bart does it all free—gratis."

Shelley's jaw dropped. "Free? But why?"

Bart gave her a generous smile. "The answer to that is quite simple. I take these boys on as a ministry. It's the least I can do for my Lord after all He's done for me."

Her eyes widening in surprise, Shelley felt a sudden appreciation for the man seated beside her. "You're a Christian?"

Though he answered, "Yes, I am," he wouldn't have needed to utter a word. The sincere look on his face said it all. Perhaps Bart Steel *was* the answer to her prayers for her son.

"I—I couldn't expect you to take Kip into your class for free," she said timidly. "Maybe I can pay you a little bit each month."

He threw back his head with a laugh. "And take a blessing away from me? No way! The Lord has called me to do this. It's my ministry. I refuse to take a penny. Your part in this will be to pray. I have a new class starting this afternoon. If you can bring Kip to The Genesis Hut right after school, we'll get him started."

Shelley couldn't contain a smile. She'd have Kip there even if she had to drag him. "I'll have him there, and thank you."

Chapter 2

"Why can't you tell me where we're going? What's the big secret?"

"You'll see. We're almost there." Shelley flipped on the turn signal, then headed the car into the already crowded parking lot. Good thing she had the day off. But even if she hadn't, Mr. Mossman, the man who owned the company she worked for—an understanding family man and a Christian himself—would have understood.

Kip straightened in his seat as he gawked out the windshield. "The Genesis Hut? What are we doing here?"

After turning off the ignition, she reached into the backseat and pulled up a gym bag. "Here, carry this for me."

He gave her an I-don't-get-it look, then crawled out of the car, taking the gym bag with him, and followed her to the door.

"We're here to see Mr. Steel," she told the attractive woman behind the counter when they entered. "He's expecting us."

Kip's eyes widened, but before he could ask any questions, Bart came through a side door, all smiles, his hand extended.

"This has to be Kip. I'm Bart Steel. Put 'er there, man."

Shelley almost laughed aloud at the expression on her son's

face as he stared, openmouthed, at their greeter, then timidly took the man's hand.

"I see you brought your bag. Good. That means we can get to work right away."

"*My* bag?" Kip glanced down at the bag in his hand. "Wow! You mean I'm going to take your class? Learn Genesis?"

"You bet you are; that is—if you're up to it. It's gonna take a lot of hard work."

Turning to Shelley, he gave her a broad grin. "You can pick him up in two hours."

Kip sent a quick, questioning glance his mother's way, probably remembering the many discussions they'd had about the family finances—or lack thereof. "Is this okay with you, Mom?"

Shelley nodded. "Oh yes, it's more than okay with me. I put everything in the bag Mr. Steel said you'd need. Enjoy your class. I'll be back in two hours."

The next two hours seemed to drag by. What if Kip wasn't interested in martial arts? Or if it was too hard? Took too much energy? And more importantly, what if he didn't like the discipline Bart said went along with it? Then what? What other options did she have? She'd watched Dr. Phil and Oprah, listened to Dr. Dobson and Dr. Kevin Leman on Christian radio. She'd heard the horror stories of how boys Kip's age had been led down a path of destruction by older boys. She couldn't let that happen to him. If only Richard hadn't fallen asleep at the wheel and hit that guardrail and left them. Kip needed his father. *She* needed him.

Finally, the two hours passed, and Kip came walking out

the door, looking tired and spent but happy.

"So? How did it go?"

"Whew, that was some workout."

"But good, right?"

He gave her a guarded smile. "I guess so."

"When is your next class?"

"Wednesday. After school. But I can ride my bike. You don't have to bring me."

Either things hadn't gone as well as she'd hoped or he didn't want to admit he was enjoying it since she'd been the one who'd arranged it. But either way, she decided not to prod and casually said, "I figured you could."

A week went by, and while Kip seemed to enjoy his time at The Genesis Hut, there was very little change in his attitude. He still barely talked to her, spent most of his time in his room, and complained about having to go to church. If anything, the relationship between the two of them had become more distant than ever. He seemed to have no respect for her, her wishes, or her feelings. The following Monday, she phoned Principal Taylor.

"Don't be discouraged, Mrs. Morris," the man said kindly. "These things take time. Give Kip some space and let Bart handle it on his end. If we don't see a change in Kip soon, Bart may want to implement phase two."

Her grip tightened on the phone. "Phase two? What is phase two?"

"I'd better let Bart tell you, but I'm sure he won't do it unless it becomes absolutely necessary."

Just the thought of phase two, whatever that was, brought thoughts of terror to her mind. *How far does Kip have to go to deserve phase two?*

Shelley hurried home from work Wednesday afternoon, planning to fix Kip's favorite supper and spend a nice evening with him, talking to him about his class, watching TV, and just hanging out together. But he didn't arrive at six thirty, his usual homecoming time after his Genesis class. Nor at seven. She put things in the oven on low and moved into the living room to wait, her frustration growing with each passing minute. Finally, at nine o'clock, she heard a car pull into the driveway, and thinking perhaps it was a parent of one of Kip's friends bringing him home, she hurried to the door and flung it open. But it wasn't a parent in the driver's seat; it was an older boy who looked as though he had maybe reached his sixteenth birthday, a boy she hadn't seen before, and in the backseat were three more boys.

Kip gave them a wave, then rushed past her into the house and headed for his room.

"Just a minute, young man! You have some explaining to do! Where were you? And who were those boys?" she called after him. But as she reached his door, he slammed it in her face. "Kip!" She tried to turn the knob, but he'd engaged the lock. "Kip! Open this door immediately."

No answer.

The sound of loud music was his only response.

"I don't have the money to replace this door, but I'll break it down if I have to."

Still no response. Shelley couldn't remember a time when

she'd been more angry and frustrated. *Please, God. Please make him open the door!*

Still the door didn't open.

"All right, Kip! Have it your way. I'm going out into the garage and get your father's sledgehammer. If that door isn't open by the time I get back, I'll break it down! I mean it, Kip. Don't push me to do something we'll both regret."

She listened for the door lock to snap open, but it didn't. Principal Taylor's words banged into her mind with such force it frightened her. *"To be effective, a parent should never make a threat without carrying it through."* Her heart began racing. "I've made a threat; I *have* to follow through with it!" she said aloud as she hurried to garage and picked up the heavy hammer. *Please, God, let that door be open by the time I get back!*

But the door remained closed. "Kip, if you're near the door, get out of the way. I don't want you to get hurt when I swing this hammer!" Sucking in a deep breath, Shelley lifted the hammer from the floor, swung it back to get the momentum necessary to break the door, then flung it forward with all her might, leaving the hammerhead on the other side of the thin, hollow-core door, the handle sticking through a gaping hole in its center. *I can't believe I just did that!*

Slowly, the handle disappeared through the hole, and the door opened, revealing the startled, drawn face of the fourteen-year-old. "You—you broke the door," he stammered, his eyes revealing total astonishment as he stood holding the handle awkwardly in his hands.

Be strong. Don't back down. Don't apologize. You're the mom here, the one in control. "Yes, and since I don't have the money to repair or replace it, it looks like you're stuck with a hole in your door," she told him unflinchingly, keeping her tone as level as she could, though her heart was still racing and her knees felt as if they were about to let her collapse onto the floor. "Come into the kitchen and eat your supper."

Though she didn't wait to see if he was going to obey, she heard his feet padding on the hardwood floor behind her as she moved into the kitchen and to the range.

"I can't believe you broke that door," Kip said, appearing to be in total shock as she placed his plate in front of him.

Fastening her gaze on his face, she narrowed her eyes. "And I'd do it again if I had to. I love you, Kip. You're my life, and I can't sit idly by and watch that life go down the tubes. Trust me, I'll knock the whole house down if that's what it takes. Now enjoy your supper. Rinse your plate and silverware when you're finished and put them in the dishwasher."

"You're not going to do it for me?"

"Nope. I would have if you'd been here on time, but not now. Not this late. You're on your own. I'm your mother, not your servant. Oh, and put the butter in the fridge and turn out the kitchen light when you're finished." Though it hurt her to not do the things she always did for him, in some ways, it felt good. *Tough love—isn't that what they called it? I know it's tough on me. I just hope it's as tough on Kip.*

At breakfast the next morning, the room was so silent that the lack of noise hurt her ears. The kitchen was as cold as if it were sitting in an igloo, with zero words passing between the two of them. Shelley wanted to talk, to say she was sorry for breaking the door down and making Kip clean up his dishes, but she couldn't. Doing those things would be counterproductive, like going backward and unraveling the few things she'd done to try to be more assertive with her son.

"Got my Genesis class again tonight." Kip gulped down his last swig of orange juice, stood, grabbed his bag, and headed for the door, ignoring her effort to kiss him good-bye.

Heartbroken, she simply nodded. "Fine. I'll expect you by six thirty. Have a good day." She waited until the door closed behind him, then glanced at the clock. "Maybe it is time for phase two, whatever that is."

"Hey, what are you doing here?" Marsha asked as she exited her car and linked arms with Shelley in The Genesis Hut parking lot. "You decide to take Bart's class after all?"

Shelley tried to appear nonchalant. No need to air her family problems. Marsha was a good friend, but she had two quiet, mousy little school-age daughters. What did she know about teenage sons? "No, not me. Kip is enrolled in one of the Genesis classes. I came over on my lunch hour to—to see how he's doing."

Marsha gave her a blank stare. "He's taking Genesis during schooltime?"

"No, after school. I—I came to see his instructor." Shelley

pulled the door open and motioned her inside.

Marsha's blank stare turned to one of confusion. "Whatever you say. Sorry, I'd like to stay and talk, but I gotta scoot. My class starts in fifteen minutes, and I have to change."

The receptionist greeted Shelley warmly, then added, "Bart said to send you in as soon as you got here. He's in his office."

She thanked the woman, then pushed open the side door leading to the office area. Through the door's glass window, she saw Bart sitting at his desk, facing his computer screen. It was easy to see why the women flocked to his Whole New You classes. He was not only good-looking; he had a gorgeous head of dark curly hair, a smile that would send any woman into orbit, and was one of the nicest, most considerate men she'd ever met.

He rose when he caught sight of her and motioned her in. "I'm so glad you called. We need to have a talk about Kip."

"He's not doing well, is he?"

"He's doing great with the physical part, but his attitude concerns me." Bart motioned her toward a chair in front of his desk, then seated himself. "He's still filled with anger, and though I hate to say it, some of it seems directed toward you."

"Me?" Shelley reared back. Those were the last words she'd expected to hear. Other than break down his door the night before, what had she ever done to anger her son?

"Yes. Kip and I have had several man-to-man talks about very personal things. He's angry because his father died. He's angry because money is tight in your home. And. . ." He paused.

"And?"

"And he's angry with you for 'treating him like a baby.' "

34

He shifted his head to one side and held his palm up between them. "I know you don't think you do, but being overprotective has to be a natural reaction for a mother who loves her son like you love Kip. Like most boys his age, he looks at your protective love as coddling. I doubt he's even talked to you about his Genesis sessions."

She lowered her head, avoiding his eyes. "No, he hasn't, though I've asked him about them."

"I'm sorry to say this, but your son looks at you as weak and totally in the dark about him, his friends, his interests—all of it. Oh, he loves you—I'm convinced of that—but you're just not hip. Can you name his favorite music group? Do you know his favorite video game? Or his average score? And clothes? I know you're on a limited budget, but do you have any idea what brand of shoes he'd buy if he had the money? If he has a girlfriend? What Internet site he frequents most?"

She gave her head a sad shake. "No, I don't know any of those things."

"Most moms don't, but if they want to have open communication with their sons, they need to. Not that you need to endorse those things, just know about them. How can you combat an enemy you don't even know exists? Some of those things I just mentioned *are* your son's enemies!"

"So what can I do? He won't talk to me."

"That's because you two don't have anything in common except your last names and the house you live in. In his eyes, you're out of the loop. You need to establish a common ground. Something you are both so interested and caught up in that you can't keep from talking about it with one another. You need to be the hippest mom around—one your son brags about to his friends."

Shelley's jaw dropped. "Me? Hip? I'm a Christian, Mr. Steel, and I know you are, too. How can—"

"Bart. Call me Bart, Shelley. If you and I are to be partners in this venture, we need to be on a first name basis."

She sucked in a breath and let it out slowly. "Okay—Bart. How can I do what you're saying and not compromise my faith and personal convictions?"

"Trust me. I'm not asking you to compromise in any way, but what I'm about to propose will take more than perhaps you're willing to give."

Shelley shook her head slowly. "Mr. St—Bart. Last night, I broke my son's door down with a sledgehammer to show him I meant what I said. If someone would have told me six months ago I could do something that ridiculous, I would have laughed in his or her face. I doubt there is anything you could ask of me that would be more demanding than that."

He gave her a sideways grin. "Sledgehammer, huh? I'm surprised you could even lift it."

She gave her chin a determined tilt. "When it comes to my son, I can do anything."

He rose, walked around his desk, and stopped directly in front of her, his eyes locked with hers. "Okay then. I'd say you're ready for phase two."

"*What* is phase two?"

"What time does Kip get up on school mornings?"

"As late as possible. Usually by seven. Why?"

"Could you meet me here at five thirty? If I promise to have you out of here by six thirty?"

"In the morning?"

"In the morning."

"I guess I could, but why?"

He gave her an impish grin. "Because we don't want Kip to know what's going on until we're ready."

Now she was totally confused. "Ready for what?"

"You'll see. Will I see you tomorrow morning?"

She shrugged. She had no idea what he had in mind, but if it had any chance of changing Kip back into the son she hoped he'd be, anything was worth it. "Okay. That's pretty early, but if you're game, so am I. I can't thank you enough for the interest you're showing in Kip. Even though he doesn't mention it, I can tell by his dedication to your class that he looks up to you."

"My pleasure. Like I told you in Principal Taylor's office, I feel working with boys like Kip is my calling from God. I look at it as my God-given ministry." He grabbed a printed sheet from a stack on his desk and handed it to her. "Bring the things on this list with you. Phase two begins tomorrow morning at five thirty."

Shelley glanced at the colorful sheet, then smiled up at him. "Okay. See you in the morning."

"The important thing is that Kip mustn't know anything about this until I say so. Secrecy is of the utmost importance. Don't slip up, or all is lost."

"Gotcha."

Shelley awoke with a start when her alarm sounded at four forty-five the next morning. She'd purposely shut her door when she'd gone to bed, something she rarely did, hoping the sound wouldn't waken Kip—as if any sound could get him out of bed any earlier than necessary. After brushing her teeth and giving her face a quick splash to get her juices flowing, she dabbed on a bit of lipstick and added color to her cheeks; ran a pick through her hair; crawled into her T-shirt, pink sweats, and running shoes; grabbed a bottle of water from the fridge; snatched up her purse and car keys; and quietly slipped through the garage door and into her car.

She had hoped to make it to The Genesis Hut early enough to have a little time to gather her thoughts before Bart arrived, but he was already there and hurried to open the door for her. Even at this early hour, he looked great and, dressed in a sleeve-less T-shirt, more muscular than she'd realized.

"Hi. I was afraid you might change your mind and not show up."

"And miss out on phase two, whatever that is? No way! You've got my curiosity up."

He gave her a quick once-over. "You look terrific in that outfit, but I hope you're wearing a tank or T-shirt under that zippered top. We're going to be working up a sweat."

She tilted her head and narrowed her eyes. "Is this your sneaky way of getting me into an exercise class?"

"Nope. No class. What I have planned for you is one-on-one. Just you and me."

For the first time, it occurred to her that she was alone in this oversized building with a man she barely knew and at an hour when very few people were about. "Look, M—Bart. I appreciate your interest in my son, but I'm still not clear about what part I'm supposed to play in all of this."

He grinned. "Sorry. It isn't that I'm trying to keep phase two a secret, but not all women can handle phase two. It's not for the fainthearted. However, with your determination and desire to help your son, I have a feeling you just might succeed."

"So—what will I be doing in phase two? From the things you had on that list you gave me, I figured it would somehow be tied to exercise. Is that it? You think I need to be more physically fit to handle my son?"

"In some ways, yes. I've done phase two with three other mothers with great success. But I also have to admit I've had other mothers who wimped out and failed. They just didn't have what it takes." He gestured toward a chair, waited until she sat down, then seated himself beside her. "From all appearances, I'd say Kip loves taking Genesis. He was a little mouthy at first, but once he realized that type of behavior wasn't acceptable here, and that if it continued he was out, he began to cooperate. We've made good progress in the past two weeks, but Kip is still sometimes standoffish with me. That boy has built a nearly impenetrable shell around himself, yet he is giving his all to my class. I think he's afraid. Has he said anything to you about being bullied? Or refusing to join a gang?"

His words brought terror to her heart. "No. Nothing."

"I've seen the look in his eyes before, in the eyes of other boys I've tried to befriend. I'm beginning to wonder if there isn't more going on in the school than the principal knows about."

"You're frightening me."

"Frightening you is not my intent. I'm not saying Kip is being bullied or has anything to do with a gang, but I think it's only wise that you are aware of what we might be dealing with." He rose, extended his hand, and pulled her to her feet. "You, milady, are going to learn the same thing Kip is learning."

"Me?" Holding her hands up between them, she backed away. "You've got to be kidding. I could never do that."

"With my help, you can, but you mustn't let Kip know until we're ready. He has a two-week start on you; most of what we've been doing during that time, though, has been background and fundamentals, and we've been meeting only three times a week. I'll guarantee you: If you will work with me every weekday morning for one hour and do the homework I assign, in two weeks, you'll be caught up with Kip, maybe even ahead of him."

"But why? Why would you want to teach me the karate moves? What would it accomplish? Am I supposed to give him a karate chop when he disobeys or comes home late?" None of this made any sense.

He threw back his head with a chortle. "No, of course not. But, if you did, the shock value alone might jar him enough to knock some sense into his head."

"Then what?"

"Remember when I told you how important it was for you and your son to have a common interest? Something that would bond the two of you together? The moves I've taken from karate and teach at The Genesis Hut can be that bond. He may not look up to you now, but how would he feel if you showed up as a new member of his class?"

She huffed. "He'd probably be embarrassed and leave. What boy wants his mother in his class?"

"Ah, but what if his mother is the best one in the class? Knows more about the background of martial arts and the moves than he or anyone else in the class knows? And all his friends are in awe of her? Don't you think he would be proud of you?"

"I—I don't know."

"What have you got to lose? You've already admitted he's on a downhill slide."

"I guess it would be worth a try."

"It'll be hard work, but you might even end up liking it."

She rubbed at her temples. "And I may hate it. I've never done anything like it before."

"I'm a great teacher." He gave her a teasing grin. "Tough, but great."

"And what do you get out of all this extra effort you put into phase two?"

"If it works, the satisfaction of a job well-done, favor from God, and, hopefully, thanks from you." He picked up her bag, then nodded toward the door. "Let's get at it. We haven't a moment to waste."

Shelley hesitated, but only for a split second. Kip *was* the most important thing in her life. If it took every ounce of strength she could muster to bring him back to her, she'd do it. Lifting her chin high and squaring her shoulders, she moved forward. "Let's do it."

On the way to the workout room, Bart explained, "The word *karate* is a combination of two Japanese characters: *kara*, meaning 'empty,' and *te*, meaning 'hand'; thus *karate* means 'empty hand.' If we add the suffix *do*, which is pronounced 'doe,' it implies karate, or Genesis as I call it, is a total way of life that goes well beyond self-defense. In traditional karate-do, we always keep in mind that the true opponent is oneself."

"How did you get started in karate?"

Bart opened the workout-room door and motioned her inside. "Same way most guys do. I was raised in Brooklyn, and as a boy, I got beat up pretty bad by an older boy because I wouldn't give him the watch my dad had given me. He actually broke my arm. I decided right then that that was never going to happen again, so I got me a part-time job at the little grocery store around the corner to pay for it and began karate lessons at our local Y." He closed the door, then moved to the center of the room.

"Did you ever have to defend yourself?"

He gave his head a shake. "Never did. Not one time, but maybe some of that was because I shot up like a weed my sophomore year in high school and ended up being the tallest guy in my class. The muscles I'd added probably helped, too. Let's move over there. We need to do some warm-ups. Watch and do what I do."

She took her stand a few feet from him and began to mirror

his movements. "Brooklyn, huh? How did you get from Brooklyn to Colorado?"

"By the time I graduated high school, I was getting pretty good in karate. I'd won a number of our area tournaments, decided I wanted to try my hand at one of the larger ones, and came with my karate master to a tournament in Denver. By the way, that karate master was the one who led me to Christ. I liked Colorado, earned a good scholarship, and came to Boulder for college. After graduation, I moved to Denver and established The Genesis Hut."

Adjusting his position, he leaned toward her. "Let me explain what Genesis is. Like I said, I became interested in karate before I became a Christian, but, as you know, karate and most other martial arts programs have their beginnings in Far Eastern beliefs. Those beginnings, and the connotations associated with them, really bothered me after I was saved, and I almost quit karate because of them. But the more I thought about it, and the nearly unequalled disciplined training that goes with it, the more I decided there had to be a way to keep the benefits of karate while still holding on to my Christian principles. After spending many long hours in prayer, I came up with the idea of Genesis, á la *new beginnings*, a program based on the karate moves but with the emphasis on God and His Word."

He eyed her carefully. "You're doing great, but don't hold your breath. Let it out naturally."

She gave him a sideways grin. "I was holding it, wasn't I?"

He grinned back. "Yeah, I'm afraid you were."

"Your explanation about Genesis makes me feel better. It

really concerned me to think Kip would be subjected to Far Eastern teachings."

"Well, you needn't be concerned. God intended us Christians to be strong. Strong but not aggressive. We have the same belt designations as karate, but our belts have godly meanings. Our white belt stands for purity. I use that color to explain how God wants us to be pure in mind, body, and spirit. The red belt reminds us of the blood that Jesus shed for each of us. I tell my students, even kids Kip's age and younger, that we are all sinners and in need of a Savior. The blue represents our royal standing as a child of the King. The brown belt stands for strength, the strength we need to face the world and stand up for our beliefs. And the black represents the evil we as Christians must fight daily and overcome to remain true to God and be a witness for Him. Each of the belts has to be earned by the student. There are no shortcuts. Once the students have earned their belts, they wear them proudly and with honor."

"Do you honestly think I can pull this off? I've never been a strong person."

He lowered his arms and gave her a kindly smile. "Shelley, in Genesis, strong doesn't mean big, muscular arms. It means being physically fit and knowing how to make the best of whatever size you are, by using defensive techniques and moves. Even a small person like you can do it, but true strength lies *within* the person who truly masters Genesis. Like I said, we're talking about discipline, a way of life. I have a feeling you're stronger than you think."

She returned his smile. "Thanks, Bart. I want to be strong.

Your encouraging words really help. I *am* going to do this thing, even if it kills me. Now, where do we go from here?"

"Did you by any chance take gymnastics or maybe some dance classes when you were a kid?"

She gave him a puzzled look. "I took a couple of years of gymnastics in my early teens, but I trained in ballet from the time I was in first grade through high school. Why?"

"Just wondered. I've found that students who have had some type of training like that take to the movements we'll be using much faster and more easily than those who haven't. Balance is of the utmost importance in practically every single one of the movements we use. If you've taken gymnastics, then I guess you can walk a balance beam."

She allowed a broad grin to blanket her face. "The balance beam was my specialty. I got pretty good on it."

"Think you could walk on it now?"

"Walk? You mean without doing the flips and fancy turns? Just walk?"

"Yeah. Just walk from end to end without falling off."

She grinned at him. "Piece of cake."

He gestured toward a semidarkened part of the room, then flipped one of the light switches on the wall. "Show me."

There, off in the corner, sat a balance beam. Though Shelley hadn't been on one in years, she ran toward it, eager to show him she was more agile than he apparently thought she was. She might be in her mid-thirties, but simply *walking* across a balance beam was like riding a bicycle: Once you'd mastered the technique, you never forgot it.

Though it was a bit more difficult to mount than it had been when she was younger, she made it and quickly stood to her feet, holding her arms out to steady her position.

Bart hurried to her side. "Be careful! I'll spot you."

Lifting her chin high and squaring her shoulders, she walked the complete length of the beam without a single slipup, even doing a quick, sure-footed turn at the other end and walking back. Feeling quite proud of her accomplishment, she smiled down at him, then dismounted. To her surprise, Bart leaped at her as her feet hit the floor, encircling her in his arms.

"Sorry, I was afraid you might fall!" He gave her a shy grin. "But it looks like you didn't need my help after all."

"You didn't think I could do it, did you?"

"You want the truth? I figured you could do it, but I thought you might take a few tumbles before you succeeded. You're good! Once you've mastered a few of the basic Genesis techniques, I have a move I want you to try. The only students who have mastered it have had an exceptional sense of balance. I think you can do it. It'll sure impress the socks off your son if you can."

Though her knees were trembling and her hands felt sweaty, she gave him a nonchalant smile. "Do you really think all of this will bring Kip around?"

He shrugged. "Maybe. Maybe not. But isn't it worth a try?"

She had to agree. Anything was worth a try, even this crazy scheme.

He rubbed his hands together briskly. "Let's get started on our first move."

For the next several minutes, they went through warm-ups and simple routines, paying special attention to their breathing, with Bart throwing in bits and pieces about the history of karate and the way it should only be used for defense, never for outright fighting to purposely overcome someone or show off one's strength. He laughed openly. "Though I doubt I'll have to worry about you on that count, but every woman should know how to defend herself."

"Often, when I've had to be out late at night and cross a parking lot by myself, I've wished I knew how to defend myself."

"We hope you never have to use the aggressive tactics you'll learn here, but you never know when a threatening situation may arise. This way, you'll be better prepared to handle it. Sometimes simply buying yourself a few extra minutes can mean a real difference." He grabbed two pristine white towels from a nearby rack, then tossed one to her with a grin. "You'll need this, lady, 'cause we're ready to get down to business and we're gonna work up a real sweat."

Smiling, Shelley caught the towel, cradling it in her arms. "You may sweat, but ladies perspire."

He gave her a mischievous grin. "Believe me, in my classes— you're gonna sweat."

She found out the hard way he wasn't exaggerating as he led her through a series of exercises, extensions, and movements she'd never done before as he gave her a demonstration of some of the techniques she'd be learning. By the time their hour was up, though in some ways she was exhilarated, she was also exhausted, but she wasn't about to let Bart know.

"You sure I didn't work you too hard?" he asked as he walked her to the lobby at the end of their session.

She gave her head a shake. "No, of course not. I'm fine." *Who do I think I'm kidding? Every muscle in my body aches.*

"See you in the morning." He pushed the front door open so she could exit, then gave her a wave.

She waved back, hoping she could make it to her car before her knees gave out. What a morning she'd had, and she had the same thing to look forward to tomorrow.

Bart watched until her car disappeared into the early morning traffic. The gal had spunk. He'd really put her through her paces, demanding more of her than he did most students, but with her, time was of the essence. Shelley was such a nice person. Good-looking, too, and she sure didn't look like she could have a fourteen-year-old son. She was exactly the kind of woman of which his mother would approve, and best of all, she was a Christian. *What am I thinking? First of all, hooking up with one of my students is a definite no-no. And secondly, I'm happy being a bachelor. Besides, that woman comes with baggage—a son with his own set of problems.* But he had to admit, it was nice to hold her in his arms, even if just for a brief second.

"What's the matter with you?" Shelley's boss stared at her as she pulled open a file-cabinet drawer later that morning.

Shelley inserted the file folder, closed the drawer, then

slowly turned to face Marvin Mossman, her boss. She felt like she'd been run over by a Mack truck. "Nothing, why?"

"You act like you've got a backache or something. Aren't you feeling well?"

"Just overdid myself a bit. That's all."

"I hope you weren't trying to move heavy furniture by yourself. My wife's back always gives her fits when she pulls that trick. Maybe you'd better take the rest of the day off, give yourself a good rubdown with a liniment, and stretch out on your bed for a few hours. Give your body a chance to recuperate."

She forced a smile. "I'm okay. Honest. Besides, I've got to get this pile of communications out in today's mail."

He shrugged. "Your call, but take off if you need to. I hate to see you hurting."

It seemed as if five o'clock would never come. The instant the long hand hit twelve, Shelley grabbed her purse and headed for the door. If she hurried, she'd have time to stretch out for a full hour before Kip got home. Her body begged to relax.

She'd barely gotten through the door to her bedroom and kicked off her shoes when the phone rang. "Hi," a deep male voice said on the other end. "I hope you're not hurting. You worked pretty hard this morning. You really impressed me with that balance beam performance."

"Oh, hello, Bart." She rubbed at her sore neck. "Don't worry about me. I'm—fine."

"I would never have worked you that hard if you hadn't told me you were used to exercising."

Maybe I exaggerated that statement a bit. "I'm going to start reading those pamphlets on nutrition you gave me as soon as I'm sure Kip is in his room for the night."

"Considering how hard you worked this morning, it might be better for you to get to bed early than spend your time reading. By the way, I know we had only planned on our sessions being Monday through Friday, but I'm always here on Saturdays. Think you could manage to come in then, too? It doesn't have to be at five thirty. I could work in an hour for you around ten."

After transferring the phone to her other hand, she sat down on the edge of the bed. "I guess Saturday at ten would work. Kip rarely gets out of bed before noon on Saturdays, so he wouldn't even miss me. But isn't that asking a bit much of you? You're already coming in early every day. I don't want to take advantage of your generosity. I'm sure you have better things to do with your time than work with me."

"Nope. You and Kip are my number one priority. I'm determined to make sure phase two works. I hate losing—at anything." He paused. "You would tell me if I worked you too hard, wouldn't you?"

Now she was on the spot. As a Christian, she wasn't comfortable lying, yet the last thing she wanted was to admit that she hurt. Surely, to reap the rewards she hoped phase two would bring, she could endure a little pain and discomfort. "I have a little soreness but nothing I can't tolerate."

"I normally take showers, but when I hurt," he went on, "I put one of my favorite Christian artist's CDs on my stereo, take a long, hot soak in the tub, go to bed early, and just relax. A good liniment helps, too, if you have one. I have one I especially like.

I'll give you a bottle in the morning."

She rubbed at her thigh. *I wish I had that liniment now!* "Thanks for the advice. A hot bath always feels good after a long day."

"Shelley?"

"Yes?"

"You're a great sport. I'm enjoying working with you. You're taking to Genesis much more quickly than the average female."

She felt a blush rise to her cheeks. "I–I'm enjoying working with you, too." *Far more than I should!*

"Get a good night's sleep. See you in the morning."

She said good-bye, then hung up the phone, more eager than ever to stretch out on her bed.

Kip arrived home right on time. Shelley rose from her bed when she heard him enter the front door and hurried to greet him. "I haven't started supper yet, but because we're going to have leftovers, it won't take long. How are the classes going? You haven't said much about them."

He tossed his bag onto the sofa, then shrugged. "Good. They're goin' good. We haven't gotten into the heavy stuff yet—but I like it so far, and I sure like Mr. Steel. That guy has some great biceps."

"Kip? What's the name of your favorite music group?"

The startled look he gave her was almost comical. "Why'd you ask me that?"

"Just curious. Tell me, what's their name?"

He scrunched up his mouth thoughtfully. "I like a couple

of groups, but I guess my favorite would be the Green Goblins. What's yours?"

She hadn't expected a question in return. "I like Point of Grace."

He let loose a snicker. "That's a Christian group? Sounds more like a lady with an odd-shaped head."

She grinned. "At least they're not green." For the first time in months, she and Kip were actually carrying on a conversation and laughing. Maybe Bart knew what he was talking about after all.

Kip backed toward his door. "I'm going to my room and work on some stretches Master Bart taught me. Call me when supper's ready."

She nodded. "Yeah. I will."

Shelley had to drag herself out of bed the next morning. Every muscle, every bone, in her body ached. "Even my hair hurts," she told herself as she pulled on her sweats and headed for The Genesis Hut.

Again, Bart met her at the door, his eyes narrowing. "Um, just as I thought, you did overdo yourself yesterday. I wondered if you had been exercising as much as you'd led me to believe. We'll take it a little easier this morning. Just remember, when you work out at home as well as here, the warming up and cooling down periods are just as important as the exercises themselves, and absolutely necessary."

"I'll remember. I promise." She flinched as she nodded her

head. Even her neck hurt.

"Shelley, Genesis is not only the disciplining of the body, it's the disciplining of the mind. You must learn to focus, block everything else out of your thoughts, and concentrate of what you're doing. Each movement is important and has its purpose."

"I'll try."

"Trying is not good enough, Shelley. You must do it. When you're home alone, tune the radio to a station you abhor. A rock or heavy metal station, then turn up the volume. Next, stand in the middle of the room balancing on one foot and read your Bible aloud."

"But I can't stand rock—"

"I know. I hate that kind of music, too, but once you learn to concentrate deeply enough on what you are doing, the music will begin to fade into the background and you'll be so absorbed in focusing on the Word that you'll no longer hear it. That's the kind of focus I'm talking about. Believe it or not, what I'm telling you actually works." He gestured toward the workout area. "Now, let's get started."

By the time Friday morning rolled around, a good portion of her soreness had disappeared. Shelley had learned to read her Bible while precariously balancing, barely noticing the loud noise of the radio, and was amazed at her progress. Bart was a great teacher, and so much fun to be with; she found herself waking up long before her alarm went off, feeling great, and had lost nearly two pounds. Of course, the healthy diet Bart had insisted on helped, and since he was also encouraging Kip and the other members of his class to eat healthy, they were both benefiting.

"Has Kip said anything about the new friends he's making?" Bart asked her as they started their warm-ups. "I heard a couple of them ask him to go to a ball game tomorrow night."

"He hasn't mentioned it."

He gave her a shy grin. "Well, if Kip ends up spending the evening with his friends, how about us going to a movie?"

"Us? You and me?"

He nodded. "Why not us? I'm sure we could both use a break. We can even make the movie a chick flick."

"Don't you have a policy in your business to never date students?"

His grin made her heart pick up its pace. "I'll make an exception with you. Although if you prefer, we won't call it a date, we'll call it a field trip. How about it?"

What was it about Bart and his wonderful sense of humor that made her forget her resolve? "A movie would be nice. I haven't been to one in a long time."

He gave her a thumbs-up. "Then count on it. If Kip goes to the ball game, we go to the movie."

Chapter 3

By Saturday morning, Shelley's body felt more like its old self. She had the warm-ups and cooldowns and most of the beginning moves down pat. "I really feel like I'm getting somewhere," she admitted as she and Bart worked out, side by side. "And I have more energy than I've had in a long time."

"Good. I'm glad to hear it. I'm proud of you. You're making great progress, but you need to learn to relax. Make your body movements more fluid." She held her breath as he stepped close to her. "Here, let me show you. Put your left hand in mine and let me rotate your arm in a slow, even movement."

She did as he instructed, only to find her face mere inches from his, his arm gently wrapped around her waist. How did he expect her to think with his blue eyes focused on hers, his warm breath bathing her cheeks?

"Better. Much better," he murmured softly, his gaze still fixed on her face. "Now the other arm."

Shelley thought she would melt out of sheer joy as they changed positions. What was the matter with her? She was a grown woman, yet she was as giddy as she'd been on her first date.

In a lightning-fast movement, he dropped her hand, turned his head aside, and stepped away from her, his demeanor back to one of strictly business. "Good. You're a fast learner. Practice that at home."

To her, he suddenly seemed frazzled, out of control, which was anything but normal for him. Shelley couldn't help wondering, *Is he feeling the same vibes? No! No way. This man is surrounded by beautiful women every day of his life. Why would he be drawn to me? He probably moved away quickly because he didn't want me to get the wrong impression.*

Eager to get her own self under control, she quickly changed the subject. "Tell me the truth. How do you think Kip's doing?"

He moved into position and began a series of slow, deliberate movements, motioning her to follow. "Other than still having occasional bouts of mouthiness, he's doing great. The other class members really like him, especially the girls. They think he's cute."

Shelley stopped still. "There are girls in his class?"

"Sure. Most of the classes have girls in them."

She let out a sigh of relief. "Then maybe it won't be such a shock when I show up. I'm still pretty apprehensive about this whole thing. I sure don't want to make a fool out of myself."

He gave her an encouraging wink. "Take it from me. I know the moves those kids have mastered. If you keep working as hard as you are now, the day you show up in class, you'll be way ahead of them."

"I hope you're right."

"Trust me. I wouldn't say it if I didn't mean it. Did Kip ever ask you about the ball game?"

"Not yet."

"I know he's planning on going. If something happens and he doesn't go, call me on my cell phone. Otherwise, I'll see you about seven. Okay?"

She nodded, then gave him a demure smile, more excited about spending the evening with him than she cared to admit, even to herself. "Seven will be fine."

"Hey, Mom, is it okay if I go to a basketball game tonight with some of my Genesis friends?" Kip asked as he came out of his room about noon in a wrinkled T-shirt, his dark curly hair looking as though it had been stirred up with an electric mixer, his face bearing sleep lines.

Shelley smiled at his overall appearance. "Guess you slept okay."

"Sure did. That Genesis stuff is hard work." He dropped down at the kitchen table and picked up the glass of juice she had waiting for him. "Is it okay if I go?"

"Need me to drive?"

He gave his head a shake. "Naw. Cramer said his mom would drive us."

She paused thoughtfully. "I guess it'll be all right, so long as you promise me you won't do anything you shouldn't."

"Mom"—Kip plummeted his fingers into his tangled hair and scratched at his scalp—"Isn't it about time you gave me some slack?"

"Freedom and slack will come when you prove to me you can be responsible. By the way, I'm glad you're enjoying your Genesis class."

A broad grin spread across his face as his hands delivered several rapid karate-like chops to an imaginary adversary. "I'm gettin' to be one mean martial arts machine. Everybody better stay out of my way."

Shelley felt a rush of excitement. She'd learned those very moves herself and longed to share them with him. "Oh? I was under the impression that moves like those were only to be used if absolutely necessary."

"You sound like my Genesis instructor." Kip shrugged, then lowered his arms to his sides. "I'm gonna go call the guys and tell them I can go."

Bart hesitated before ringing Shelley's doorbell. The last thing he wanted was to cause more trouble between her and her son. Maybe he should have left well enough alone and not even mentioned the movie. Too late for that—she was expecting him.

He did a double take when she opened the door. Other than the business suit she'd been wearing at the principal's office, he'd never seen her in anything but sweats. She looked good, and she smelled good, too. Kind of flowery. Try as he might, he couldn't keep his eyes off her. During the short time he'd known her, she had kept her hair tied back in one of those ponytail things, but not tonight. Tonight, it hung wavy and free, clear to her shoulders, and it was as shiny as if she'd just washed it and put some kind of sparkle stuff on it. He wanted to reach out and touch it, then realized what a stupid move that would be. She'd probably slap him.

When her blue eyes looked up at him and she said, "Hi, come on in," he thought he would melt. *Come on, Bart, you're a grown man,* he reminded himself. *You were even engaged once. You're acting like a schoolboy on his first date!*

Unable to resist taking in another whiff of her perfume, he leaned toward her and awkwardly whispered, "Thanks for coming with me."

"Thank you for inviting me."

Was she batting those baby blues at him, or was he only hoping she was? Shyly pulling his hand out from behind his back, he handed her a single pink rose. "I stopped to see my folks on the way here. This is from my mom's garden."

Shelley took the flower from his hand and lifted it to her nose. "Umm, it smells wonderful. Oh, Bart, thank you. I've tried to grow roses but haven't had much luck. Simple zinnias and marigolds are more my speed. I'm ready, but give me a minute to put this lovely flower in some water before we go. I wouldn't want it to wilt."

He nodded, pleased that she'd been happy about the rose, and stepped inside. Her house was exactly like he'd thought it would be. Homey, inviting, and filled with light. Several pictures of Kip stood in strategic areas about the room. Some of him alone, some with Shelley, and some with a handsome man he assumed was Kip's father.

"There, that should do it." She placed a vase containing the rose on the coffee table, then stepped back to admire it. "Okay, now I'm ready."

Apparently, many people had been looking forward to the release of the movie they'd chosen. Nearly every seat was occupied. They finally located four empty seats about halfway up and took the two on the aisle.

"I'm glad you decided to come. Though you probably don't make a habit of attending karate films, I think you'll enjoy this one," Bart explained, motioning toward the screen. "Now that you've been attending class, you'll recognize a number of the moves."

She glanced at the empty seat beside them. "I wish Kip was here with us. I know he'd enjoy it. He loves everything you've been teaching him at Genesis. He practices all the time."

"He'll probably come another evening with some of his friends. Would you like something to drink? And some nice, hot, buttery popcorn?"

"Not now. Maybe later."

They sat in silence as the movie started, watching the screen without a word until the hero was attacked by three men late one night as he walked to his car. "Watch that guy," Bart said in a low voice while he leaned close to Shelley, warily slipping his arm around her shoulders. "He'll make quick work of those villains." He smiled to himself, thankful she hadn't pushed his arm away.

"Could one man actually do all of that if it weren't staged?" she whispered.

Bart nodded. "Probably not quite as easily as that, but one

man *could* do it if he was well-trained, mentally alert, and physically fit. Hopefully, no one will ever have to defend themselves against three men at the same time, but it always helps to be prepared."

She leaned into his arm and smiled up at him. "Could you do it?"

He screwed up his face. "Defend myself against three men? I'd like to think so, but I hope I never have to find out. While what we learn is good for defense, it should never be used to show one's strength. I think of karate or Genesis as a competitive sport. The fact that what you learn could be used to defend yourself is an added benefit."

"You mean like a policeman carries a gun, knows how to use it, but hopes he never has to shoot it?"

He gave her shoulder a little squeeze. "Exactly."

Though Bart was enjoying the movie, both his thoughts and his gaze kept wandering to the lovely woman beside him.

To Shelley's surprise, the movie contained not only a number of karate scenes, but the plot was about a karate instructor who fell in love with one of his students. She poked Bart's arm in a teasing way. "Have you ever done that? Fallen in love with one of *your* students? Some really gorgeous women take your classes."

With a muffled laugh, he grinned down at her. Even in the dim light of the theater, she could see mischief brewing in his eyes as he tightened his grip on her shoulders. "Not yet, but it's a distinct possibility."

Shelley sucked in her breath and held it. Exactly what did *that* mean?

After a few moments, he whispered in her ear, "Have you ever fallen in love with *your* Genesis teacher?"

His reversed question startling her, she struggled to find an answer, finally deciding to answer him as he'd answered her. "Not yet," she said, smiling, her mouth quivering as she spoke. "But it's a distinct possibility."

After that little repartee, she had a hard time keeping her mind on the movie as the words that had passed between them kept playing and replaying in her mind. To her, their relationship, though they'd known each other for only a short time, was becoming serious. To him, no doubt, it meant nothing, just one of those things that happened over and over—probably with each new female student who caught his eye. The man had never married. Did that mean he made this kind of play for women, then dropped them when someone better, prettier, with a more sparkling personality came along? Deciding she'd better cool it and keep her guard up, lest she get hurt, she turned her full attention toward the screen, eager to see if the heroine got the hero in the end or if he left her for another woman.

"I thought sure those two were going to get married—or at least engaged," Bart said, twining his fingers with hers as they left the theater and walked to his car. "I don't know about you, but I like happy endings. Wanna get a sandwich? Or a cup of coffee?"

She glanced at her watch, deciding it would be best if she

put some space between herself and this man who seemed to be everything she'd want, *if* she ever decided it was time to move on with her life. "Thanks, but not tonight. Kip will be home soon, and I need to go over my Sunday school lesson again. I'm filling in tomorrow for our regular teacher."

"I've never asked: Where do you go to church?"

"Clark's Point Community Church. It's over on—"

"That's where I go!"

Her jaw dropped. "You go there, too? Which service?"

"The eleven o'clock."

"Kip and I go to the nine o'clock service and then to the set of Sunday school classes at eleven."

"No wonder I haven't seen you there before. Of course, with a church as large as ours, I can go months without seeing some of my friends. It's wonderful the way our church is growing, but it'll sure be nice when we can build that bigger sanctuary and not have to have two separate morning services and two sets of Sunday school."

"Do you go to Sunday school?"

His face brightened. "Yeah, I do. I'm in the Men in the Word class at 9 a.m. Pastor Glendale is our teacher. His Sunday morning schedule allows him to teach only that one class since he preaches at eleven. Which class are you in?"

She smiled. "Women in the Word, taught by Pastor Glendale's wife."

"This is uncanny! Maybe I could skip Pastor Glendale's Sunday school class this once and we could sit together."

"And let Kip discover we know each other?"

He quirked up his brows. "Not a good idea, I guess. At least, not yet."

There were those two words again. *Not yet.* Her life seemed to be an ongoing series of *not yets.*

"I may go to the early service tomorrow anyway and catch up with some old friends I've been missing, but I promise I won't sit with you."

When they reached his car, they crawled in and headed toward her house, their conversation filled with references about the pastor and his wife and the influence those two dedicated people had on their lives.

"Thanks for the movie," Shelley told him after he'd taken her key and unlocked the front door. "I had a great time."

She waited, but he made no effort to leave. "I hope the weather is as nice tomorrow," she said for lack of something profound to break the silence.

His face took on a somber expression as he stood staring at her, his brow creased. "I—I. . ." Leaping forward, he pulled her into his arms so suddenly it almost frightened her. "I've wanted to kiss you," he said breathlessly before planting his lips on hers.

She stood there, stiff as a statue, wide-eyed, staring at his face, her arms at her sides, locked in place by his embrace. *Is he teasing me, playing with my emotions? I want to kiss him back, but should I? This may mean nothing more to him than a simple good night kiss, but to me, it means much more. Even though I am attracted to this man, I have to guard my heart.*

When their kiss ended, he pulled back slightly, one hand

still splayed across her back, keeping her captive. "Guess I ought to say I'm sorry, Shelley, but I'm not. And no—in case you're wondering—I don't make a habit of kissing my students. You probably won't believe me, but you're the first one. Actually, you're the first woman I've kissed since my fiancée left me."

How could someone as handsome and popular as he was, a man who was constantly surrounded by beautiful women, be telling the truth? She wanted to say she didn't believe him but, since he'd seemed so sincere, couldn't bring herself to do it.

"I've tried to stay away from you, Shelley; honest I have. I know you've got a lot on your plate with Kip and all, and though I could really mess things up if he knew about us, I couldn't stay away even though I've tried. You're—different from most of the women I meet. There's something about you, something that draws me to you and keeps you on my mind. I don't know what's the matter with me. I think of you day and night." He paused. "If I had my way, I'd kiss you again."

Shelley gazed up at him, his sweet words penetrating and pulverizing the shield she'd attempted to place between them, until it was no longer there. She, the woman who had vowed she'd never get involved with another man until Kip was out of high school, was already hopelessly in love with Bart—and there was nothing she could do about it. Slipping her hand behind his neck, she drew his head to hers, so close she could feel the warmth of his cheek. She closed her eyes and lifted her face toward his, then whispered, "What's stopping you?"

Bells rang, stars darted across the sky, and firecrackers sounded as their lips met. Only this time, instead of a hurried stolen kiss, their lips met slowly, tasting and teasing, before they finally melded into one long, delicious kiss that Shelley knew she'd remember forever. Though the stark reality of life might come with morning's light, this one delicious moment was hers and his. Theirs.

"Wow," Bart uttered as he slowly backed away from her. "I'm sure glad I barged ahead and you didn't slap me. I'd hate to think I passed up an opportunity to kiss you."

One look at his eyes, and Shelley knew this had been no ordinary kiss for him either. What she saw reflected there convinced her that this man was for real. He wasn't out to play some silly game, make a conquest he could later brag about to his friends. This man loved the Lord. He'd been as afraid of getting involved with someone who didn't share his faith as she was, and her heart sang. "I—I'd better get inside, but thank you for a lovely evening."

He took her hands in his and pulled them to his lips, kissing her fingers one at a time. "The pleasure was definitely mine." Then, backing away, he moved out into the stillness of the night, leaving Shelley with feelings she hadn't experienced in years.

She watched for Bart at church the next morning, hoping to at least get a glimpse of him. She finally spotted him coming out of one of the other aisles as she and Kip moved into the grand foyer at the close of the worship service. He looked more handsome than ever in his eggplant-colored dress shirt, floral eggplant and avocado green tie, and beige trousers.

Kip gave her a nudge, his face brightening as he, too, spotted Bart. "Hey, look, Mom. There's my Genesis Master. I didn't know he went to church here. Let's tell him hi." Without giving her time to respond, Kip surged on ahead.

By the time she made her way through the crowd to where they were standing, Kip and Bart were already engaged in conversation. Trying to still the quickened beat of her heart, Shelley swallowed hard and uttered a simple, "Hello," as their eyes met.

Bart casually responded, "Hi," but, to her, the look he gave her said far more than his mere greeting. Though Kip chattered on about one of the moves he was trying to master, Bart's attention kept flitting toward Shelley.

"Well, I'd better get moving. I told my mom I'd come by, then stay for lunch. Dad hasn't been feeling well. Mom's fixing her famous barbecued brisket. I wouldn't want to miss that." He extended his hand, and to her surprise, Kip took it and gave it a generous shake. "Good-bye, Kip. See you tomorrow." Then turning toward Shelley, he nodded. "Good to see you again, Mrs. Morris."

"It was good to see you, too." She watched as he hurried out one of the exit doors, then put her arm around her son's shoulder. "Barbecued brisket. That sounds good. How about having lunch at Hog Wild, that barbecue place near the mall, after our Sunday school class?"

He smiled at her. "Yeah, that sounds great. Wow—Master Bart attends our church."

She smiled back. "Pretty neat, huh?"

"Yeah, pretty neat. I can't wait to tell the guys in my class. They're really gonna freak out."

"I'll just bet they will." *Thank You, Lord, thank You!*

Chapter 4

Bart grabbed Shelley's hands, then stood gazing into her eyes when she entered The Genesis Hut the next morning. "I don't know what's happening to me. We've only known each other for a month now, but I think about you constantly and can hardly wait to see you each day. Yesterday, when I was at my folks' place for lunch, my mom asked me what was going on in my life. She said I seemed happier and more alive than I've been in a long time." He gave her hands a squeeze. "I—I told her about you. She and Dad are anxious to meet you."

Shelley's emotions ran the gamut from unexcelled joy to confusion and fear. Never had she been more elated or more filled with trepidation. Bart was everything she could ever hope for in a man and she cared deeply for him, but even if *he* was ready for a relationship, which she doubted, was *she*? Though Richard had been gone for a number of years, she still felt an allegiance to him and still wore her wedding ring. And what about Kip? He seemed to be in awe of Bart as a Genesis Master, but how would he feel if he knew sparks were flying between his mother and his teacher? Since she'd given her son no reason to expect her to date again until he was older, the two of them had never discussed the possibility that she actually might find herself attracted to someone. She had no idea how he felt about such things. But no matter what she might want out of life, Kip and his happiness were her first priority. If Kip wasn't ready to have another man in his life, neither was she. That was the way it had to be, even if it meant giving up her own chance at happiness.

"My mom was surprised when I first told her about you, and that you had a son," he went on, oblivious to the war raging inside her. "But knowing how much you've come to mean to me, and especially that you and I share the same faith, she encouraged me to let you know how I feel." He gave her hands another squeeze. "So I am. I'm crazy about you, Shelley."

Startled yet thrilled by his words, Shelley gazed up at him, her heart ricocheting with love for this man. "I–I'm crazy about you, too, but—"

His finger pivoted around the wedding ring on her finger. "Don't you think it's time you took this off?"

She nibbled on her lip. "Even if I could, Bart, there's still Kip. I don't know how he'd feel about the two of us dating if he knew."

"He may not be as opposed to it as you think. He's making real progress in class, his anger is becoming manageable, he's excited about Genesis, and I think he likes me."

"I'm sure he likes you. In fact, he's in awe of you. But he has no idea you and I are—"

"Drawn to each other?"

"Yes. I'm afraid he's going to be furious when he finds out I've deceived him."

"You haven't deceived him. You just haven't told him about us yet. Kip isn't a baby, Shelley. You have to quit treating him like one. The boy is nearly fifteen and well on his way to manhood. In a few years, he'll be off to college."

A shudder coursed through her body. "Don't remind me. I'm already dreading that day."

"Look, let's just go on with our original plan and see how he reacts when I bring you into his class. In the meantime, I have no intention of giving you up now that I've found you. If Kip decides he doesn't want me around once he finds out about our relationship, I'll back off, even if I have to wait until he's off to college, but I refuse to give up on us. What you and I have is too special to let go."

She lifted misty eyes to his. "You'd really be willing to do that? Wait nearly four years?"

He bent and lovingly kissed her forehead. "Whatever it takes, but I pray it won't be that long." He kissed her again, then tugged her toward the workout room. "We have one more week before you make your debut. I hope you're ready for some real work and lots of homework, because, as your Genesis Master, I'm going to expect your very best. Are you ready?"

"Ready!"

The next week went by quickly, almost too quickly, as Bart pushed Shelley through the final movements she needed to perfect before she stepped onto the floor and faced Kip and his classmates.

Since Kip's friend had invited him to go on a weekend trip with him and his parents the next weekend, Shelley and Bart were able to spend all day Saturday and Sunday together, even further perfecting the moves Shelley had worked so hard to learn, polishing up her technique, and just enjoying one another's company.

"Look what I found in my locker! A brand-new Genesis uniform in just my size!" Shelley pivoted around like a model when the two of them met in his office Monday afternoon before the first class she would attend with Kip. She rose on tiptoe and kissed his cheek. "Oh, thank you, Bart. It fits perfectly, and I especially love the white belt and all it stands for. But I should report you for cruelty. You really put me through my paces over the weekend."

"You look beautiful in it." He gave her a shy grin. "If you're trying to make me feel bad for overworking you, you're succeeding. But I'm proud of you, sweetheart. Not once did you complain. Though you've only been working at this thing a short time, you're way ahead of Kip and the others in his class. I can hardly wait to introduce you. As soon as everyone is here, we'll do it."

She grimaced. "I'm nervous. What if Kip is furious?"

"He may be a little upset at first, but once his friends start making a fuss over you, I think he'll come around. We've prayed about this. We have to trust God to make it work. We can give it all we've got, but only God can touch his heart."

She shrugged. "You're right. I *am* trying to trust God and put Kip in His hands, but sometimes it's hard. He's my baby.

I just want to jump in and help Him."

Bart huffed. "That's the built-in mother instinct in you. God placed it there, so I doubt He's surprised when you try to take control."

"I really do want God's will for Kip's life, and for mine, too, whatever it may be."

"And I'm praying God will let me be a part of both yours and Kip's life." He gave her shoulder a reassuring pat, then lowered his head and closed his eyes. "God, Shelley and I are asking You to help us through these next few minutes. You know our hearts. This whole crazy plan of ours was conceived to help Kip. We've done all we can; now we're asking You to soften his heart and prepare him for the shock he is about to receive. We love You and praise Your name."

Though she tried to hold it back, a tear rolled down her cheek.

Bart brushed aside her tear with the pad of his thumb as he gazed into her lovely face. He knew she was nervous; he was, too, but all the work they had accomplished in preparing for this moment had been done to help her son. His crazy plan had worked with three other teens. He only hoped it would work with Kip. For, in addition to his concern for the boy, he knew if Kip was angry and ran away from him Shelley would run away from him, too, and he couldn't bear the thought. Gathering her up in his arms, he pulled her close, kissing her with a kiss he hoped wouldn't be their last. "Hang on, babe.

Give me two minutes, then come on out. Remember, chin up, head held high, exude confidence. You're a child of the King." Backing away slowly, he left his office, closing the door securely behind him.

Kip and his class were already in place and warming up. The minute they saw Bart approaching, they formed a line that would have made any drill sergeant proud.

"At ease, class. I hope you've all had a good weekend," Bart began, eyeing each member as he slowly walked up and down the line, scanning each one's face. "Today begins our fifth week of training. I'm proud of each of you. You've come a long way, but you still have a lot to learn. Normally, I don't allow a new student to be added to our class once a session has begun, but today I'm going to make an exception. The student I'm referring to has been working long and hard to catch up to where you are now. I think she'll be a great addition to our class."

Kip leaned toward the boy next to him and whispered something Bart couldn't hear. "Would you like to make your comment to the whole class, Morris?"

Kip responded with a sideways grin. "All I said was, 'Great. Another girl.'"

Bart let out a chuckle. "I take it that means you have no interest in girls?"

The other students snickered.

Kip glanced around nervously, obviously embarrassed. "They're okay, I guess."

"Well, don't underestimate girls, Kip. As I'm sure you've noticed, since we have several girls in this class, girls do quite well with Genesis. Let me assure you, our new girl is as enthusiastic about learning Genesis as you are. You could learn a few things from her."

He turned and gestured toward the side door. "She'll be joining us any minute now." *Come on, Shelley. Don't back out on me now!*

To his relief, the door opened and Shelley, looking absolutely gorgeous in the new outfit he'd given her, appeared, chin lifted and head held high, just like he'd told her.

Kip let out loud, "Yeow! That's my mom!"

Chapter 5

Ignoring Kip's surprised outburst, Bart motioned for Shelley to join them. "Class, I'd like you to meet our new student, Shelley Morris."

"Is she really Kip's mom?" a boy standing near the end of the line asked.

Her heart pounding furiously in her chest, Shelley held her breath. *Please, God, don't let Kip be angry.* But from the look on Kip's face, she could tell her entrance had been an absolute blockbuster.

"Yes, she is Kip's mother, but to us, Shelley is merely another class member." He gestured toward Shelley. "Normally, I call each of you by your last name, but since we now have two people named Morris, we'll call our new student by her first name, Shelley."

Bart hitched his head toward the center of the room. "Everyone, take your circle positions. Since you've already warmed up, we'll do a quick round-robin. When I point to you, I want you to perform whatever move I call out."

Everyone hustled into position. Shelley hesitated a moment before crossing the room and taking a place opposite Kip. She wanted so much to go stand by him, but she opted for a place farther away, hoping to give him a chance to adjust to her being there before they actually confronted each other. She tried to keep her eyes off her son as the round-robin began, but she couldn't. Much to her dismay, he avoided eye contact with her. *He's furious with me, just like I thought he'd be. Oh, God, please don't let this cause an even bigger wedge between me and my son. He was just beginning to open up to me.*

As Bart randomly moved from student to student, barking out the name of a move like a commanding general, each person he pointed to did that move to the best of his or her ability, some responding more slowly than others. Some more quickly. Some as though they weren't sure what they were doing. When Bart called out, "Morris! Prepare!" then gave his command, Shelley held her breath. But to her amazement, Kip responded immediately, executing the move exactly as Bart had taught her it should be performed. She almost wanted to applaud.

He called out another student's name, then, whirling around, pointing his finger toward her, he barked out, "Shelley! Punch, drive!" Her response was quick, accurate, just as they'd rehearsed it dozens of times.

"Good job." Bart gave her a thumbs-up.

"Not bad for a girl," one of the bigger boys commented with a tinge of sarcasm.

Bart glanced around the circle. "Anyone think they can do it better? If so, you're welcome to try."

No one offered. For a moment, Shelley was afraid Kip might be the one to challenge her, but he remained in his place, his expression stoic. Bart continued around the circle. "Let's try something else. I want to see how well you remember the things I've told you. Can anyone tell me what the word *karate* means?"

Nearly every hand went up.

"Good. Just to make sure you all remember it, let's say it together. Emp–ty hand," he said slowly and distinctly, with each person joining in. "Now, let's try something a little bit more difficult. Who said, 'Mind and technique become one in true karate'?"

Before Shelley could stop it, her hand shot up, but seeing no other hands lifted, she quickly pulled it down.

Bart pointed toward her again. "You, Shelley, didn't I see your hand go up?"

She winced. "Yes, sir."

"If you know the answer, tell us. Whose quote was that?"

She glanced around the circle and found everyone staring at her, waiting for her answer. Even Kip. "It was Shotokan founder, Gichin Funakoshi, sir."

"Excellent. Can anyone tell me the Japanese names for the three aspects of karate practice?" No one responded. "Come on, people. We learned this the first week." Spinning around toward Shelley again, he asked, "How about you, Shelley? Can you name them?"

She blinked hard. "*Kihon*, which means 'basic,' *Kata*, which means 'forms,' and *Kumite*, which means 'sparring,' sir."

He smiled at her. "Good job, Shelley. I'm glad someone remembered her homework."

"She might know stuff, but I'll bet she can't do the crane

movement!" one of the tougher-looking kids wearing a smirk called out.

"We'll see." Bart walked slowly toward her. "Are you familiar with the crane movement?"

She nodded. "Yes, sir. I think so, sir, though I've only practiced it a few times."

"Then move into position and give it a try."

She *knew* how to do it, had done it successfully in her practices at home as well as at Genesis, but could she actually do it with all these kids staring at her? She hated to make a fool of herself in front of them. Especially Kip. What he was asking of her was not easy.

Bart took one step toward her. "Shelley, go ahead. We're waiting."

The words he'd drilled into her flooded her mind. *"Remember, Genesis is a blending of body and mind. You must put everything else out of your thoughts except what you are doing. Your mind and body have to work together in one fluid movement. Don't let anything or anyone distract you."*

Shelley closed her eyes and mentally replayed the crane technique exactly the way she'd practiced it, the way Bart had shown her it should be done. Then, as swiftly as a well-aimed arrow, she performed the move, landing firmly on one foot in perfect balance.

All sorts of *wows*, *fantastics*, and other exuberant, descriptive terms echoed throughout the group. But no words of praise came from the boy she loved more than life itself.

"Good job, Shelley." After giving her a thumbs-up, Bart

raised his hand and the room instantly became silent again. "At ease, everyone. I'm quite sure Kip's mother's joining our class came as a surprise to you, a pleasant one. I met Shelley several weeks ago, and after hearing she had an interest in beginning an active exercise program to maintain good health, I encouraged her to sign up for this class. However, knowing Kip was already enrolled in Genesis, and not wanting to embarrass him if she couldn't keep up or learn the moves as quickly as the rest of you, she declined. I hated to see her give up so easily, so I offered to work with her, make sure she could do it, and try to bring her up to speed."

After a brief pause, he continued. "Let me assure you, she has worked harder than any of you to get to this point. I'm sure after seeing her performance you all agree she deserves to be here." He gestured around the room. "If any of you have parents who would be interested in Genesis, have them give me a call. Who knows—we might end up with a parents-only class." He gave his hands a slight clap. "Let's take a five-minute break, then get back to work. We have a tournament coming up in a few months. I expect to see some winners from this group, okay?"

Shelley glanced toward Kip, hoping to have a few words with him, but he was surrounded by a cluster of his peers who, no doubt, were talking to him about her.

"Good job, sweetie," Bart whispered with wink as he casually passed by on his way to the drinking fountain. "Couldn't have done better myself."

After what seemed an eternity to Shelley, the class ended

and everyone headed for the locker rooms. With the many enthusiastic compliments she received from the girls in the class, she could only imagine the conversation going on in the men's locker room as she changed into her street clothes. Was Kip proud of her? Or was he laughing and making fun of her behind her back? *Please, God, I've worked so hard for this day. Make Kip realize I did it all for him.*

When she finished changing, Shelley waited in her car, impatiently watching the front door of The Genesis Hut for Kip's appearance. "Good session," she told him, trying to sound casual when he finally crawled in beside her. "Want to stop at Hamburger Haven for supper? I don't know about you, but I'm famished."

Kip stared at her. "I thought you said their hamburgers were too greasy."

She feigned a laugh. "They are greasy, but they sure taste good."

He slumped in his seat, his eyes focused on the traffic entering and exiting the parking lot. "Why'd you do it, Mom? Why my class? You could have joined the women's exercise class. Wouldn't that have been better?"

Shelley chose her words carefully. "You're right. I could have. I—I guess that means you'd rather not have me in *your* class. Your friends didn't seem to mind. Some of them even told me how great I'd done, and you should have heard the girls in the locker room."

"It's kinda embarrassing when your mom is in your class. Sorta like you're checking up on me. Besides, you're too old to be in my class."

Taking her eyes off the road for only a second as she merged into the outgoing line of traffic, she gave him a sideways glance. "Oh, honey, my intention was not to check up on you. I just wanted to share in something you were interested in. It seems you and I have had very little to talk about this past year. If that's the way you feel, I'll quit the class right now."

He spun his head toward her. "No, you can't!"

"Why? I thought you didn't want me there."

"The rest of the guys thought it was cool. You know—you being there and doing all the stuff you did."

"Do—do you think it's cool?"

He shrugged. "Yeah, I guess so."

After a quick glance in the rearview mirror, she pulled the car over to the side, shoved the gearshift into PARK, and turned to Kip. "Look, sweetie, next to God, you're the most important thing in my life. I mean it, Kip, if you want me to drop out of your class, I will. I'm only interested in Genesis because of you. If I simply wanted to exercise, I could buy a secondhand treadmill."

Kip shrugged again. "Naw, you can stay, I guess. I was a little freaked out at first, but I'm okay with it now." He gave her a slightly teasing grin. "Actually, you were pretty good. Better'n any other girls in the class."

Shelley couldn't contain an audible sigh of relief. "You think maybe the two of us could work out together at home sometime?"

Kip laughed. "Only if you teach me that last move. That was great."

"You got it!" After a backward glance, she pulled the car out onto the street and headed toward Hamburger Haven, feeling better about her relationship with her son than she had in a long time. Maybe this crazy Genesis scheme of Bart's would work after all.

"But, Mom, I don't get it," he said as soon as they'd ordered their burgers. "When did you have time to learn all that stuff? You're at your office all day, and you were always home evenings."

"Mornings, before you got out of bed. Five thirty to six thirty, to be exact. That shows how much I love you. You know how I hate to get up any earlier than I have to. And I practiced for at least an hour after you went to bed each night." She sent him a quick smile. "You know, I figured I'd hate Genesis, but I ended up loving it. Though I've only been doing it for a few weeks, I haven't felt this physically fit in a long time, plus I feel strong, powerful, and more confident about myself and my capabilities. Is that the way you feel?"

"Yeah, I do, and I like Mr. Steel. He's a real cool guy."

Shelley grinned. "Yeah, I like him, too."

"So, how do you think it went?" Bart asked Shelley when he phoned later. Since he'd been the one to talk her into this risky idea of his, he'd almost hated to dial her number, afraid her unexpected appearance in class might have caused even more trouble between mother and son.

"Good. It went good. Kip wants me to stay in the class."

Relieved, he leaned back in his chair and propped his feet

on the desk. "You have no idea how thankful I am to hear those words. I knew you were apprehensive, and nervous, too, but you sure did a great job. I was proud of you."

"Thanks for the compliment. If I did well at all, it was because of you and your patience with me. I guess all the money my folks spent on my ballet lessons and gymnastic classes paid off. But I'm sure, especially at first before I got up on that balance beam, you thought I'd be a real klutz."

From the tone of her voice, he could almost see the smile on her face. "Klutz? Never. You were good right from the start. You're the one who did all the work to perfect the techniques. I only guided you. Besides, working out mornings with you has been the highlight of my day. You're not going to stop coming in early and deprive me of your company, are you?"

"You think I should continue?"

"Selfishly, yes. I like starting out my day with you."

"I like starting my day out with you, too, but now that I've caught up with Kip's class—"

"You've become important to me, Shelley. I'm really going to miss our private times together." Gathering up his courage, he plodded on. "Of course, if you'd rather not get up so early, there is an alternative. We could officially start dating."

There was a pause on the other end. "I've really enjoyed our times together, too, the movie and all, but I'm just not sure how Kip would feel about us spending time together, now that it's no longer necessary. I've told you about the promise I've made to him."

"Don't you think that promise is a bit extreme? Boys need

a positive male influence in their lives. I know I did."

"I'm not sure about that. I've seen what can happen when a new man enters a boy's life. Several of my friends with boys Kip's age, who have either dated or remarried after losing their husbands, have had nothing but trouble. Most of them say if they could do it all over again they wouldn't have remarried, or even dated, until their children were grown. God entrusted Kip into my care, Bart. I have to do what's right for him."

"Even if it means forsaking your own happiness?"

"Yes, even then."

He gave his head a shake. "Before taking such dire measures, maybe you should get Kip's opinion."

"Maybe. But I'm afraid even bringing up the subject might make him think I was considering breaking my promise. Especially now that his attitude is changing and the two of us are beginning to get along like a mother and son should."

"So you're telling me it's over between us? For at least the next four years? We can't spend any time together? The only time we'll see each other is in class?"

The silence on the other end of the phone gave him his answer even before she spoke.

Though it broke Shelley's heart to have to be truthful with Bart, it wasn't right to string him along when, as far as she was concerned, the relationship they both longed for had to be put on hold. "Yes, Bart. As much as I hate it, I guess that's what I'm saying. Please try to understand. It's not that I'm not in love with you. I am. I'm crazy in love with you, but, at least for now, Kip comes first—in everything."

He harrumphed. "Then I guess we'd better say good night. I'll see you in class tomorrow. That is, unless you've decided you're putting some kind of hold on that, too."

"All I'm trying to do is delay things. For how long, I don't know. Kip wants me to stay in class, so unless you'd prefer I didn't, I'll be there." She said good-bye, then slowly placed the phone back in its cradle. *Lord, if I'm doing the right thing, why am I so miserable?*

Though Shelley laughed and put on a happy face as she joined in with Kip and the others in class the next day, inside she was heartsick and a bundle of nerves. Bart treated her just like any other student, taking her to task when she did things wrong and giving her routine words of praise when she did something right. It was apparent she was no longer his *special* student but merely, like everyone else who attended, one of the group.

Other than the few times she found him gazing at her, it was as if the love between them had never existed. Wasn't that the way she wanted it? Hadn't she been the one to tell him their love had to be put on hold? How could it be put on hold if they continued to see one another, kiss, and hold each other in their arms? She wanted to run out of there, put on her street clothes, get into her car, and never look back. But when class was over and she and Kip were in the car riding toward home, and he turned to her and told her how glad he was that she was taking

Genesis with him, her desire to escape suddenly disappeared.

"I mean it, Mom," he went on, his face bearing evidence of his enthusiasm. "You should have heard all the kids at school talking about you today. Even the girls were impressed that my mom is taking Genesis. I told them you were going to enter the tournament."

Shelley nearly choked. "Enter the tournament? Me?"

Kip grinned at her. "Yeah. The one Master Bart hosts at the end of each session. You're pretty good. Maybe you'll win a plaque or one of those gold cup things."

Her grip tightened on the steering wheel, her forehead creasing into a scowl. "I don't think so, sweetie. I didn't get into this thing to enter a contest—only to be with you."

"But, Mom, you *could* win. I know you could. If we work out together at home, maybe we'll both win plaques. Wouldn't that be great? We could put them on the mantel."

Shelley cast a quick glance his way. For the first time in months, he seemed happy. Honestly happy. How could she deny him this one simple request? She'd hoped, since temporarily breaking things off with Bart, that after a few weeks she could silently drop out of class and get back to her normal routine of being a working mom, her newfound amicable relationship with her son would continue, and things between them would be fine. Entering a tournament had not been in her plans. "Yeah, great, but I—I don't know—"

"Come on, Mom. Say you'll do it. It'll be fun." He grinned over at her, his smile beaming like one of those toothpaste ads. "You've got to. I've already told the guys."

You're in this far—you can't back out now, she tried to convince herself. *Not with Kip singing your praises and begging you to compete.* "Okay, I'll do it. *But my heart will be breaking each time I look at Bart.* "Just promise you won't be too disappointed if neither of us wins."

"I promise." Kip held up his hand, palm toward her. "Give me five, Mom."

The next eight weeks were filled with both agony and ecstasy. Agony, as Shelley faced Bart in class three afternoons a week, knowing she'd pushed aside the finest, most decent man she'd met in a long time. And ecstasy, as she watched her son mature into the caring, respectful, well-disciplined young man she had hoped he would become. And Bart, with his godly example, was the cause of both.

Each day as she gazed at this man of power and strength, her heart ached. It was all she could do to keep from running to him, throwing her arms about his neck, and kissing his handsome face. She wanted nothing more than to tell him how wrong she'd been to put a hold on the love they shared. But she couldn't. Just the thought of what might have happened if she'd gone back on the promise she'd made to Kip and he'd responded negatively was enough to keep her aching in silence.

"It's only two weeks until our tournament," Bart reminded his class as he stood before them, carefully eyeing each member. "We still have a lot of work to do. Many of the karate schools we will be competing against think the Genesis technique is for sissies, that it is only for those who are too weak and inept to learn karate. Our goal is to be a testimony for our Lord and show them they're wrong—we're strong in Him and because of Him. I'm expecting great things from each of you, but let me warn you, the competition will be fierce. Those competing against us have had excellent training, and they want to win as much as we do. Though winning isn't everything, it *is* a symbol of the many hours of practice and hard work you have put in to getting where you are today. As I've told you before, it's not always the person with the most strength who wins. The true opponent is one's self." He gave his hands a loud clap. "Now, let's get busy."

Shelley took her place near one of the older girls, distancing herself from her son who was still reveling in his new set of friends.

"Shelley, watch your form!" Bart barked out, his gaze zeroing in on her. "You're rushing things and leaving yourself wide open!"

She gave him a nod, then watched as he moved across the room, coming to stand directly in front of Kip, perching his hands on his hips. "Morris, how many times do I have to tell you to keep that left hand up? This is no time to get careless. Remember, we'll be representing our Lord at that tournament."

Instantly, Kip raised his hand a bit higher.

"No, not like that!" Bart moved in close, coming nearly nose to nose with the boy, grabbing hold of his arm. "Like this, and keep your eyes trained on your opponent. Your work is getting sloppy. You have to be ready at all times. Remember the things I've taught you."

Shelley felt her anger rise nearly to the bubbling-over point.

Was Bart deliberating picking on her and Kip? It seemed every day he was finding more fault with them than with the others. She wanted to rush across the room and tell him to bug off her son or she'd—she'd what? She was no match for him. Instead, she clenched her fists at her sides, bit her lip, and bottled up the words she'd like to say. Rushing to her son's aid like a mother hen would only embarrass him and might cause her to lose whatever ground she'd gained.

Unfortunately, the remainder of the week was no better as Bart continued to be on both hers and Kip's back. Finally, when she could stand it no longer, she decided to speak to Kip about it.

His eyes widened with surprise. "You think Master Bart is picking on me?"

"Don't you?"

He gave his head a shake. "No. I'm glad he tells me when I goof up. He's always telling me he thinks I have the makings of a champion. The guy really knows what he's doing, Mom. He's a great teacher. Have you seen all the awards and plaques in his office?"

She gave her chin a haughty tilt. "That doesn't give him the right to embarrass you."

He shrugged. "Embarrass me? Why should I be embarrassed? He's only trying to make me better."

She decided to let the subject drop. It was obvious Kip was too in awe of Bart to even notice. Saying more would only upset him.

At the end of Monday's class, Bart motioned her into his

office. "Shelley, you have got to quit coddling Kip. I think you're the reason he holds back and loses his focus."

Her jaw dropped. "Me!"

He nodded. "Yes, you. I see the look on your face when you're afraid he's going to get hurt or lose a match. The other boys have seen it, too, and they're beginning to tease him about it. You're much too possessive with him. Like it or not, Kip is well on his way to becoming a man."

Jutting out her chin, she firmly planted her balled-up fists on her hips. "You pick on him, Bart! You pick on me, too. What are you doing? Trying to drive us both out of your class?"

His gaze softened. "Is that what you think I'm doing?"

"Aren't you?"

"Of course not. How can you say such a thing?" He moved toward her and reached for her hand, but she pulled it away. "You're the one who turned *me* away. And it hurt, Shelley. You have no idea how much it hurt. I could never turn you away. One indication from you that you want me to wait for you is all I ask and I will. I don't care how long it takes. I love you. I want to marry you, sweetheart. I want us to be a family." He sent an impatient glance toward the nearly closed door where one of the boy's faces peeked through the open crack. "What is it, Benningfield? Can't you see I'm busy?"

The boy screwed up his face. "Sorry, sir. My mom washed my uniform. I—I left it at home."

"Call your mother and see if she can bring it over." He gestured toward the door. "And close the door behind you."

Not sure exactly how to respond to Bart's words, Shelley

moved toward the door, needing to put some space between them, but he caught hold of her wrist. "Not so fast. We're not through yet."

"I'm sorry, Bart. Maybe I did overreact, but you know how concerned I am about Kip."

"We have to talk about this, Shelley. I can't go on behaving as though there is nothing between us. I, at least, have to see you, spend time with you." He relaxed his grip. "I've been giving our situation a lot of thought. Kip likes me; I know he does. I think he'd be more receptive to the two of us dating than you think."

"Look, Bart. I've considered that possibility time and time again. And you're right. At first he might be receptive, maybe even happy about the two of us dating, but what about later on, after the newness has worn off and he begins to resent you for taking my time? Time he feels belongs to him?" She tried unsuccessfully to tug her arm away from him. "Don't you see, Bart? I may be a woman who desires the love of a good man, but first and foremost, I'm a mother. I can't risk losing my son. Not when we've come this far. If we did see each other, behind his back, and Kip found out, it could be disastrous. I can't take that chance."

His gaze softening, he let go of her. "Have you prayed about it, Shelley? About you and me? Or have you decided *you* know better than God what is best for the three of us?"

His question hit her right in the gut and took her breath away. Though for weeks nearly every waking thought had been of Bart, her prayers had been that Kip wouldn't discover her relationship with Bart and be upset about it. As usual, *she* had been deciding what God should do. In all honesty, she really hadn't asked God to reveal *His* perfect plan for their lives. But her pride wouldn't allow her to admit it to Bart. "I have to go. Kip's waiting for me."

"Shelley, if you're half as crazy about me as I am about you—"

"Please, Bart. Don't even say it. I can't—we can't—" Fighting back the explosion of tears that threatened to erupt, she pushed past him, nearly knocking over a chair. "I've got to go. Kip is waiting for me." Before he could respond, she hurried through the door, shutting it firmly behind her.

The day of the tournament finally arrived, with the students from three other Denver martial arts schools participating. Shelley was as nervous as a first-time parachutist as she warmed up side by side with Kip and the other members of their class.

"Hey, Kip, too bad your mom turned Master Bart down when he asked her to marry him," Jimmy Wright, one of the boys, said mockingly, giving Kip a slap on the shoulder. "He'd make a great dad."

Shelley caught a quick intake of breath. How did Jimmy know? They'd been so careful.

Kip let out a snort. "Come on, Jimmy, quit the joking. My mom barely knows Master Bart. Besides, she never dates anybody."

"That's not the way I heard it. My big sister saw the two of them at the movies. And remember that weird little redheaded guy who bugs us all the time? He said he heard Master Bart ask her to marry him a couple of weeks ago when he went to his office to tell him he'd forgotten his suit."

"Don't you think I'd know if my mom was dating someone?" Kip literally snarled the words.

Shelley stood as still as a stone, her pulse racing.

Jimmy shrugged. "That's what I heard. Maybe you'd better ask your mom."

Kip whirled toward his mother. "That's not true, is it, Mom? You haven't been dating Master Bart, have you?"

He'd asked her an outright question. She couldn't lie to him. "It's—sorta true."

He gave her a cold stare. "You promised you weren't going to date anyone, and you've been dating my teacher?"

"It was only once, and it wasn't exactly a date. Just a movie."

"Okay, everyone," Bart said into his megaphone, unaware of the conversation taking place. "Get to your places. We're ready to start."

Shelley leaned toward Kip. "It's not what you think, Kip."

Narrowing his eyes, he glared at her. "You lied to me."

"I didn't lie, Kip. I just didn't—"

Giving his head a shake, he moved along with the rest of the class, leaving her standing alone, her heart wadding up into a thick ball.

Shelley hurried to join their group, then took the only empty seat left in their section as the tournament began. If only she could talk to Kip, try to explain, but he avoided all eye contact with her.

It seemed like hours before their division was called. Finally, Kip's name was announced. Shelley held her breath as he walked toward his opponent. The boy he'd been matched up with was a good three inches taller and bigger boned. *Lord, protect my son, please! Don't let him get hurt.*

After the two bowed to one another, the match began. Though the boy was the bigger of the two, Kip's quickness and agile footwork seemed to give him the advantage. Shelley cheered with all the others when he scored the first point. It looked like he would score the second point, too, but when he ended up doing all the wrong things, the point easily went to the other boy. For the first time, Kip glanced in her direction. Shelley could tell by the way his shoulders sagged and by the sadness in his eyes that his mind wasn't where it should be. It was still on her deception.

"Come on, Kip! You can do it! Concentrate!" she yelled out, wanting him to win so badly she could taste it.

But Kip didn't do it, and his opponent scored a second point. Though Kip danced around and made a few jabs, none of them protected him when the bigger boy moved in for the finish and sent him to the mat, claiming the winning point.

Shelley ached for her son. What disappointment he must feel. He'd worked so hard for this moment—trained for it—and he'd been good. Even with the size difference, he should have been able to win. But he hadn't. Kip had lost, and there was no doubt in her mind she was the cause of it. If only Jimmy had kept his mouth shut, at least until after the tournament. But in her heart, she knew the blame for Kip's loss hadn't been with

Jimmy. The real question was, why hadn't she been honest with her son? She glanced Kip's way, hoping to get his attention and at least be able to mouth *I love you* to him, but he was sitting scrunched down in his seat, his hands cupped around his head, staring at the floor.

To her surprise, they called her name out next. "We're behind, Shelley. We need your win," Bart whispered as she passed him in an almost daze. "Even if you don't want to do it for me, do it for Kip and our school."

She gave a slight huff. The only reason she'd consented to this crazy scheme was to help her son, and he'd lost. And, from the look on his face, ended up angry and devastated. Why should she even bother to compete?

She was about to throw her hands up in defeat and frustration and leave the floor, conceding her match before it began, when a chant broke out behind her. In unison, the members of her class were saying, "Go, Shelley, go. Go, Shelley, go. Go, Shelley, go." How could she let them down? Every day, she'd worked out beside these kids, made friends with them, struggled to achieve with them. She looked around for Kip, but his chair was empty. Where was he? Had he gone to the restroom? Or was he off nursing his wounds, maybe waiting in the car in the parking lot, too embarrassed by his overwhelming loss to face everyone?

Drawing in a deep breath, Shelley moved to take her place in front of her opponent, a stocky-looking girl with a long, dark ponytail, heavy eyebrows, and squinted eyes that said she meant business. The girl stared at her as if she were dirt, then snarled, "Hey, Granny, who let you out of the care home? Where'd you park your wheelchair?"

Shelley bit back the snappy retort just waiting to escape her lips as Bart's words again came to her mind. "In Genesis, we must always keep in mind that the true opponent is oneself." *I have to do this. I have to. Those kids are counting on me. Bart's counting on me. Concentrate, Shelley. You can't wimp out now, not when you've put so much into this thing. Erase everything else from your mind. Even Kip's loss. This is your time to prove yourself. Win—or lose—give it your best shot. Don't let your son think of you as a quitter.*

Keeping her face devoid of expression and lifting her chin high, she bowed low to her opponent, her heart pounding so loudly she was sure the girl could hear it and sense how afraid she was.

"Remember what you've learned!" she heard Bart say from the sidelines. "You can do it. I know you can!"

Though she concentrated with all her might, the first point went to her opponent. Though unnerved by the sudden blow she'd experienced, keeping her guard up, she backed away to regroup.

"The next point is yours! Go for it!" she heard Bart say. His confidence in her gave her new courage. *I can do this. I know I can.*

Using some of the footwork she'd learned, she danced her way around her opponent, all the time jabbing, keeping her opponent at bay, looking for that tiny window of time to make her move, as Bart had emphasized in every class she'd taken from him. After ducking to avoid a driving thrust that set her opponent momentarily off balance and open, Shelley made her move.

"Point!" the referee said.

She'd done it. The score was tied!

Her opponent gave her an empty stare, apparently shocked and surprised that she'd moved so quickly. Seemingly fazed, for one brief second, the girl let her guard down again, giving Shelley another chance for a quick jab, and a second point became hers.

"One more, Shelley!" Bart's excited voice boomed out. "One more, and the match is yours!"

Trying to clear her mind of thoughts of Kip and his loss, Shelley moved to the edge of their area. After a deep, cleansing breath, she took a few quick steps, then lunged forward, hoping to land another unexpected jab. But the girl was ready for her and sidestepped. She had to change her strategy. But how? What move would win her the next point?

"Use your specialty!" Bart's voice came from the sidelines.

Backing quickly away, Shelley sent a quick glance his way; then, her gaze locking on her opponent, her eyes daring the girl to come at her, she moved several steps backward, lifted her arms high, her hands drooping from her wrists, and balanced herself on one foot. Just as Shelley hoped, the girl came at her with all her might, determination to keep her from scoring the winning point evident in her eyes. She waited until the teenager had nearly reached her before using the power of her balancing leg to thrust herself into the air and contact the girl with her free leg with such force it knocked her to the floor.

"Point!"

She'd done it! She'd won her match! And although she was hysterically happy to be the winner, the *mother* instinct in her made her go to her opponent and assist her to her feet. "Sorry," she said, meaning it from the depths of her heart as she reached out her hand. "I hope I didn't hurt you." She hated it that someone had to lose in order for her to win.

The girl looked at her as if she had three heads, then, avoiding her hand and giving a growl, headed back to her chair, her face distorted with anger and disappointment.

"Great job, Shelley," Bart told her proudly as he wrapped his arm around her shoulders and they moved back to the area assigned to her class. "You did everything just right. Your winning match put us in a tie for first place. With a couple more matches yet to come, we may even surge ahead."

At that moment, his praise meant nothing to her, nor did the praise of her class members. All she had on her mind was her son. "Where's Kip? Have you seen him?"

Bart shrugged. "I don't know. I haven't seen him since he left the floor."

Her win paled at his words. She had to find her son. Without waiting to watch the final match, Shelley hurried toward the locker rooms. "Where's Kip?" she asked the man who had been assisting the boys with their uniforms.

He lifted his shoulders in a shrug. "Don't know. He came running through here after his match, but he never stopped. He was pretty upset. I figured he was headin' for home."

A WINNING MATCH

Shelley rushed into the women's locker room long enough to grab her purse and her clothes, then headed for her car, but Kip wasn't there either. Frantic to find him, she leaped behind the steering wheel and raced toward their house.

But the house was empty.

Where was he?

Chapter 6

Shelley startled as the phone rang, then snatched it up, expecting it to be Kip. "Kip! Where are you?"

"It's not Kip. It's me. I saw you rush out. I was hoping he was with you. Some of his friends said he was really upset."

"Oh, Bart, I have no idea where he is, and he's furious with me." Despite her efforts to hold them back, tears of concern gushed forth. "I'm the reason he lost his match."

"You? Why? Why would he blame you? The poor kid must have lost his confidence. He did everything wrong. He can't blame you for that."

"I should never have let myself get involved with you." Shelley grabbed hold of the desk for support. "He knows, Bart. Remember that boy who came to your office about leaving his suit at home? He overheard us talking and told another boy, and that boy told Kip everything, right before his match. I heard him."

"Did Kip ask you about it?"

"Yes. I—I couldn't lie."

"Whew, no wonder he did so poorly. That sure explains it. He's got to be upset with both of us. Do you have any idea where he might be?"

100

Shelley swallowed at the lump nearly blocking her airway. "No, and I'm so worried. You didn't see the look on his face. He trusted me, and I let him down."

"Stay by the phone in case he calls or comes home. I'll see if I can find him. Maybe he's gone somewhere quiet to think things over. And, Shelley—"

"What?"

"Pray and have faith. Ask God to be with him. Call my cell phone if you hear anything."

With a heavy heart, she trudged her way toward the window and pulled the curtain aside, all the while praying for her son's safe return. Although a light rain had been falling most of the day, the wind had picked up, and the rain had turned into a downpour. The sky had filled with black ominous-looking clouds, and it was beginning to get dark. Had Kip worn a jacket? She couldn't remember. "Come home, Kip. Please come home!"

She switched on the desk lamp, then grabbed the phone book and called the home of every friend of Kip's she could think of, but no one had heard from him. After dialing Bart's cell phone and learning he hadn't heard from him yet either, she fell to her knees, begging God to bring her boy back to her.

Eight o'clock came, then nine. Still no Kip. She was ready to phone the police when she heard the front door open. Turning quickly, her heart thundering, she gazed into the saddened eyes of her son. "Kip, where have you been? I've been worried half out of my mind!"

Bart stepped inside, closed the door behind him, then put a hand on the boy's shoulder. "When I stopped by my place to get my raincoat, I found him. He was sitting on my porch steps, drenched through to his skin."

Shelley grabbed Kip's hand. "Why did you go to Bart's house? You should have come home."

Kip lowered his eyes, avoiding her gaze.

"He wanted to talk to me, Shelley. To see if what that boy had told him was true. I explained the whole thing. How the two of us met in Principal Taylor's office, arranged to have me teach you Genesis, and how you joined the class, about the movie, all of it." Bart gave her a shy grin. "Even the part about me falling in love with you and asking you to marry me."

She felt breathless, as if the wind had been knocked out of her.

"I explained that the entire thing had been planned with his good in mind. Our intention was to create a better relationship between the two of you. That was all. Neither of us expected the attraction that developed between us. It just happened."

Moving up close to her son, Shelley met his gaze at eye level. "I love you, Kip. The last thing I'd want to do is hurt you; don't you realize that?"

Kip continued to stare at the floor. "You lied to me, Mom."

"I didn't exactly lie. I just kept things from you. Bart and I only went out together that one time. To see a movie about karate."

Kip nodded. "Yeah, I know. Master Bart told me all of that."

"Why go to Bart, Kip? I would have told you the same thing if you'd asked me."

Bart's brow creased. "Kip had something else on his mind, too."

Shelley looked from Kip to Bart and back again. What else could there be? Had something happened she didn't know about? Was Kip in some kind of trouble?

Bart gently grabbed hold of Kip's forearm. "You want to tell her, or you want me to?"

Kip bit at his lip. "Naw, I'll tell her." Lifting his chin and squaring his shoulders, he looked directly at Shelley. "Mom, I owe you an apology. I let you, Master Bart, and my whole team down this afternoon. I admit I was mad at both of you when that kid told me what he'd found out about you guys, but I knew how important winning that tournament was to everyone. I had no right letting my anger get in the way. I should have remembered what Master Bart had told us over and over again. 'In Genesis, we must always keep in mind that the true opponent is oneself.' That kid didn't defeat me. I defeated myself by not keeping my mind focused on what I was doing. I could have won that match if I had. I know I could. I've already apologized to Master Bart, and I'm going to apologize to the others at our next class." He paused and swallowed hard. "I know how hard you worked, Mom, and I blew it for you, Master Bart, and everyone else. Can you forgive me?"

In that instant, Shelley realized Kip was no longer a child but well on his way to becoming a mature young adult. Unable to resist, though she feared her actions might embarrass him, she threw her arms around him and kissed his cheek. "Of course I forgive you, sweetie. Can you forgive me for not being up-front with you? I swear I'll never do anything like that again. From now on, it'll be just you and me. Just like I said it would."

He nodded. "But I *want* you to date Master Bart, Mom. He's the coolest guy I've ever met. Besides, he's a Christian. That should make you happy."

Shelley did a double take. "You want us to date? Really?"

A smile played at Kip's lips. "Yeah, really." Then glancing up at Bart, he added, "I wouldn't even mind having him as a stepdad."

She felt herself blush. "Let's not rush things. I know you respect Bart as your teacher, but—"

Bart released his hold on Kip and circled his arm around her waist, smiling down at her. "Kip and I have talked this whole situation over, man-to-man. I told him the last thing I wanted was to come between the two of you. I promised if you would agree, since Kip says he's okay with us dating, we would take it slow and easy. But, if at any time he was uncomfortable with us being together, I'd back off and get out of your lives."

"And I want us both to stay in Master Bart's Genesis class, Mom. He said you won your match. I'm really proud of you. I should have stayed to watch instead of running off like that." The smile Kip gave her warmed her heart and assured her everything was going to be okay. "In the next tournament, I'm gonna win, too."

Bart tightened his arm, giving her a little squeeze. "And I'm sure he will. By the way, in case either of you are interested. . ." He paused, his face taking on a gigantic smile. "We did well in every division. Thanks to the hard work of all our students, The Genesis Hut won the tournament!"

Kip let out a "Yee haw!" and then gave Bart a high five.

His happy response made Shelley happy, too. The points she made had contributed to their win.

Later, after Kip had gone to take a shower and Bart prepared to leave, he took Shelley's hands in his and gazed into her eyes. "There for a while, I thought we'd gone too far when we'd implemented phase two, but I guess God used it despite our bungling. From here on out, I think the three of us are going to get along just fine, Shelley."

"I've made so many mistakes," she confessed, her heart thudding inside her. "Instead of trusting God, I was trying to do everything by myself. You were right, Bart. I *was* coddling my son. Trying to keep him a baby, I guess. It's a wonder he had anything to do with me. Poor guy probably felt like he was being smothered."

"You were only doing what you thought was right. Raising a son alone has to be an awesome job. I'd like to share that responsibility with you." Lifting her face to meet his, he gently kissed her lips. "I really do want to marry you, sweetheart. And Kip needs a man in his life. I want to be that man. I love you, Shelley Morris."

For the first time in months, Shelley felt at peace—with God and with herself—and relieved to have their relationship out in the open. She'd turned everything over to God now, like she should have done in the first place. Whatever happened from here on out was in His hands. "I love you, too, Bart. And

I love God for bringing the two of us together."

"I'm going shopping for an engagement ring tomorrow, my love," he whispered into her ear as he held her close. "The day you tell me you're ready, I'll slip it onto your finger."

For Shelley, the next few months were sheer bliss as she and Bart spent every possible moment together, laughing, talking, enjoying one another's company, and getting to know every little detail about each other. As often as Kip could, when his homework or school activities didn't get in the way, he was with them, too. In some ways, to Shelley, it almost seemed as if they were already a family.

When her birthday came, the three of them gathered around a table at Tom's Pizzeria to celebrate.

"Happy birthday, sweetheart," Bart told her, once their pizza had been consumed. After a wink to Kip, he handed her a beautifully wrapped box. "This is from Kip and me. We went shopping for it together."

Kip grinned at her, his eyes filled with anticipation. "Yeah, Mom, open it. I think you'll like it."

She eyed first one, then the other. The thought of the two men in her life shopping together for her gift brought tears to her eyes. Swallowing her emotions, she untied the filmy red ribbon and opened the lid. "Oh, it's a new Bible!"

Kip let out a snicker. "We got a red one 'cause a Bible is supposed to be read. Get it, Mom? Red? Read?"

She rolled her eyes. "Yeah, I get it, and I love it. My old

Bible is in pretty bad shape."

Bart gave her arm a nudge. "We kinda figured that, especially when all those loose pages fell out and fluttered into the aisle during the morning service at church last week."

Shelley grabbed her son's hand, then Bart's. "Thanks, guys. I love it, and I promise I'll take good care of it. Each time I read it, I'll think about the two most important people in my life who were thoughtful enough to give it to me."

Kip pointed to a spot in the lower right-hand corner of the Bible's cover. "The man at the bookstore said after you and Bart get married that you can bring it in and he'll put your name on it. We didn't think you'd want Shelley Morris on it when you're gonna be Shelley Steel soon."

Shelley let out a little gasp. "You're ready for us to get married?"

Ignoring her question, he grinned. "We've got another present for you, too." Kip nodded toward Bart. "Go ahead. Give it to her."

Bart reached into his pocket and pulled out a small velvet box.

Just the sight of it made Shelley's heart sing and rendered her speechless.

"Kip helped me pick this out, too." His expression filled with love, Bart slowly opened the lid and pulled out a lovely engagement ring with several sparkling diamonds set into a simple gold band. "I love you, Shelley, and I want nothing more out of life than to spend it with you. Will you marry me? Become my bride?"

Kip grabbed her arm, his face beaming with happiness. "Go ahead, Mom; say yes!"

Shelley felt faint. This was all too much to comprehend.

"Shelley! Sweetheart! Are you okay?" Bart quickly circled his arm around her and drew her close, his expression one of concern.

Sucking in a big gulp of air, she smiled up at him. "I'm fine. Just a little shaken. I—I never expected this—so soon."

Kip squeezed her arm impatiently. "Mom, are you gonna say yes or not?"

Taking in another gulp of air, then smiling so wide she thought sure her lips would crack, Shelley reached her left hand toward Bart and spread her fingers wide. "I'd love to marry you, my darling."

With Kip looking on as though he were about to grab the ring himself if Bart didn't hurry, Bart placed it on Shelley's finger. "This is a symbol of my love and devotion, dear Shelley, my precious one. Each time you look at it, may you be reminded of the man who loves you and wants to spend the rest of his life with you." Pulling her into his arms, he kissed her as she'd longed to be kissed from the first time their lips had met, with a long, slow kiss that sent a tingle rushing through her head, making her woozy.

"Yes!" She heard Kip shout as she reveled in Bart's embrace. Next, she heard applause. Opening one eye, she caught sight of a whole table full of pizza eaters, each enthusiastically applauding. Soon all of the restaurant's patrons were applauding.

Slowly pulling away from her, Bart, his face bearing a slight blush, took several long, low bows. "Thank you, one and all. This lovely woman just allowed me to place an engagement ring on her finger. I'm sure each of you wishes us the greatest of happiness. Now, if you don't mind, I'm gonna to kiss her again."

"Attaboy!" Kip hollered. "Go for it, Master Bart."

And Bart did.

"Okay, when are we gonna have this wedding?" Kip asked when the three piled into Bart's car and headed for home.

Bart grinned at Kip's image in the rearview mirror. "When do you think we should have it?"

"How about next week?"

Shelley let out an audible gasp. "Next week? No way. Planning a wedding takes months."

Bart reached across and grabbed her hand. "I'm with Kip. Next week is fine with me!"

"You two are incorrigible."

Kip snapped his fingers loudly. "I've got it! You guys got engaged on Mom's birthday. How about getting married on mine? It's two months away."

Shelley gave it some thought. "That'd sure be better than next week."

Bart shrugged. "I've waited this long. I guess I can wait two more months."

"Then it's settled. The wedding's gonna be on my birthday. I think we should invite everyone at The Genesis Hut. Students, teachers, parents—everyone."

"Whoa there, partner. That's a whole bunch of people. We'll

want to invite the members of our church, too," Bart added. "As well as family members and business associates. Let's not get carried away."

"You're not going to wear one of those dumb, long, white dresses with all that stuff on it, are you, Mom?"

She struck a thoughtful pose. "Um, they say it's not proper to wear white for your second marriage, so maybe I'll wear beige or pale pink."

Bart frowned. "This may not be *your* first wedding, but it's mine. I always envisioned my bride wearing a beautiful white gown." He sent Kip a teasing smile. "The *big* white one with all that stuff on it."

Shelley gave him a playful swat. "Let me think it over. We don't have to decide right now. I'll call Callie Norton, the wedding planner from Blest Be the Tie, and get her opinion. I've heard great things about her."

Bart sent her an adoring smile. "Whatever kind of wedding you want is what I want, too, and wear whatever you like. White, pink, purple—even red. As long as you say 'I do' when Pastor Glendale asks, that's all I care about."

"Yeah, Mom, I agree with what Master Bart says."

Bart gave his head a shake. "Kip. You have got to stop calling me Master Bart. That's okay in class, but we're going to be a family now. Drop the *Master* part, okay?"

Kip grinned. "Okay—Bart."

"It'd look kind of silly for my best man to be calling me Master Bart."

The boy did a double take. "Your best man? Me? Really?"

"Can't think of a better guy for the job." Bart turned his head and smiled at Kip. "You will do it, won't you?"

Kip beamed. "You bet! Wait'll the guys hear about this. It's gonna blow them away."

Shelley grabbed Bart's arm. "You really didn't have to ask Kip—"

"Hey, I wouldn't have asked him if I hadn't wanted him."

Shelley smiled to herself as she leaned back in the seat, remembering the day she'd walked into Principal Taylor's office and met Bart—and how resentful she'd been when he was invited to sit in on their session. Yet he'd been the very one who had brought Kip out of his funk and taught him discipline and respect. *The Lord works in mysterious ways, His wonders to perform,* she told herself with an appreciative glance toward her son. *Only God could have thought to work things out this way. And now we're going to be a family.*

The following weeks were filled with a flurry of happy activity as Shelley spent as much time with Bart as possible, making sure there was still plenty of time worked in for Kip, as well. As her son had requested, the two of them continued to take Genesis lessons from Bart, which, to Shelley's joy, brought the three of them even closer together.

"I know you're trying to keep expenses down," Callie Norton told her as the two sat in her office going over the budget Shelley had set for their wedding. "But a lot of people are going to attend this wedding. If I were you, I'd skip some of the frills, like using too many attendants, banking the church with too many flowers, giving extravagant gifts to your wedding party, extra fancy and expensive invitations, that sort of thing. Most people don't remember those things anyway, but they will remember how you look in your beautiful white gown and how handsome Bart will look in his tuxedo."

Shelley screwed up her face. "You *really* think I should wear white? Since this isn't my first wedding? I—I don't want to upset people."

"I'd say if Bart wants you to wear white, that's all that matters. I wouldn't worry about it. Brides wear all sorts of weird things these days, but a traditional white gown is always acceptable."

Shelley gave her a demure smile. "Then white it is. White, with lots of beads and lace."

"How's your son taking all of this? Kip? That's his name, isn't it?"

"I've never seen him this excited about anything. All he can talk about is the fact that he's going to have a father. And he's really excited that Bart wants him to be his best man."

"That's a wonderful tribute to your son." Callie opened a big book containing pictures of wedding cakes and pushed it across the table toward her. "From all I've heard about the man you're marrying, he's going to make a wonderful father for your boy."

Shelley gazed dreamily at the elaborate cakes on the page. "He is. Having Bart in Kip's life is exactly what he's needed. I only wish I'd been smart enough to realize it."

Callie cupped her hand over Shelley's. "You're a Christian.

You know how important God's timing is. Maybe this is the right time for the three of you. The time of God's own choosing."

Smiling up at Callie, she bobbed her head. "Those were Bart's very thoughts."

With Kip at his side, Bart wandered into the formal shop, then glanced around, amazed at the selection. He'd had no idea tuxedos came in so many styles and colors. To him, plain old black would have been a great choice, but not to Shelley. She wanted white.

"There you are. You're early."

He spun around as a pretty young blond approached him. "You must be Callie."

She nodded. "Guilty. And I take it you are Bart and this is Kip. Have you two had a chance to look over the tuxedos?"

Bart groaned. "Not really. Can you imagine? Shelley wants us to wear white ones. She said if she's going to wear white, we have to wear white, too." He nodded toward Kip. "Neither of us is too thrilled about it, but if that's what she wants, white it is."

"White is always nice. Let's take a look at some of the choices."

"Whew," Bart said later, placing his hand on Kip's shoulder as they seated themselves in his car. "I had no idea picking out tuxedos was going to be so difficult." He glanced down at his chest. "Somehow, I can't see myself in a ruffled shirt, especially a pink one."

Kip frowned. "Yuk. Me either."

"But we don't want to disappoint your mom."

"I know."

"So, I guess it's white tuxedos and pink ruffled shirts, old buddy."

"Unless—"

Bart turned toward him. "Unless what?"

The boy's face lit up. "I have an idea that I think will make all of us happy!"

Quickly caught up in his future stepson's sudden excitement, Bart smiled back. "So? What is it? Tell me. I'm wide open to suggestions."

Chapter 7

Happy birthday, sweetie." Shelley placed a breakfast tray on her son's bedside table, then moved to open the blinds, letting in the sunshine of a beautiful morning. "Time to rise and shine. This is a big day for both of us."

Kip sat up in bed, rubbed his eyes, then gave her a teasing smile. "What'd you get me for my birthday? A car?"

"Dreamer!" She lifted the tray, then carefully placed it on his lap. "But I might start letting you drive mine once in a while, with me at your side, of course."

Kip rolled his eyes. "Mom, I'm fifteen now."

She tousled his hair. "All that means is you're one day older today than you were yesterday. Now eat."

Noting Bart's name on the caller ID when the phone rang, she eagerly snatched it up. "Hi, sweetheart. Our day is finally here," she said brightly, her heart doing a sudden flutter. "Did you check to make sure the tuxedos are going to be delivered to the church in plenty of time?"

"What? That's all you're going to say? No 'I love you'? 'You're the most important thing in my life'? 'I can't live without you'? All you're concerned about is tuxedos?"

Though the tone of his voice was teasing, Shelley felt bad.

"I'm sorry, honey. It's just that there's so much yet to be done, and our wedding is only a few hours away. I *do* love you, and you *are* the most important thing in my life. Next to God and Kip, that is," she added, her own voice teasing. "Just chalk my stupidity and thoughtlessness up to me being a nervous bride. I just want everything to go right, without any unexpected hitches."

Kip leaned toward the phone and cleared his throat loudly, as if he wanted Bart to be able to hear his response to her statement.

Bart laughed. "Tell Kip I heard that and I got his message. And tell him 'happy birthday' for me. I'll give him his present later."

Shelley frowned. "Message? What message? He didn't say anything."

"Forget it. Just remember that in less than six hours you'll be Mrs. Bart Steel, my wife."

She let out a contented sigh. "How could I forget such a wonderful thing? I can hardly wait. I love you, Bart."

"I love you, too, precious. See you at the church." He let out a chuckle. "Don't forget—the magic words are '*I do*.' Love you, babe. Bye."

After hanging up the phone, she turned to Kip. "Bart said to tell you happy birthday and he got your message. What was that all about?"

As if he were trying to hold back a grin, Kip shrugged. "Beats me."

From the expression on Kip's face, she could tell something

was going on between those two but neither was ready to let her in on their secret. What could that secret be?

Shelley stood in front of the triple mirror in the bride's room at their church, gazing at her reflection. Was this day really happening, or had it all been an incredible dream?

Callie stepped up behind her and peered over her shoulder. "You look lovely in white. I can hardly wait to see Bart's expression when you come through those double doors."

"I'm so nervous I can barely remember my name. What if I trip up the aisle? Forget my vows?"

"You'll do fine. Don't worry about it. God has taken care of you so far—He won't fail you now. Just take your time and forget about everything else, except that this is your day—your wedding day."

"Have you seen him?"

"Bart?" Callie adjusted Shelley's veil, then smiled at her approvingly. "Yes. I peeked in the side door a few minutes ago. He's in his place near the altar waiting for you." She let out a slight giggle. "He looked almost as nervous as you do."

"And Kip? Was he there, too?"

"Yes, and looking quite handsome, I might add. With his hair all slicked down with gel."

"The gel was Bart's idea. I'm amazed at how close those two have become since we announced our engagement." She turned when the door opened and Marsha appeared.

"Wow! You're gorgeous!" Marsha hurried inside, quickly

closing the door behind her. "I know you already have something old, something new, something borrowed, and something blue, but I couldn't resist giving you this." Smiling, she reached out a tiny white box.

"Marsha, you've already given me so much. You've been to all three of my bridal showers. By the way, you look fantastic in that pink dress. As my matron of honor, you may outshine me."

"With the way you look in that magnificent white gown, there's no chance of that. Now, open my gift."

Shelley lifted the lid from the box and pulled out a gold ring. Frowning, she gazed at her friend. "A wedding band?"

Marsha threw back her head with a laugh. "No, silly, it's a toe ring! They're all the rage with the young and hip. Slip off your sandal and let me put it on you."

With an amused giggle, Shelley stepped out of the white satin sandal and held out her foot. "I'm neither young nor hip, but I love it. Thank you, Marsha. Only you would have thought of a toe ring as a gift."

Callie cast an approving glance at Shelley's foot. "What a delightful gift, but we'd better hurry. Bart's parents have already been seated. Your boss and the rest of your wedding party are anxiously waiting in the foyer. Are you ready?"

Shelley began routing around in her makeup bag. "My earrings! I forgot my earrings! Where are they?"

"On your ears, silly." Marsha grabbed her hand. "Relax, kiddo. Everything is under control—except you."

Shelley blinked her eyes a few times, then sucked in a deep

cleansing breath. "I'm ready. I guess." Raising her free hand, she fingered her lips. "Do I have on too much lipstick?"

"Your lipstick is perfect." Marsha let loose her grip. "You're gorgeous."

Stooping, Callie carefully picked up the long, lace-trimmed train, then nodded toward the door. "Let's go, beautiful lady."

Shelley wanted to cry as she moved into her place at the end of the line and slipped her hand in the crook of Mr. Moss-man's arm. She was glad her boss had agreed to give her away. He was such a nice man and had been amazingly good to her all the time she'd worked for him, allowing her to take time off whenever she needed to.

"You look lovely, Shelley," he told her, patting her hand. "I'm honored to be giving you away in the absence of your father. I know he and your mother are looking down from heaven, watching you on this most special day. I'm sure the two of you, or should I say the *three* of you, will be very happy."

"Thank you, Mr. Mossman. Your words mean a lot to me." Her gaze went to Marsha, her two bridesmaids, and to Bart's precious little niece who had consented to be their flower girl. They all looked too beautiful for description in their flowing pink dresses and fresh flower headpieces. And the ring bearer— Shelley panicked. "Where's the ring bearer? Isn't he here yet?"

Callie shrugged and appeared almost amused. "He's here. Bart wanted him to stay in the sanctuary with the men until it was time for him to go down the aisle."

"But why? Why would he do such a thing? Callie, is there

something you're not telling me?"

Again, Callie shrugged. "I guess you'll have to ask Bart about that, but don't worry. He has his reasons."

Shelley gave her head a shake. Bart had asked so little of her, insisting their wedding be as *she* wanted it. The least she could do was let him have this one thing his way. Maybe he thought the boy, one of the younger members of his Genesis school, would be more comfortable being in the sanctuary with the men, instead of all the women in the party. She stiffened as the organ began to play. *Please, Lord, don't let anything go wrong. Make this day perfect.*

"You first," Callie, who was standing by the doors leading into the sanctuary, told the little flower girl, giving her a slight forward shove. "Remember, sweetie, take your time. Step, together. Step, together. Step, together, and don't forget to sprinkle the rose petals as you go."

Shelley wished she could see the adorable child as she moved down the aisle. The ring bearer, too, but Callie had cautioned Shelley to stay at the end of the line so she wouldn't wrinkle her train.

Callie sent an amused glance Shelley's way and whispered, "The ring bearer is following the flower girl, and he looks so-o-o adorable!"

Shelley felt a sense of relief. So far, everything was going according to plan.

Callie gestured toward the bridesmaids. "Okay, ladies, you're up next. Take it slow and easy, and don't forget to smile."

After they'd moved down the aisle, she nodded toward

Marsha. "Okay, pretty lady, now you."

Lifting her head high, Marsha turned and gave Shelley one last reassuring smile before moving on to join the rest of the wedding party.

Shelley sucked in a deep breath. She felt faint, as if her knees were going to fold up beneath her.

"You okay?" Mr. Mossman sent her a look of concern.

Callie, who was watching the progression of Shelley's attendants as they moved down the aisle, turned quickly toward her. "Don't be concerned, Shelley. Nearly every bride goes through the same thing about this time. Marriage is a big step. It's only reasonable you should be nervous. You're about to commit the rest of your life to Bart. Do you need a glass of water?"

"No, nothing. I'm fine. Honest I am. It's just that I'm so—so happy!" Before she could stop them, tears of joy misted her eyes. Using the dainty, lace-trimmed handkerchief she was carrying, the "something old" her mother had carried at her own wedding, she dabbed at her eyes. "Oh no! I got mascara on it!"

Callie laughed. "If your mother were here, I doubt she would be concerned about a little mascara smear. Don't worry about it. With a drop of detergent, it'll come right out. Now. . ." She paused and lowered Shelley's veil over her face, gently fingering it into place as the strains of "Here Comes the Bride" filled the sanctuary. "Go marry the man of your dreams. He's waiting for you."

After sending a quick, inaudible *Thank You* up to God, Shelley, holding tightly to Mr. Mossman's arm, stepped forward and into the open doorway. Though there were hundreds of friends and loved ones filling the pews on both sides of the aisle, she had eyes for only one person.

But when she saw him, she let out a loud gasp!

Chapter 8

Her loud gasp was followed by an outright laugh.

Instead of the traditional white tuxedo she'd expected him to be wearing, Bart was dressed in his pristine white Genesis uniform, his black Genesis belt tied smartly around his waist, and he was grinning that amazing grin at her.

And Kip, the two groomsmen, and even the ring bearer were wearing their Genesis uniforms! That was why he'd wanted the ring bearer to remain with the men. So she wouldn't see him ahead of time. It all made sense now.

Though Shelley tried to maintain the "Step, together. Step, together. Step, together," slow, steady rhythm brides were supposed to maintain as she moved toward Bart, she couldn't. Everything in her made her want to run up the aisle and leap into his arms.

Why not? she asked herself. *This is my wedding! There's no law that says it has to go as we'd planned! Didn't Bart say this wedding should be however I wanted it?*

Turning loose of Mr. Mossman's arm, she, who rarely did anything impetuous, tightened her grip on her bridal bouquet, grabbed her tiara, and ran up the white satin runner toward

Bart, leaving Mr. Mossman behind, her long train billowing out behind her like a silk parachute.

When she reached him, she flung herself into his arms. The startled look on her beloved's face only heightened her joy of doing the unexpected.

Bart, his look of shock quickly replaced with a broad smile and his eyes taking on a shine that seemed to light up his entire face, held on to her like there would be no tomorrow. "I love you, Shelley."

Though his voice had been merely a whisper, Shelley heard it as clearly as if he'd used his megaphone. "I love you, too," she murmured before pressing her lips to his, so caught up in her love for this man she nearly forgot the sanctuary full of people who were staring at them in amazement.

"You are truly a gift from God, my love. I'll praise Him every day of my life for allowing me to be your husband." Then, to the applause of those who had gathered to witness their vows, Bart whirled her around in a complete circle before gently setting her down, her billowing train fluttering into a heap at their feet.

"And I praise Him for letting me be your wife."

Still smiling, Bart reached into his pocket and pulled out a small plastic bag. "I have something for you."

Shelley leaned forward, trying to get a peek as he pulled something from the bag.

"Since the rest of our wedding party and I are wearing our Genesis belts, it's only fitting that you should wear yours." Grinning, he unfolded the white Genesis belt she normally wore with her uniform and wrapped it loosely about her waist, tying it with the knot he'd taught all her classmates to tie, ending by ceremoniously kissing her on the cheek. "This knot symbolizes the tying together of our two lives, my love. I'm glad you're wearing white. You make a beautiful bride. Thank you for saying you'll be mine."

Shelley looked down at the belt and lovingly fingered the knot he'd tied before gazing back up at him. "Oh, Bart, darling, may our union never be broken. I love you more than words can express."

After giving her a wink, Kip leaned toward her and gave her a high five. "Way to go, Mom!"

Grinning, Pastor Glendale loudly cleared his throat. "Now that the, uh, *preliminaries* are over, could we please get on with this wedding? That is, if Bart and Shelley are ready and have no other surprises for us."

With a giggle, Marsha scurried to straighten Shelley's long train, then hastened back to her place.

After a quick, loving glance at his bride, his face still beaming, Bart turned and gave Kip a high five, then nodded toward the pastor. "Yes, sir! We're ready. All three of us."

Downhill

Dedication

To my eldest daughter, Dawn Lee Johnson,
whom I love dearly.
Life is a slippery slope.
Many times we fall, have to pick ourselves up,
get back on our feet, brush the snow from our knees,
and take out on the downhill run again,
as we attempt to reach our goal.
Though sometimes the vision of that goal is cloudy,
we must forge ahead.
I pray that good things will happen to Dawn Lee,
an example of what the ideal
mother and grandmother should be,
and that God will see her through the rough spots,
show her His perfect will for her life,
and give her the desires of her heart.

Chapter 1

Stormi McNeil breathed a frantic gasp, then lowered her head and grabbed her coworker's arm as a group of laughing and talking skiers crossed the Keystone Lodge lobby, headed toward the hotel's registration desk. "I know I'm up next, but you'll have to check them in for me, okay?"

Renee's eyes widened. "All of them? There has to be at least a dozen. Can't you help me?"

"Please, Renee. I'll explain later." Her head still lowered, Stormi spun around and moved as quickly as her body would take her into the little storage room at the far end of the hotel's granite-topped counter and closed the door behind her, her heart thumping like the beat of a drum. *Not him. Not now.*

After sucking in a few deep breaths in an attempt to gather her thoughts and regain her composure, she opened the door a crack and cautiously ventured a peek. It *was* him. No doubt about it. The moment he'd walked through the front door, she'd recognized that handsome face, despite the beard generously covering its lower half. She watched, narrowing her eyes, as an absolutely gorgeous woman, a blond with long, straight hair that swished from side to side as she tilted her head and talked in an animated way, smiled up at him and batted her long, heavily mascaraed lashes. *Flirt! And I'm sure he loves every minute of it.* She strained to see if the attractive woman had on a wedding ring, but the blond's hands were still clad in gloves.

Pulling her gaze away from the couple, she scanned the faces of the others standing in line with them and found them each to be as she'd expected. The men—handsome. The women—beautiful. And every one wearing the latest, most fashionable skiwear. *Must be nice to be one of the "in" crowd.*

From her secretive vantage point, Stormi watched as Renee struggled to register the big group alone, all the while hoping the hotel manager wouldn't happen to stroll by and wonder why Stormi wasn't at her post helping.

Though she couldn't hear every word as each skier moved up to the desk and presented his or her charge card, she could make out most of what each was saying. The first four registered two to a room. Two men together and two women together. The next two each requested a single room. She held her breath as *he* stepped up to the desk, hoping he wasn't going to ask for a room for himself and the blond. Remembering the way he'd been in the past, that was exactly what she expected him to do. But to her surprise, he didn't even mention a double. He asked for two rooms with an adjoining door. *Humph. Is that supposed to make it proper?*

The cell phone attached to her waistband rang, causing her to flinch and hurriedly back away from the door. She snatched it up quickly, fearing a hotel guest had called the manager and reported the long line waiting at the registration desk. "Hello, front desk," she spoke into it in her most businesslike manner.

"This is Stormi. How may I help you?"

"Can you tell me how late the lifts run today?" a woman's voice asked.

Stormi breathed a sigh of relief. It was only a hotel guest. "Yes, ma'am. The lifts to take people up the mountain remain in operation until three, our usual time, and continue to run until everyone is off the mountain. But don't forget we have night skiing. Area 51 is open and well lighted for skiing from 8:00 to 10:00 p.m."

"Oh, I see. Night skiing. My sons will like that. Thank you."

"You're welcome. Is there anything else I can do for you?"

"No, that's it."

"Have a pleasant day." Stormi clipped the cell phone to her waistband, then moved back to her spying place, hoping to get another glimpse of *him*, but *he* was no longer in the line. Neither was *she*—the blond. She shrugged. *Looks like he's the same old guy. A real womanizer. Nothing's changed.*

Renee strode over to her, her brows raised. "Okay, what was that all about?"

"Just someone I knew in my past and didn't want to talk to. That's all. Thanks for covering for me. I owe you one."

"You bet you do. Big time. Just be thankful we didn't get caught with that many people in line. You know the rules."

Stormi nodded. "Yeah, I know them; I really hated to put you on the spot like that, but believe me, it was necessary."

"You wanna talk about it?"

"Not now. Maybe later. How long are they staying?"

"The ones I just checked in? A week."

"A full week? Oh, Renee, please tell me you're joking."

"Nope. No joke. They'll be here until next Sunday. If there is someone in that group you're trying to avoid, it's gonna be tough. Seven days is a long time."

Stormi's fingers rubbed at her temples. "Tell me about it."

"Now it's your turn to cover for me. I'm going to take a nice, long, well-deserved break." Renee tugged off her navy blazer, placed it on a hanger, then hung it on the coatrack alongside the other office employees' jackets bearing the embroidered Keystone Lodge emblem on the pocket. "Be back in fifteen or twenty minutes."

The first thing Stormi did when she returned to her accustomed place at the registration counter was look up the number of the room that had been assigned to *him*, hoping the woman had given her name, too. Not that it mattered what the woman's name was, but she was curious.

"Hey, Stormi."

She glanced up and found the head bellman standing at the counter, an amused look on his face. "Hi, Bill. What's up?"

"Would you call the man in 711 and tell him I found his black leather gloves? He thought sure he'd had them in his pocket when he came into the hotel, but I found them in the parking garage. Tell him I'm bringing them up to his room, okay? Maybe he'll give me a big, fat tip. He was sure anxious to find those gloves."

She nodded. "Yeah, sure. I'll call right away." But as Bill headed for the elevators, the number 711 took on a sudden importance—711 was *his* room. Stormi glanced around the lobby, hoping to see Renee or another one of the hotel's office staff, but no one was around. *What difference does it make if I call him? I'm the last person he'd expect to be working at this hotel and calling his room.*

With nervous fingers, she dialed the number. *He* answered on the first ring. Just the sound of his hello sent shivers down her spine. "This is the front desk," she said, trying to mask her voice by lowering it and speaking softly. Was she stuttering, or was it her imagination? "One of our bellmen found your gloves in the hotel parking garage. He's bringing them to your room."

"Oh, great! Those were my favorite gloves. I can't believe I dropped them. I'm usually not that careless. Maybe they fell out of my pocket. Thanks for letting me know."

You were probably so caught up in conversation with your little blond you never noticed when you dropped them. "You're quite welcome, sir."

As she lowered the phone, he spoke again. "I haven't stayed in your hotel before. I'm wondering. Are there any good Mexican restaurants in this area?"

His question didn't surprise her. He'd always loved Mexican food. Still keeping her voice pitched a bit lower than usual and very businesslike, she answered, "If you're looking for an upscale restaurant with lots of atmosphere and good food, Little Mexico is quite popular."

"Is Little Mexico your favorite?"

That question did surprise her. "I like it. The food is typically Tex-Mex, but it's a bit out of my price range."

"So, if you were going out for dinner and you wanted Mexican, where would *you* go?"

"The Mexican Hat Dance. It's a quaint little restaurant tucked up in the mountains. A lot of the hotel employees go there, but it doesn't have the authentic decor of Little Mexico."

There was a pause on the other end of the line. "You weren't the one who checked us in, were you?"

"Ah, no, sir. That was probably Renee."

"Oh? Somehow your voice sounds familiar. I thought perhaps I'd met you at the desk."

"No, sir. I just came back on duty a few minutes ago."

"Well, thanks for your call. I'm sure the bellman will be here any minute."

"You're welcome, sir." How strange it felt to be calling *him* *sir*. At the beginning of their relationship, *honey*, *sweetie*, or *dear* had been appropriate. But by the end of their relationship, words like *traitor*, *liar*, and *two-timer* had taken their place. Now she was calling him *sir*. Of all the fine hotels in the area, why did *he* have to pick this one?

The rest of the morning, no matter how busy she was or how many guests were waiting to be checked in or out, Stormi kept her gaze anchored to the row of elevators at the end of the corridor, watching for *him* each time a set of doors opened. Finally, at one o'clock, he emerged, and anchored to his arm was the gorgeous blond.

Hurriedly taking two awkward steps to the right, Stormi hid herself behind a large column. *Doesn't look like he's changed one bit. He always was lured by a pretty face.* Was she going to have to hide like this for the next seven days? If she didn't need the money, she'd be tempted to ask for the vacation time she'd been saving, take off work, relax, and try to forget about *him*. But she couldn't. That time was already planned. She'd promised the owner of the little sandwich shop, where she worked a second job on her off-hours, she'd fill in for him in a few weeks, when he and his wife went to New Jersey to help celebrate his parents' fiftieth wedding anniversary. If she used her vacation time now, she'd have to disappoint him. Something she'd never do. Her boss was too nice to be treated in such an uncaring way.

When *he* glanced in her direction, she quickly stooped behind the counter.

"What *are* you doing?"

Startled by the bellman's voice, Stormi whirled around and began scanning the floor, "Ah, I thought I heard my pen drop. I was looking for it."

Bill frowned. "You're holding it in your hand."

Embarrassed at offering such a stupid excuse for hiding behind the counter, she forced a giggle. "I am, aren't I? I was sure I heard it hit the floor."

As Bill moved away, he called back over his shoulder. "By the way, thanks for calling that man in 711. He sure was glad to get his gloves back. Gave me that good tip, too."

"You're welcome." Stormi turned her attention back to the elevator corridor, but it was too late. *He* was gone.

She almost felt a sense of relief when her shift ended at five. She'd made it through the entire day without having an encounter with him. After a quick stop at her tiny apartment to change into her green polo shirt and khaki trousers, the uniform she wore for her second job, she bundled up against the cold and walked the two short blocks to Abe's Soup and Sandwich shop. The place was filled with happy customers, all devouring Abe's delicious sandwiches and laughing about the wonderful day they'd had on the Rocky Mountain slopes. Even though she was fifteen minutes early, Stormi hurriedly took off her coat and gloves, hung them on a peg, then washed her hands and pitched in by filling orders as quickly as she could.

"Thanks, kiddo." Abe gave her a playful nudge with his elbow. "I was hoping you'd be early. That new waitress didn't show. We've been swamped all day, and it looks like this evening is going to be the same."

"No wonder. Your soups, sandwiches, and homemade breads are the best in town. Not to mention your famous cheesecake. Don't worry. We'll manage."

Abe grinned. "You're biased. How's the hotel business?"

Stormi checked the orders, then sliced off ten thick slices of pumpernickel bread and slathered them with Abe's secret-flavored mayo. "Doin' good. Full up. Not an empty room available the rest of the week."

"I can't believe you live in one of the best ski areas in Colorado and you don't ski. Don't you ever get a yen to climb into a pair of boots, strap on some skis, and give it a try?"

"Nope. Besides, I'm too busy." After placing five of the slices of bread into five paper-lined baskets and adding several tall layers of honey ham to each slice, she topped them with colorful purple onion rings and sweet peppers, added lettuce that had been shredded with carrots and red cabbage, a hearty slice of tomato, a slice of Monterey Jack cheese, another slice of bread, then anchored the entire concoction together with an oversized toothpick. Three slices of dill pickle and a fresh radish rose placed alongside each sandwich as a garnish, and the baskets were complete. She checked the order one more time, then, after placing the sandwiches on a tray, added one simple lettuce salad with low-cal dressing. "Besides, it's a lot more fun working here with you, creating these spectacular sandwiches."

Abe filled five paper trays with piping hot curly fries, then slid them across the counter toward her. "Uh-huh. Sure it is. You think I believe you? There's no way a beautiful young woman like you would want to spend her evenings and weekends with a bald-headed, irritable old man when she could be out with people her own age having fun. You need to live a little, Stormi."

"I'm doin' okay. Don't worry about me." She sprinkled generous shakes of salt to each mound of fries, then added them to the large round tray she'd already laden with the sandwiches. "Hate to leave your good company, but I want to get this order to your customers at table 12 before their fries cool off."

"Don't forget to come back. I need you to help me fill some more orders."

She gave him a nod. "I'll be back just as quick as I get these delivered. I promise."

After months of consistently maneuvering her way through

the crowded tables and chairs, she easily wiggled her way through the crowd to table 12, unfolded a little rack single-handedly, and lowered the tray onto it. *This is going to be easy. Other than the one person who ordered the lettuce salad, everyone else at the table ordered the same thing.* "Now, who ordered the salad?" she asked, smiling as she lifted the salad plate.

"Stormi? Is that you?"

Recognizing the voice instantly, Stormi froze.

It was *him*!

Chapter 2

She couldn't respond even if she'd wanted to. The muscles in her neck refused to lift her head, and her tongue rebelled at forming words—as if she could think of any words to say, which she couldn't. Like she'd been so many times in her life when she'd been around *him*, she felt tongue-tied.

He stood to his feet and circled the table, his hand coming to rest on her arm. "I've tried so many times to find you. You just disappeared, and no one knew where you were."

Willing herself to behave normally, rather than like some babbling lovesick schoolgirl, even though her head was spinning and her stomach was doing the cha-cha, Stormi swallowed through her tight throat, squared her shoulders, and lifted her eyes to meet his. "Hello, Mark." Then, trying to appear nonchalant, she lifted the salad and sent her gaze around the table. "Which one of you ordered the small dinner salad?"

Mark took the salad plate from her hands, set it down in front of the blond she had seen him with earlier, then grabbed hold of Stormi's hand. "Tell me where you're staying. Give me your phone number. We have to talk."

Ignoring his requests, she tugged her arm away and began distributing the sandwiches and trays of fries.

Mark followed her around the table. "I mean it, Stormi. I'm not letting you get away this time."

Grabbing hold of the serving tray, then folding up the little rack, she did a quick glance at those seated at the table. "Is there anything else I can get for you? Does anyone need drink refills?"

Mark took hold of her arm again. "I really do mean it, Stormi."

Keeping her voice low and hoping to avoid a scene in front of Abe's customers, she leaned toward Mark and said in an almost whisper, "You may have been able to order me around at one time in my life, but not now." Tugging her arm away, she added, "I have work to do."

It seemed like the sanctity and safety of the kitchen was a mile away, instead of perhaps only thirty feet, as she made her way through the tables. She knew without looking back, her words had upset Mark. He was not a man to accept *no* from anyone. This wouldn't be the end of it. Though she hadn't told him her address or given him her phone number, and he hadn't yet realized she worked at the hotel, he knew she worked at Abe's. He might not know what hours she worked, but that wouldn't keep him away from her. Or would it? She hadn't been that important to him in the past. What made her think she'd be that important to him now? But her refusal to listen to him had probably embarrassed him. If, for no other reason, he would probably seek her out to chastise her for making him look foolish in front of his friends.

Maybe she should take her vacation time at the hotel after

all. But that wouldn't be fair to Abe. His parents' anniversary was special to him.

❧

"What took you so long?" Abe shoved three unfilled orders across the counter as she burst through the kitchen door. "We didn't mess up someone's order, did we?"

She let out a long, slow sigh. "No, nothing like that."

"What is it, Stormi? You look upset. Did one of our customers bad-mouth you? Get out of line?"

She picked up the top order on the stack and scanned it without really seeing the words. "No. I'm just a little tired, that's all. We had a busy day at the hotel, too."

Squinting, Abe waved his long bread knife at her. "You work too hard. Wish I could tell you to go on home and get some rest, but I can't. I'd never keep up without you."

Donning a fake smile, she used the back of her hand to push the flat of the knife to one side. "I haven't eaten all day. Maybe that's my problem. As soon as the crowd thins out, I'll eat one of our delicious sandwiches, and I bet I'll be as good as new."

His eyes narrowed. "You wouldn't lie to old Abe, would you?"

With a laugh, she gestured toward the unfilled orders. "You'd better worry about your business and forget about me. I'm fine."

"Stormi—"

"Abe."

"Okay, you win, but I think there's something going on in

your life you're not telling me about. I won't say any more about it, but if you ever need to talk, I'm here."

"I know." For the next hour, the two worked nonstop filling orders. Finally, a much-needed lull came. As promised, Stormi fixed herself a sandwich, and after making sure the table where Mark and his group had been seated was now empty, she moved to a far corner of the room to enjoy it in privacy. *I still can't believe Mark is here in Keystone. Why, of all places to ski in Colorado, did he turn up here? And he's staying at the Keystone Lodge? Unbelievable.*

She glanced up as one of the waitresses scurried toward her. "Someone left you a message. We've been so busy I haven't had time to give it to you. Great-looking guy. Left me a terrific tip, then added five dollars to it after I promised I'd get this note to you."

"Thanks." As Stormi reached out and took it, she noticed her hand was trembling. She hadn't seen Mark for five years. She had thought she was finally over him. *Apparently not.*

After carefully unfolding the napkin on which he'd written his message, she read it silently.

Stormi, we have to talk. I need to see you, if only to apologize. I'm staying at the Keystone Lodge. Room 711. Please call me.

Mark

The sandwich, which had tasted so good, suddenly lost its appeal as her stomach twisted into a knot. *Mark? Apologize?* That was a new one. The Mark she knew would never admit to doing anything wrong. Was this apology thing his subtle way of wheedling his way into her life again? To get even with her for disappearing like she had? Well, she wasn't about to let that happen. Not again. She was back on her feet now, and even though she was still in debt, she'd made great headway by working her two jobs—jobs she loved—and she wasn't about to let him mess up her life again.

When her shift ended, she buttoned up her collar against the cold Colorado night air, wrapped her wool scarf securely about her neck, pulled her stocking cap down over her ears, and tugged her gloves on before telling Abe good night and stepping out into the heavy snow that had begun to fall. But before she took a step, her gaze did a quick sweep of the area. She'd always felt safe walking the few blocks to her apartment when getting off work late at night; however, there was always that one chance, and she had to be ready. But like all the other late nights she'd walked home, she reached her apartment without incident.

The light on her answering machine was blinking when she opened the door. *Mark? No, it couldn't be.*

She punched the PLAY button and waited. "Stormi, this is Andrea at the hotel. Renee phoned me a few minutes ago. She was going to take the early shift in the morning, but she thinks she's coming down with the flu. Could you come in at five instead of nine tomorrow? I know that's early and you work a second job—but we have three buses checking in about eight, and we really need you to help preassign rooms and get the keys ready. Call and leave a message if you can't reach me.

Thanks, Stormi. It's nice to have someone dependable like you we can count on."

Stormi checked her watch, then gazed at the answering machine. It was already after eleven. After her unexpected encounter with Mark, she'd planned to go to bed, pull the covers over her head, and sleep until eight. Now she'd have to be up by four in order to take a shower and blow-dry her hair.

Even though she wished she could beg off, she picked up the phone, dialed Andrea's number, and said into the mouthpiece after the beep sounded, "Andrea, this is Stormi. I got your message about Renee. I'll be in at five."

There were already people waiting to register when Stormi arrived the next morning. It was always that way during the peak ski season. Some folks drove all night just to make sure they could check in and get a full day of skiing. Sleep could come later. Not being a skier herself, she could never understand people's overexuberance for sliding down the mountain on a bone-chilling day, on a pair of slats, with snow blowing in their faces. But if it weren't for them *and* their overexuberance, she wouldn't have a job. Two jobs, as a matter of fact.

She had barely taken off her coat and donned her Keystone Lodge jacket before Andrea appeared, all smiles. "I can't tell you how much I appreciate your coming in early. I really hated to call you, but with three buses arriving at the same time, we're all going to have our hands full. Housekeeping has promised me they'd be ready. I hope they make it."

"It's okay. Don't worry about it. I don't mind, really." Actually, being busy kept her mind occupied with thoughts other than those of Mark. She wasn't used to sleeping late, anyway, and would have probably lain there awake, remembering the good times she'd had with him and ending up in a crying jag.

"Good morning, sunshine."

Stormi grinned at Kirk Benner, one of the catering managers, as he ambled toward her, his usual broad smile on his face. Did the man never have a bad day? "Hi, Kirk."

"Got any plans for Saturday night? A bunch of the hotel staff are going ice-skating." He gave her a flirtatious smile. "I'd like to take *you*. Maybe we can have dinner afterward."

"Sorry, I have to work, but thanks for asking."

"I can ask them to switch your hours around."

This time, she gave her head a shake. "I'm not scheduled for duty here that night. I have to work at my second job. Saturday nights are Abe's busiest nights. He needs me there, but thanks for the invitation."

Kirk leaned his elbows on the counter and rested his chin in his palms. "Are you really working that night, Stormi, or is that your nice way of telling me you don't want to go out with me?"

"No, that's not what I'm saying at all. I like you, Kirk. You're a real gentleman. But I don't have time to date you or anyone. My two jobs take all my time. There's nothing left over."

"There's more to life than work, Stormi," he countered. "Is working two jobs really that important?"

She bobbed her head. "I've made some foolish mistakes in my life, costly mistakes, and I'm about to get them all paid off.

I want things in my life, Kirk. I want my own house, a car, money in the bank for a rainy day. The only way that's going to happen is if I keep doing what I'm doing now. Working two jobs."

Kirk backed away but kept his gaze locked on her. "I admire you for working so hard to achieve your dreams, but what is life without a little fun?"

"I'm still young. I have plenty of time for fun later. Right now, reaching my goals is my entire focus."

His broad smile returned. "Okay, I hear that. But promise me when and if you ever find time for an evening out on the town you'll let me know. My invitation stands. It has no expiration date."

Feeling more than flattered, she returned his smile. "Believe me, when and if that happens, I'll give you a call."

She watched as he moved across the lobby and into one of the waiting elevators. He was such a nice man; if she wanted to date, he'd certainly be a candidate, but dating was the last thing on her mind. At this point in her life, she had goals to reach, and that required tunnel vision. No one, not even the tempting Mark Denton, could persuade her to change her mind. She'd gotten out from under his spell once, and she had no intention of falling for him and his line again.

"Excuse me, ma'am. Can you tell me where to find the gift shop?"

Turning toward the voice, Stormi found herself staring into the pale blue eyes of Mark's beautiful blond. "Certainly," she answered politely, hoping her staring wasn't as obvious as it felt. She almost envied the woman's thin body and her long, manicured nails. "It's at the end of the elevator corridor. You can't miss it."

"Do they carry a line of elegant perfumes? I want something really—alluring."

"I'm not sure, but I would imagine they do." *What's the matter? Isn't your present fragrance enticing enough?*

The blond started to leave but paused, turning to look at Stormi. "Do I know you? You look familiar."

Hoping the woman wouldn't remember her as the person who had exchanged words with Mark the night before and report to Mark she'd seen her working at the hotel, she forced a pleasant smile. "I don't think so. I have one of those nondescript faces that looks like everyone else."

Unfortunately, her answer didn't seem to satisfy the woman's curiosity.

"Did I perhaps see you in the ski shop yesterday?"

"No, although I live in Keystone, I'm not a skier, so it couldn't have been me."

The woman narrowed her eyes and cocked her head to one side. "I rarely forget a face," then smiling, she added, "even a nondescript one. I'm sure I've seen you before."

"Perhaps we've passed in the hallway."

The blond gave her head a slight nod. "Perhaps. Thank you for the information about the perfume. I'll check out the gift shop."

Glad their conversation had come to an end, Stormi called out, "Have a nice day!" as the woman moved into the elevator corridor.

"Pretty lady," Andrea said as she came out of her office and stepped up behind the counter. "Wish I looked like that."

"Yeah, me, too, but I don't have the willpower to live on salads and low-calorie dressings."

"What makes you think she does?"

Stormi smiled to herself. "Just a hunch."

Though she kept an eye out all day for Mark, their paths never crossed. Being an avid skier, he'd probably made the first chair when the runs opened that morning and had been out all day. Strange, his cute little blond hadn't accompanied him. Maybe the woman didn't really like to ski and was only a trinket he'd brought along for company.

At five that evening, Stormi made a beeline for her apartment, to freshen her makeup and slip into her night-job uniform, then headed to Abe's. As usual, the place was packed.

Abe grabbed her arm and nearly dragged her into the kitchen when she walked through the door. "Whew, glad you're here. That new girl didn't show up again. Can you help me with the orders?"

She gave him a big smile. "Sure. You're the boss."

"Oh, by the way." He reached into his apron pocket and pulled out a small piece of paper. "Some guy has called here at least three times today, saying he needs to reach you. Here's his number. You better call him before you get busy."

She didn't have to look at the paper to know who'd called. "Thanks. I'll call later. I'm sure there's no hurry."

Abe gasped as she stuck the little paper into her pants pocket. "He sounded like it was urgent."

"Believe me, it's not urgent."

He harrumphed. "How do you know? You didn't even look at the paper to see who called."

Stormi scooted past him to the sink to wash her hands. "Trust me, Abe. I know whose name is on that paper, and I have no interest in talking to him."

He leaned toward her with a raised brow. "Old boyfriend?"

She glanced at his reflection in the little mirror over the sink. "What makes you think that?"

"Honey, I've learned over the years there are few things that get the kind of reaction you gave me when I handed you that paper. The guy is either a bill collector, a blast from your past you'd rather forget, or an old boyfriend."

Giving her head a shake, Stormi forced a giggle. "That silly theory won't hold a drop of water. Keep your day job, Abe. With that hokeypokey kind of analyzing, you'd make a lousy therapist. You wouldn't even make a good carnival fortune-teller."

"So you're saying that guy is neither a bill collector nor an ex-boyfriend?"

Stop putting me on the spot! "Get to work. We've got orders to fill."

Abe picked up the top order and began assembling the makings of two meatball sandwiches. "Look, kid, I don't mean to pry; I know your private life is none of my business, but I hate to see you go through life alone. You need to meet some nice guy and have a good time. Just calling the guy doesn't mean you have to marry him."

But I wanted to marry him! That's the problem. He didn't want

149

to marry me. "I'll date—eventually, just not now, and not the man who called me. He's—he's not my type."

"He sounded really nice on the phone."

"Voices can be deceiving."

"I'm gonna tell you one time; then I'm gonna shut up and make sandwiches. Call the man—now."

Stormi fingered the little paper in her pocket. "I can't, Abe. It wouldn't be good for him or me."

Abe lifted up his hands in defeat. "Okay, I'm a man of my word. 'Nough said."

Every time she heard the little bell on the front door jingle, Stormi glanced in its direction, half hoping, half fearing it was Mark, but it never was.

Since they were shorthanded, even though she was so tired and sleepy she could barely keep her eyes open, she offered to stay past closing time and help Abe with the cleanup. It was nearly midnight when she wearily pulled on her coat, stocking cap, and gloves, and stepped out into the cold.

"You sure keep late hours."

Startled by both the voice and having a man step out of the shadows, Stormi's hand flew to her mouth, her heart thudding against her chest like a ricocheting hardball. "Mark! You scared me."

He took hold of her hand and slipped it into the crook of his arm. "Sorry. Scaring you was not my intent. When you didn't return my calls, I figured my best shot to get to see you was to come and wait until you got off work. I never expected you to work this late. You don't have a husband waiting for you at home, do you? I noticed you're not wearing a ring."

"No, no husband."

"Good."

She pulled her hand from his arm and frowned up at him. "Good? What's good about it?"

"Look, Stormi, I didn't come here to start an argument and open old wounds. I was hoping we could go somewhere and talk. We can take my car or yours. Whichever will make you more comfortable."

She wished she could jerk away from him and run, but what good would it do? As physically fit as he was, he'd catch her before she got fifty feet. "I don't have a car. I walk to work."

He eyed her warily. "You're kidding, right?"

"No, it's the truth. I don't live very far, and the exercise is good for me."

"As if you don't get enough exercise working at this place." He glanced up and down the street. "This is my first time at Keystone, so I don't know the area very well. Where shall we go?"

"Nowhere, Mark. We have nothing to talk about. The past is exactly that—past. I'd like to keep it that way."

The garish outside lights at Abe's suddenly went out, plunging the area into semidarkness; then Abe appeared in the doorway. "I thought you'd gone on home, Stormi." His glance going toward Mark, he asked, "Everything okay?"

Figuring this was her one chance to avoid getting into Mark's car and breaking her resolve, Stormi grabbed Abe's arm. "That offer to take me home still stand?"

Abe sent a confused glance from her to Mark and back again. "Sure."

"Okay then. I'm ready."

"My car's right there."

She sent Mark a menacing stare. "Thank you, but Abe already offered. Enjoy your week at Keystone."

Mark's eyes narrowed. "How did you know I was going to be here all week? I never told you."

Caught! "I—I just assumed since—ah—most folks come for a week, you—"

"Stormi, is there something you're not telling me?"

She rubbed at her temple with her free hand. "Look, Mark, I'm tired and I'm sleepy. There's nothing I'd like better than a hot shower and a good night's rest. Like I said, we have nothing further to discuss. Good night." Turning away from him, she nearly shoved Abe in the direction of his car.

Once they'd settled into their seats and Abe had started the engine, he turned to her, his expression one of deep concern. "Okay, out with it. Was that man the bill collector or your ex-boyfriend?"

Stormi scooted down in the seat, then stared out the window. "Smart man that you are, I think you've already figured that one out."

"The man who phoned today and wanted you to call him, right?"

"Right."

"Then my guess would be ex-boyfriend."

"Bingo! You win the prize."

Abe switched on the windshield wipers and watched as they pushed the fresh buildup of snow first right and then left, sending a powdery fluff of white into the air. "You still have feelings for him?"

For a moment, Stormi remained silent, listening to the rhythmic *swish-swish* of the blades. "I'm not sure. I've worked so hard at putting all thoughts of him aside and moving on with my life. I thought I'd succeeded. But now, after seeing him again, I—I don't know. But I have to stay away from him, Abe. He's not good for me. He laughed in my face once, and it nearly killed me. I can't let him toy with my feelings again. My life has finally begun to settle down. I can't let him disrupt it."

"Then you have to be firm. Tell him you want him to get out of your life and stay out."

"I already have. He's not listening."

As Abe shifted the lever into DRIVE and inched the car forward, she sent a guarded glance back toward the sandwich shop. There was Mark, his hands buried deep in his pockets, his shoulders hunched against the cold night air, and he was watching them. Stormi slammed her eyelids shut, pressing them tightly together. But it was too late. His handsome image was already etched deep into her heart.

Though she spent a sleepless night, she crawled out of her bed when the alarm went off without even bothering to hit the SNOOZE button. "Day three," she said to her image in the bathroom mirror. "I have to be strong. Only four more days, and he'll be gone."

"Hey, thanks for covering for me while I was sick," Renee

told Stormi when she joined her behind the counter at eight that morning. "I really thought I was coming down with a bout of flu. Turned out it must have been food poisoning. A bunch of my friends and I ate supper at that greasy little diner. We all got sick, but I'm over it now and as good as new. How have things been going?"

She shrugged. "Okay, I guess."

"Did you ever talk to whomever it was that you were trying to avoid?"

"Yeah, a couple of times."

"I'm your friend. You gonna tell me who it was?"

"Just someone from my past. That's all."

"Male or female?"

Stormi looked up from the computer screen. "What difference does that make?"

"Well, if it was a woman, I'd say perhaps she was either an archrival or an old friend who betrayed you. And if it was a man, it'd have to be an old boyfriend."

"It was a man."

"Then it was an old boyfriend?"

"I didn't say that."

Renee tilted her head, her gaze kind and understanding. "You didn't have to say it. It's written all over your face. Looks to me like you still have feelings for the guy."

Stormi shrugged. "Is it that obvious?"

"Probably only to me since I know you so well. Maybe you two could work out whatever problems had caused you to separate."

"Not likely. It's been five years. Even though my old feelings for him have resurfaced, I doubt he's given me a thought in all that time. Not only that, his girlfriend is here with him."

"Um, not a good sign. Did he know you were working here?"

"No. In fact, he still doesn't, although he does know I work nights at Abe's. He showed up there last night at closing, but Abe rescued me and drove me home."

Renee's eyes narrowed. "He's bound to run into you here at the hotel."

"I know, and I'm dreading the moment. Once he knows I'm stuck here at this desk all day every day, I'm at his mercy. I sure don't want him to make a scene and cause me to get fired."

"They'd never fire you. You're too good of an employee. But I don't understand. If his girlfriend is with him, why is he pursuing you?"

Stormi gave her head a shake. "He wrote me a note saying he wants to apologize for treating me the way he did."

"So? Let him apologize, and maybe you'll both feel better."

"Um, he may feel better, but not me. A simple apology might ease his conscience, but that apology won't make the hurt I suffered go away, so what good would it do? No, the less I see of him, the better. Each moment I'm near him just prolongs the agony of seeing him walk out of my life again." She lifted her chin, crossed her arms resolutely, and leaned her back against the counter. "I refuse to spend any time with him. If he wants to apologize, he can do it with a Hallmark card."

Renee snickered. "Now you've got my curiosity up. I wish

I could remember what the men in that group looked like, the ones you insisted I check in for you. Your ex was in that group, wasn't he?"

Stormi nodded.

"He must be quite a guy to have swept *you* off your feet like he did." Renee paused. "Uh-oh. One of the hotel's guests is coming across the lobby, and he's headed straight for us. Do you want to take care of him, or do you want me to?"

Stormi straightened up, then adjusted her collar. "I'll do it. Why don't you check with housekeeping and make sure the rooms for that large group coming in at noon will be ready in time?"

"Oh, good idea. We sure don't want to have all those people sitting around the lobby waiting for rooms. I'll take care of it right now."

"Wait." Stormi hurried to the end of the counter, picked up an envelope, then handed it to her. "Someone left this for the head housekeeper. Probably a tip for good service."

"Miss, can you tell me where the gift shop is? I need to get a copy of the Denver paper."

Stormi felt the blood rush to her head.

It was Mark!

Chapter 3

Turning slowly, she found herself staring into the blueness of his eyes. "Hello, Mark."

"Stormi?" His startled gaze went to the Keystone Lodge name tag pinned to her jacket. "You work here, too? That's how you knew I'd be here all week?"

"Yes," she mumbled softly, too shaken by his sudden appearance to say anything more.

"And you work at Abe's, too?"

"Yes."

"But—why?"

"To make a living. Why else would I work around the clock? I've already confessed there isn't a husband in my life."

"Sorry, I shouldn't have made such a big deal out of it. Your financial condition is none of my business."

She gave him a haughty tilt of her chin. "You're right. It isn't. As to your other question? The gift shop is at the end of the elevator corridor."

"Forget the gift shop. What I want is to know when the two of us can get together and talk."

"First of all, we have nothing to talk about. Second, as you've discovered, I work two jobs, which means I have no time to talk to you." She backed away from the counter, putting some space between them, then, in a very businesslike manner asked, "Is there anything else I can do for you?"

"Stormi, please."

Narrowing her eyes and trying to appear in control, even though her heart was frantically clamoring inside her, she said softly, "Mark, this job is important to me, and I don't want to jeopardize it by making a scene. I want you to leave me alone, okay? I've finally gotten over you. I want you out of my life—for good."

He leaned toward her, resting his palms on the edge of the countertop. "I'm not the same man you once knew, Stormi. You have to believe that."

"You really expect me to believe that I'm-not-the-same-man thing? I wonder how many gullible women have heard that line, believed it, and ended up hurt all over again. Well, I can tell you one thing—I'm not going to be one of them. Now, unless you have a hotel request I can take care of for you, I have other duties to perform."

Mark lifted his hands in surrender, then backed away. "You *will* talk to me, Stormi. I don't know where or when, but it will happen. Even if I have to extend my stay, I'm not leaving Keystone until we have some time together."

"You said you wanted to apologize. Why don't you just do it and get it over with? I'm here. I'm listening."

"I do want to apologize; but there's so much more I want to tell you, and I don't want to do it here. Just give me half an hour. Thirty minutes. That's all I ask."

He seemed so sincere. Not at all like the Mark of five

years ago. "How about five minutes?"

"No, I can't say all I want to say in five minutes."

"Fifteen?"

He shook his head. "It has to be thirty."

She stared into his eyes. Instead of the flirty, overly confident look his face had boasted all those years ago, his current expression was almost contrite. Humble. But did she dare trust him? Spend thirty minutes with this man she'd loved so deeply that his rejection had nearly sent her over the edge? "I'll think about it, but don't get the idea that means it's going to happen, because it probably won't."

"Thanks, Stormi. That's all I ask. Thirty minutes, and then, if you prefer it, I'll never bother you again. You know my room number. I'll be expecting your call. If I'm not there, leave a message. I'll meet you anywhere, anytime you say. It's important to me that we talk. I hope it will be important to you, too, once you hear me out." He gave her a pleasant smile, turned, and headed for the elevator corridor toward the gift shop.

She watched until he was out of sight, then sank onto the stool behind the counter. It looked like the only way she was going to get him out of her life was to meet with him. But— thirty minutes? The few minutes she'd already spent with him had unnerved her and weakened her resolve. What would thirty minutes in his presence do?

"Anything exciting happen while I was gone?" Renee asked when she returned from her meeting with the housekeeper.

"*He* was here."

"He? The man you told me about?"

Stormi nodded.

"I hope you two didn't have a loud argument."

"No, we didn't. Actually, our conversation ended quite peaceably. He says if I give him thirty minutes, he'll get out of my life and never see me again."

"Whoa, that's some proposition. Are you going to do it?"

Stormi expelled a deep sigh. "I told him I'd think about it. He said we could meet anytime, anywhere. It was up to me."

"I don't know what's going on between you two, but maybe you should do it."

"And maybe that wouldn't be too smart. I seem to be putty in his hands. He says he's changed."

Renee put a consoling hand on her shoulder. "Maybe he has. You said it's been five years. A lot can happen in that length of time."

"I know I've changed," Stormi confessed. "I like to think I'm not at all that person he knew."

"See, what did I tell you? Why don't you give him the benefit of the doubt? Meet with him and see what he's got to say."

Stormi put a finger to her cheek thoughtfully. "I'm considering it." Their conversation ended as the bellman ushered three hotel guests to the counter to be registered.

"So are you gonna do it?" Abe reached past Stormi and grabbed a clean towel. "Maybe the guy *has* changed. He seemed nice enough to me."

Stormi almost wished she hadn't told Abe about the

conversation she'd had with Mark. But when she'd reported to work, Abe had asked her, point-blank, if she'd seen him. Maybe she should ask Abe's advice. After all, he was one of the few people she knew who had her best interests at heart. "You think I should see him? For thirty whole minutes?"

"So long as you pick the place and time, what could it hurt? Maybe meeting with him is what it will take to rid your life of him."

She nodded. "Yeah, maybe."

"You could meet him here, but it's much too noisy. How about at the hotel? Surely there's someplace there."

She shook her head. "Too cozy."

"Your place?"

"Even more cozy. I don't want to be alone with him, Abe. It needs to be some public place, yet a place where we can talk uninterrupted."

"Why don't you call him and see if he can meet you on one of those benches down by the lake? It's a beautiful night. There'll be plenty of skaters out. You'll be surrounded by people, yet there's a lot of space for privacy. I can hold down the fort here. Go ahead. Knock off a couple of hours early. Meet with him and get it over with."

His idea had merit. "You really think you can handle things without me?"

He grinned. "I can try. Go on. Call him."

"He's probably out somewhere having dinner."

Abe motioned toward the phone on the wall. "Quit procrastinating and call him."

Stormi stared at the phone, which had suddenly turned into a big scary monster. If anyone would have told her a week ago she'd be calling Mark and making plans to meet with him, she wouldn't have believed it. After sucking in a deep breath and letting it out slowly, she moved to the phone and dialed the hotel's number, asking for room 711. She nearly fainted when he answered on the first ring. "Mark, this is—"

"I know who it is, Stormi. I recognized your voice. Does this mean you're willing to meet with me?"

"Abe said I could take off early. Can you meet me down by the skating area at the lake about eight thirty?"

"Sure. Anything you say. I'll be there."

"Thirty minutes—that's all the time I'm giving you. I mean it."

"Thirty minutes, I promise. Thanks, Stormi. You don't know how much this means to me."

Why did she feel she was walking into a web that would ensnare her and play havoc with her feelings? "See you at eight thirty."

For the next hour, Stormi was a bundle of nerves. She messed up three orders, broke two drinking glasses, and spilled mustard down the front of her clean uniform. By eight o'clock, Abe was jokingly telling her to get out of the place before she set it on fire.

Her hands trembled all the way to their meeting place. She wished she would have had time to change her clothes before meeting with Mark. She felt all tacky and sticky in her mustard-stained uniform. *Mark has always been a smart dresser. No doubt he will be dressed that way tonight, and look at me.* Though the evening wasn't as cold as most nights, it was still cool enough to wear her coat buttoned. Perhaps he wouldn't notice the mustard stain.

After walking the short distance to the hotel, she made her way through the lobby and down the stairs to the doors leading out onto the lake, pausing when she caught sight of Mark sitting on one of the benches at the far end. Maybe meeting with him wasn't such a good idea after all. *Go on, get it over with. There'll never be a better time.* She tried to convince herself as she tugged the door open and stepped back out into the night air.

He rose to his feet and grinned when he saw her approaching. "I was afraid you'd change your mind."

Why does he always look so handsome? "No, I said I'd be here, and here I am." His expensive-looking parka made her feel that much more dowdy.

He gestured toward the bench. "Come, sit by me."

Moving warily, she sat down.

"There's so much I have to tell you." Smiling, he glanced at his watch. "Are you going to time me? Do I need to set the alarm on my watch?"

She gave him a weak smile. "I don't think that's necessary. I'm a pretty good judge of time."

He reached for her hand, but she pulled it away. "Please, Stormi. Let me hold your hand. I want you to look into my eyes as I say what I am about to say. I want you to know I'm speaking from my heart."

Reluctantly, she put out her hand.

"First, I must apologize for the last time we were together. I treated you like dirt and said many things I shouldn't have said. Most of which weren't even close to true. I don't mean to use it as an excuse, but I'd been drinking heavily that day. I'd had trouble at work the entire week, my dad had been on my case, and all you could do was talk about marriage. As with almost every other woman I'd dated, I felt you were trying to pin me down, take away my independence—and I wasn't ready for it."

"But you—"

"I know. I said I loved you, and I did. Sorta. I'd also thought I'd loved several other women before you. But when I began to feel crowded and broke things off with them, there was always someone just around the corner waiting to take their place, and I soon forgot about them. I thought it was going to be the same way with you, but I was wrong."

Ouch. Mark admitting he was wrong? That's a first. "I hated it when you drank. Alcohol made you change from the most attractive guy I knew to a bigmouthed monster." *But I loved you anyway.*

He frowned, countering, "You drank, too!"

"Only because you kept urging me to do it. I never really liked it. I only did it to please you. But, like you, I became addicted, and I ended up drinking way too much of that stuff, especially after you dumped me. It took me more than a year to wean myself away from the booze. Even now, there are times when I'd like to take a drink, but I don't."

"Oh, Stormi, knowing my drinking affected you that way makes me feel all the more guilty for breaking up with you like

I did. I was dumb and stupid and cared for no one but myself. It was only after I sobered up and realized what I'd done that I came to my senses."

Though his revelation took away a small measure of her pain, it didn't go very far in repairing the deep, deep hurts she'd suffered. "You may have been too drunk to *exactly* remember what you said that day, but I remember every word. Every voice inflection. The hateful expression on your face. You laughed at me when I asked you when we were going to be married. You told me, in no uncertain terms, that you had never loved me, that I was only one of your many play toys and you were tired of me. You said I was an insignificant little nobody who would never amount to anything. Your parting words were, 'Get out of my sight. I never want to lay eyes on you again.' Those words literally shredded my heart, Mark. You were my everything. I would have done anything for you, and you treated me like pond scum."

"I actually said all those things?"

Fighting tears and losing the battle, she nodded. "That and more I don't even want to repeat."

Mark pulled a small pack of tissues from his parka pocket and handed it to her. "I'm so sorry, Stormi. So, so sorry. I was pretty arrogant before I began drinking so heavily, but once I got a little alcohol in my body, I guess I turned into a mouthy, conceited monster. I'm ashamed to say I gave my mom and dad many sleepless nights. Is there any way I can make it up to you? I hate myself for what I did. I've been praying so hard I'd find you."

Praying? Mark? She flinched when he warily slipped his arm around her shoulders but, being eager to hear what else he had to say, decided not to make an issue of it.

"This burden of guilt has been eating at me and ruining my life. I know it's asking a lot, but I have to have your forgiveness."

Praying? Forgiveness? She hadn't even realized those two words were in Mark's vocabulary. Was this the same man who'd wronged her? He didn't sound like the Mark she knew. This Mark was either a stranger, a good actor, or he was drunk again. But what did he have to gain by apologizing? Asking for forgiveness? It was all so confusing. "What about the alcohol? Are you still drinking?"

"No. It's no longer a problem for me."

She gave him a dubious frown. "I'd only been drinking a short time, and I had a real battle kicking the habit. How could you drink as long and as much as you did and whip it so easily?"

He glanced at his watch. "There's so much yet I have to tell you. I've barely scratched the surface, but I promised you thirty minutes, which means I have only fifteen minutes left. I want to keep my promise."

"Go ahead. Tell me. Abe isn't expecting me to come back, so I don't have to rush off."

"You're sure?"

"I'm sure."

He scooted a little closer and began. "I'm afraid some of my story isn't very pretty, but I'm telling it to you just as it happened. After you disappeared on me, I was upset with myself for talking to you like I had and upset with you for leaving without a word to anyone. My friends were fed up with my arrogant behavior and deserted me, my mom and dad were at their wits' end, I was flunking out of college, and I'd racked up all sorts of bills and couldn't pay them off. My life was a mess. If those things weren't enough, the loan company repossessed my car, the owner of the apartment where I lived evicted me, and the city of Colorado Springs was after me for unpaid parking and speeding tickets. I looked around, evaluated my circumstances, and decided there was only one thing I could do. Join the army."

Stormi's jaw dropped. "*You* actually joined the army?"

"Yep. Mom and Dad took care of paying off my speeding and parking tickets and my horrendous MasterCard bill. I'd lost everything else, so the army seemed the best idea at the time."

"Wow. I can't imagine the great, independent Mark Denton as a soldier."

He huffed. "I was a pretty bad one at first. Nearly got court-martialed for a few shenanigans I pulled. But then I met a man who changed my life. Ron Dawson, the army chaplain. That man was a big one. He could have taken me down with one hand tied behind his back, but he was the kindest, most gentle man I've ever met."

Stormi eyed him suspiciously. "That doesn't sound like the kind of man who would impress you."

"He didn't at first. But he went to bat for me, saved me from being court-martialed, and became my best friend. I figured, being the chaplain, he'd try to stuff religion down my throat, but he didn't. In fact, he didn't even like the word *religion*. Said it confused people. To him, being a Christian wasn't a religion, it was a way of life, a personal relationship with God Himself."

"You make the man sound like a saint."

Mark's eyes shone with a softness that made Stormi think he might be telling the truth.

"I've never known anyone like him, Stormi. He was tough as nails but as gentle as a whisper on the wind. I've seen that man arm wrestle the strongest guy in my division and win without a struggle, and I've seen him hold an enlisted man's newborn baby and cuddle it to his chest as gently as if he were its mother. I've heard him bark out commands like a drill sergeant, and I've watched him shed tears with a family whose child was sick. He never asked for anything but gave everything. You couldn't be around him for five minutes without feeling the presence of the Lord."

The Lord? Now she really had her doubts. Was this *Lord* thing another ploy of his to regain her confidence? And if it was, why would he go to all the trouble? What did he have to gain by it? And what about his drinking problem?

"You're probably wondering why a tough, foulmouthed guy like me would have anything to do with a man of God." He allowed a small chuckle to escape his lips. "I didn't have much to do with Chaplain Ron at first. In fact, I was downright rude to him. But he recognized I was a drunk the first time we met. At one time, he'd been a drinker himself. After I had my first run-in with the military police, he offered to help. I agreed to let him only to avoid the brig. First thing I knew, he and I were friends. A few months later, he became what he called my 'accountability partner.' Whenever that old drinking monster came knocking at my door, all I had to do was contact Chaplain Ron and he was right there by my side, encouraging me and helping me meet my demons head-on."

Stormi still didn't get it. "You mean it was that easy to quit drinking? All you had to do was meet with that man?"

"No, just meeting with him didn't do it. Actually, the first time I met with him, I ended up getting so mad at what he said to me, I spouted off a few things I'm ashamed to admit and stormed off in a rage. Did he get mad? Tell me to get lost and quit wasting his time? No! Anybody else would have taken me on or been offended, but not him. All he did was assure me he'd be praying for me and he would be available 24-7 when I was ready to talk."

Stormi suddenly felt chilled. The night was much colder than she'd anticipated when she'd mentioned meeting him by the lake. She should have worn her parka instead of her coat.

"You cold? Maybe we'd better go inside."

She gave her head a shake. "I'm okay."

He pulled off his muffler and looped it around her neck, then scooted closer, closing the gap between them. "You won't slap me if I wrap my arms around you to help keep you warm, will you? I sure don't want you catching cold."

She gave him a slight smile. "It might help." She held her breath as he drew her close and pulled her to the warmth of his body.

"That better?"

"Much better. Thanks. Tell me more about this miracle man of yours. His words must have been mighty powerful to make *you* stop drinking. Some people go to therapy for years and still never kick the habit."

"He was a brilliant man, but the words he used weren't *his* words."

"Oh, I see. He was using the 12-step program?"

"No, Chaplain Ron used words right out of the Bible. I'll never forget the first time he told me I was a sinner. I almost decked him. But there was no self-righteousness in his eyes. No holier-than-thou attitude. Only love and a real concern for me—a rebellious man who was little more than a stranger to him."

Stormi's eyes widened. "He actually called you a sinner?"

Mark nodded. "Yes, and the sad part was—he was right. I knew I was pretty ornery and had done some things I should have been arrested for, but I'd never thought of myself as a sinner. I'd always thought of sinners as people who robbed banks or committed murder. But Ron took his big tattered Bible and showed me where God said *all* men are sinners. No one had ever spelled it out that way to me before. I tried to argue the point with him, but he reminded me he wasn't the one who had said it. It was God—and there was only one way to make things right with God, and that was to acknowledge I was a sinner, confess my sins to Him, and ask for His forgiveness. The worst sin of all was that I had turned my back on God, refusing to accept Him and His deity."

Narrowing her eyes, Stormi stared at him for a moment before responding. "I can't imagine you being interested in anything having to do with God."

"You know, Stormi, I couldn't imagine it either. I'd assumed the only people who believed in God were the weak ones, ones who were gullible enough to believe anything. That is, until I met Chaplain Ron. Ron was a man's man. Nothing weak about him. In fact, he was the strongest man I'd ever met, both physically *and* spiritually. I found myself wanting to be just like him." Mark let out a sigh. "That sounds funny coming from me, doesn't it?"

Stormi lifted her face and gazed up into his eyes. "What are you saying, Mark? You quit drinking because you found God?"

Mark's eyes misted up. "Yes, that's exactly what I'm saying. The day I asked God to forgive me and take over my life, I poured six unopened bottles of vodka down the drain and I've never had another drink. I'm no longer a slave to alcohol. Oh, like you, I won't say the desire isn't there sometimes. It is—but I turn those temptations over to God, and He gets me through. Now I can go months without even thinking about taking a drink. I know, with God's help, eventually that desire will be completely gone."

Mark nestled his chin in her hair. "That's why I wanted to meet with you, Stormi. To apologize for my terrible behavior and ask for your forgiveness, but also to tell you about my Lord and Savior, and the change He has caused in my life. I *am* a changed man. God changed me."

Stormi sat stunned. *Mark found God! Amazing!*

"My faith in God was put to the test a few months later," he went on, "when my company was sent to Iraq. Stormi, I'd been pretty rough around the edges all my life, but I wasn't prepared for the many atrocities I saw there. Death was around me every day. Innocent people were tortured or killed for no reason at all. I had buddies who lost an arm or leg, some their sight, some who died. I prayed every day for safety. I was a changed man before I went overseas, but the experience of going over there and knowing where I would spend eternity if I was killed gave me a new appreciation for life and the God who created me. I've done a complete turnaround. Being the dedicated Christian man God wants me to be is my number one priority now."

"You seem so—sincere."

"I am sincere, Stormi. I'm trying to right as many wrongs in my life as possible. The way I treated you is one of them. Ever since the day I accepted God, I've been asking Him to send you back into my life. The night I saw you working at Abe's, I bowed my head and thanked Him for allowing me to find you. I had to ask for your forgiveness."

Her head was spinning. His humble words had come as a complete surprise. If she hadn't been staring into his face, she wouldn't have believed he was the same man. "I–I'm not sure I can forgive you. You really hurt me."

"I know I don't deserve your forgiveness. I get sick to my stomach every time I think about the way I took you for granted, toyed with your emotions, and treated you like a possession in-stead of a person. It wasn't your fault you expected our relation-ship to end in marriage. I led you on, let you believe I wanted you to be my wife because I knew that's what you wanted to hear, when all the time marriage was the last thing on my mind."

His words pierced her heart and made her gasp for breath as tears flowed down her cheeks. "I loved you, Mark, and I thought you loved me!" Pressing her palms against his chest, she struggled to push herself away from him. "What a fool I was. How you and your friends must have laughed at me."

He held her fast, refusing to let her go. "Wait! Hear me out. I did love you!"

"First you said you didn't love me; now you're saying you did?" She ceased struggling and, through misty eyes, gazed up into his face. "If you're trying to confuse me, Mark, you're doing a good job of it. Are you here to hurt me a second time?"

"I did love you, Stormi. I just didn't realize it until I'd lost you! Other than my mom and dad, I guess I'd never truly loved anyone. You were always there. I took you for granted, never giving you the respect you deserved. It seemed no matter how badly I treated you, you took it and never left me. But that day was different. I guess you'd finally had more of me and my ways than you could take, and I'd pushed you over the edge. When you walked out on me, I told the guys, 'She'll be back. She always comes back,' but you didn't. Being the proud, conceited jock that I was, I didn't bother calling you for nearly two weeks, figuring *you'd* come crawling back eventually, apologizing for upsetting *me*. But when that didn't happen, and I finally called and found your phone had been disconnected, it dawned on me that I'd gone too far that time and you'd actually left me. I rushed to your apartment and was shocked when a total stranger opened the door and told me she was the new tenant, and that you had moved without leaving a forwarding address. I'd heard the word *heartache* before, but I'd never experienced its meaning until you were no longer a part of my life."

In total awe of his unexpected confession, she carefully pondered his words. Up to now, she'd wallowed in her hatred for this man, letting it consume her thoughts, her actions, and—yes—her attitude toward all men. Now, here he was, asking for her forgiveness. No, he was *begging* for it, and she wasn't sure how she should respond. Because of him, she'd endured five years of low self-esteem, debt, and heartache. She'd been cast aside like last year's calendar. Why should she let him off the hook by forgiving him? And why should she believe his story about becoming a new man? She'd only spent a short time with him. The whole thing could be an act. He always was good at telling people just what he wanted them to believe. Maybe after their evening ended, he'd go back to his group and laugh about how gullible she'd been and how he'd once again been able to pluck the strings of her heart to any tune he wanted by turning on his charm.

"So, Stormi? I know it's asking a lot—and I don't deserve it—but will you forgive me?"

Chapter 4

Stormi shuddered as she relived their final moments together before she'd run out of his life those five long years ago. He had put her through agony. He talked about how miserable *he'd* been? She doubted he had any idea of what *she'd* been going through.

Pulling away from him and rising to her feet, she crossed her arms and glared at him. "No, Mark. I can't forgive you. I doubt your pain has been anything compared to mine. You'll have to soothe your conscience some other way. Maybe your newfound God can forgive you, but I can't. I trusted you once, and look where it got me. Why should I listen to you now?" Her heart banging against her chest, she turned to move away, but he stood, grabbed her, and held her fast.

"I deserve every word you're throwing at me, and more. But I *need* your forgiveness, and I think letting go of your hatred toward me will help you, too. Look, I have an idea. I've told you I'm a changed man. I'd like to prove it to you. Let me introduce you to the new me." Freeing one hand, he lifted her face to meet his. "Give me a chance, Stormi. The love I had for you has never died. I'd like to think there is a small corner of your heart that still has a soft spot for me. I'll be here the rest of the week. I know you're busy with your two jobs, but you have to eat. Surely you can work in an hour or so a day to spend with me."

"I really don't think—"

He put a finger to her lips. "Let's start all over again. Miss Stormi McNeil, would you do me the honor of sharing lunch with me tomorrow?"

She gulped hard. "Lunch with *you*? What about your girlfriend? Won't she mind?"

He gave her a mystified stare. "Girlfriend? What girlfriend?"

Come on; don't play innocent. "The one in the room next door to you. You did ask for a room for you and a second one with an adjoining door, didn't you?"

"Yes. A room for me and one for my mom."

She felt her eyes widen. "Your mom? She's here? I haven't seen her."

"She's sharing that room with a friend of hers. No wonder you haven't seen her. Would you believe it? Those two women are taking beginner skiing lessons during the day, then ordering room service for supper and spending their evenings in the hot tub. Mom's having the time of her life. *I've* barely seen her."

"So the little blond you checked in with wasn't your girlfriend?"

"Her? No, of course not. She's engaged to a friend of mine. Due to a business commitment, he couldn't make it up to Keystone until today, so she rode up with our group. I promised him I'd take good care of her until he got here. She's nice, but she's definitely not my type, even if she wasn't engaged. Now, back to my invitation, do we have a date?"

"I'd like to but—"

"Please, Stormi, say yes. If I say or do anything to offend you, all you have to do is tell me to get lost. I promise I'll go away peacefully, and you'll never hear from me again. All I'm asking is a chance to prove myself."

She gazed up into his face. He may have changed inwardly, but in some ways, he'd changed outwardly, too. There were crinkly lines at the corners of his eyes, and his bearded face bore signs of maturity. Even his hair was different. He'd worn it long before, nearly to his shoulders; now it was cropped short in an almost-military cut. His well-trimmed beard added even more to his good looks. "You really mean it? You'd leave if I asked you to?"

Using his free hand, he crossed his heart. "Absolutely."

I have to think. Do I really want to do this? I've spent five years recovering from our last encounter. Dare I put my heart on the chopping block again?

"I'll meet you at one of the hotel's restaurants tomorrow for lunch. Your pick. We'll get acquainted all over again."

What could a few more minutes with him hurt? We'll be in the hotel. "I—I guess we could try it. I'll meet you at the Edgewater Café about one."

Mark snatched her up and swung her about in a complete circle before setting her feet back on the ground. "I can't tell you how happy this makes me. I promise I won't disappoint you."

As soon as she felt secure enough to stand alone, she backed away from him. "I really need to get home. I'm due in at seven in the morning."

Mark grabbed hold of her hand, and the two walked silently up the stairs to the lobby. "I'll drive you."

"I can walk. I do it every night."

He smiled down at her. "Not with me around."

Without protesting a second time, she followed him into the elevator, to the garage level, and to his car. It took only minutes until his car rolled to a stop in front of her building. Before she could say good night, he was out of the driver's side and opening her door.

"You really don't need to walk—"

He grinned. "I know I don't *need* to walk you to your door, but I *want* to."

She pulled her key from her purse and hurried up the one flight of stairs to her apartment with Mark at her heels, all the time wondering if he was going to try to kiss her. She hoped not. The old Mark would, but she wasn't ready for it and might never be.

Once she had the key inserted in the lock, Mark bowed low, then backed away. "Good night, Stormi, and thanks for spending time with me. It means a lot. See you about one to-morrow. Sleep tight."

Before she could answer, he was gone. She'd let Mark back into her life.

Hopefully, she wouldn't be sorry.

Without explaining to Renee where she was going, Stormi slipped away from her position at the hotel's registration desk a few minutes before one and hastily made her way down the stairs to the Edgewater Café. She'd been in a tizzy all morning just thinking about meeting with Mark again. Though she'd had no choice but to wear her uniform, she did take extra time that morning, applying her makeup and even using the curling iron on her hair.

"Wow, you look beautiful," he told her, rising as she joined him at the table he'd selected in a far corner of the busy restaurant.

She felt a blush move to her cheeks as she lowered herself onto the floral upholstered chair he'd pulled out for her; then she said demurely, "Thank you."

"I was hoping you wouldn't change your mind about coming."

She lowered her gaze to avoid his eyes and began perusing the menu. "I considered it." Goose bumps rose on her arms as he reached across the table and placed his hand over hers.

"I'm glad you came."

They glanced over the menu and, after deciding on the soup and sandwich of the day, sat silently gazing at one another. Finally, Mark spoke. "You said you didn't ski, but how about going ice-skating with me after you get off work this evening? I know you used to ice-skate."

She gave her head a slow shake. "I don't know. I haven't skated in years."

He responded with a hearty laugh. "Neither have I. We may have to hold each other up, but it'll be fun. Come on. Say yes."

She *had* agreed to spend time with him, and skating in a

public place would mean they wouldn't be alone. "Okay, but don't be surprised if I spend most of my time falling down."

He laughed. "We'll probably both be falling down, but at least we'll be together. That's the important part. I want these next few days to be the beginning of a whole new relationship, Stormi. I know you're gun-shy and afraid to trust me—and I can't blame you—but I'm hoping by the end of the week you'll realize I'm worthy of your trust." He gestured toward their meal as the waiter placed it on their table. "Mind if I pray?"

Unsure of how to respond or what to say, she simply nodded, then, once he'd said a simple prayer, focused her attention on her soup. "The soup is good," she said for lack of something else to say. "I've never eaten at the Edgewater Café before. In fact, I haven't eaten at any of the hotel's restaurants."

"Then we'll have to change that. We'll try out each one."

She shook her head. "No, Mark, we can't. They're all terribly expensive."

"You let me worry about that. We're dating, remember?"

"But I can't let you—"

"Indulge me, okay? If I couldn't afford it, I would never have suggested it." He took hold of her hand again and gave it a squeeze. "Now, tell me all about yourself. I want to know everything. How long you've been living in Keystone. The plans you have for your future. All of it."

She glanced at her watch. "I have to be back to work in twenty minutes."

He grinned. "Guess I'll have to settle for the condensed version."

"Actually, there's not much to tell. After our breakup, I decided I wanted to get as far away from you as possible. I found an ad in the Denver newspaper that said this hotel had an opening for a night desk clerk. I answered the ad, got the job, and here I am. I doubt you ever knew how many debts I'd run up, trying to impress you. I'd paid top dollar for that new red convertible I'd bought, had gotten way behind in my rent on my fancy apartment, run both my Visa and my MasterCard to their limits—buying clothes, shoes, perfume, and joining that swanky health club you liked so much. Even though I felt my life ended the day we parted company, I had an obligation to pay off those debts. So I took a consolidation loan at an extremely high interest rate and have been paying on it ever since."

"Which is why you're working a second job at Abe's."

"Right. I started at Abe's about a week after I started work at the hotel. In a few more months, I'll be debt free."

He let out a sigh. "I had no idea you'd racked up that kind of debt. And you did it to impress me? Why?"

"In some ways, I was kind of from the wrong side of the proverbial tracks. You and your family had social standing and were accustomed to having the finer things of life. I wasn't. I would have done anything to fit in and be able to compete with the other women who wanted you as much as I did. I know now it was a dumb thing to do, but I didn't want to lose you."

He turned his head away and bit at his lower lip. "Now I feel even worse."

"Don't. It was my feeble attempt to keep hold of you, but I lost you anyway."

"Knowing this gives me even more reason to apologize. I'm so sorry, Stormi. It's no wonder you have such hatred for me."

"I don't exactly hate you, Mark. I hate what you did to me, and I hate myself for allowing it." She did a quick glance at her watch. "I'm sorry. I have to go. Thank you for the lunch."

He rose as she sprang up and moved away from the table. "What time do you get off work tonight?"

"Nine!" she called back over her shoulder as she headed for the exit.

"I'll pick you up!"

Rather than wait for the elevator, Stormi hurriedly took the back stairway. When she reached the registration desk, her heart was pounding a mile a minute—not from her race up the stairs, but from her unsettling conversation with Mark.

The new Mark.

The contrite Mark she'd never met before.

And she found herself in awe of him.

"So you're really gonna spend time with him?" Abe asked as he added sauerkraut to the two Reuben sandwiches he was preparing. "I like the guy."

"I like him, too. That's the problem. He's—different, Abe. I'm almost tempted to believe him."

"I'm glad you told me about him and the way he says he's turned to God. Maybe what he's got is the real thing."

"Maybe. He actually bowed his head and prayed for our lunch." Stormi pulled a bag of shredded cheese from the big cooler, unzipped the top, and dumped it into an oblong stainless steel container. "Mark admitting he was a sinner really threw me. I never expected the arrogant, self-centered Mark Denton to utter those words. He said the Bible says all people are sinners."

"I'm afraid I'm one of them." Abe wiped his hands on his apron, then stood staring at her. "I never told you, but another kid and I robbed a little gas station when we were seventeen. Didn't get much money. Didn't even have a gun, just flashed our pocketknives at the guy behind the counter. He was so scared he nearly threw the money at us. I'll never forget the amount. Thirty-seven dollars and forty cents. The police caught us in less than two hours. Someone had become suspicious when he saw us run out of the store. He took down our license number and called the police. Good thing we weren't eighteen, or we'd have been in real trouble." Abe huffed. "I think that would qualify as sin, don't you?"

She nodded. "I guess breaking any law would be a sin."

"I did a lot of other bad stuff, too, but that was the worst."

"From the way Mark explained it to me, the worst sin a person could commit is turning his or her back on God and refusing to accept Him and His deity."

Abe's eyes widened. "Uh-oh. In that case, I'm in big trouble."

Stormi nodded. "Me, too."

"I heard Billy Graham say that same thing on TV a couple of times. I was always gonna get our Bible off the shelf and look it up for myself, to see if God really said that, but I never did. But I doubt Billy Graham would have said it if it wasn't in the Bible. I respect that man."

Stormi filled two cups with coffee and handed one of them to Abe. "I wish I'd gone to Sunday school and church when I was a kid. I know so very little about God."

Abe blew into his cup. "Guess it's never too late to learn. Does that boyfriend of yours go to church?"

"He hasn't said, but I'm sure he does."

"Like I said, Stormi, I like that man, and it's obvious you still have feelings for him. If I were you, I'd give him a chance. He might be telling you the truth."

The rest of the evening, no matter how busy she was or how many customers were clamoring for their order, Stormi kept mulling her conversation with Abe over and over in her mind. If Mark *was* telling her the truth and she didn't believe him and turned him away, she might be making the biggest mistake of her life. But dare she continue to give him a chance to prove himself?

"See, you're a better skater than you thought," Mark told her as they held hands and skated in a counterclockwise manner around the outdoor rink.

After nearly losing her balance when a young boy cut across in front of them, Stormi giggled. "Only because you're holding me up."

A playful frown creased Mark's brow. "Me holding you up? All this time I thought you were holding me up!" Releasing her hand, he slid his arm about her waist. "I'd forgotten how much fun it is to ice-skate."

"It is fun, isn't it?"

"Maybe ice-skating wasn't such a good idea, though. You've worked two jobs today. I'll bet you're exhausted."

She smiled up at him. "Actually, the exercise and the fresh mountain air are exhilarating."

He glanced upward. "Look at that moon. Isn't that a beauty?"

Stormi released a dreamy sigh. "It's fabulous."

"Just imagine how God must have felt when He hung the moon in the sky and flung the stars into space."

Her gaze went to his face. "You really are into this God thing, aren't you?"

"I told you I was." His grip tightened about her waist. "He's everything to me, Stormi. Everything."

Remembering the conversation she'd had with Abe, she asked, "Do you go to church now?"

"Yes, every Sunday. I know you're going to laugh when you hear this, but I serve on the board. I'm a deacon in my church."

"You're kidding! A deacon?"

He laughed. "Yep, and a good one, if I do say so myself."

"You *have* changed! I doubt the old Mark would have even entered a church, much less served on its board."

His expression became somber. "My change is real, Stormi. That's what I've been trying to tell you. I've become a new creature in Christ. Old things have passed away. All things have become new."

"I want to believe you, Mark, but it's so hard."

"I'm sure it is. I hate to even think what I was like in my

early twenties. The best thing that ever happened to me was joining the army and meeting Chaplain Ron. I just wish you could have met him, too."

"I do, too. Do you see him often? Now that you're no longer in the service?"

"No, but we talk occasionally on the phone. He's career military and still in Iraq."

They skated another hour, then moved to the sidelines to take off their skates and put on their shoes. "How about lunch again tomorrow at the hotel, about 1:00, and a late dinner at that place you told me about after you get off work?" he asked after they'd turned in their skates and headed for his car.

"You sure you want to do the lunch thing again? I thought you came to Keystone to ski."

"I did, but that was before I found out you were here. I'll still be able to ski from ten till noon." He gave her a wink. "I'd much rather have a date with my best girl than ski."

She laughed, then frowned up at him. "Your best girl?"

"I'd *like* for you to be my best girl."

She thought of a retort but decided to keep it to herself. He'd done nothing to antagonize her and didn't deserve it. "Lunch would be nice."

"Good. I'll meet you at your desk, and we'll walk over to the Great Northern Tavern."

"That place is pretty fancy. I'd really look out of place in my uniform."

"Then bring a jacket or sweater you can slip into if it'll make you more comfortable. Some of my friends have eaten there, and they said the food is quite good. I'd like to try it."

"It's probably expensive! You're already planning on taking me to The Mexican Hat Dance tomorrow evening."

He grabbed her by the shoulders. "Stormi, I don't care if the food is good or bad, if it is expensive or cheap. Going to those restaurants is only a reason to be able to spend time with you. Don't you see? I want to be with you, enjoy your company, get to know the woman you are now. I like being with you."

"I like being with you—"

"Good. Spend time with me. Give me a chance. That's all I ask." He assisted her into his car, and they headed for her apartment. At her door, although he held her hand and gazed into her eyes for a moment, he simply said good night and left.

"I thought sure he'd at least give me a peck on the cheek," Stormi said to her reflection in the mirror as she applied night cream to her face. "If he had kissed me and did it without asking, should I have slapped him? Stood rigid and acted like I was offended? Or should I have melted into his arms and happily participated like I'd like to?" She shrugged. "Guess I won't know unless it happens."

Lunch the next day at River Run Village's Great Northern Tavern was more delicious and fun than Stormi had imagined it would be, and Mark was more handsome than ever in his beige Irish knit sweater and dark trousers. She was thankful she'd taken her burgundy ruffled-front blouse to replace her uniform top when she'd left home that morning. With the addition of a pair of gold hoop earrings and a simple gold chain about her neck, she actually looked like one of the restaurant's patrons, rather than the clerk from the nearby hotel.

"I'm glad I insisted we come here," Mark told her, appraising her appearance. "You're beautiful. I'm sure I'm the envy of every man in this place."

"Thank you," she replied, her hand going to finger the gold chain about her neck. "Even if you don't mean it."

"Stormi, I'm not flattering you. I'm telling you the truth. Remember—you're sitting opposite the new Mark Denton. This man doesn't lie to gain a girl's confidence."

"Are you ready to order, or would you like drinks first?" the waiter asked as he stepped up beside their table.

"We'd prefer to order," Mark answered without missing a beat. "We don't have much time."

After they'd ordered, he smiled at her across the table. "My mom loves it that I'm seeing you again. She always liked you, Stormi. She was really upset with me for letting you get away."

"I liked her, too. I hope I get to see her before she leaves. But I didn't exactly *get away*, Mark. You sent me away."

He swallowed hard. "Don't remind me."

She felt bad for bringing up the past again. "Are your mother and her friend still enjoying themselves?"

"Oh yes. I don't think there is a corner of Keystone they haven't explored. They're planning to take the hotel shuttle to some of the shops again this afternoon. I offered to drive them, but they said they didn't want a man hanging around, bugging them to hurry up."

"I think it's wonderful you brought your mother with you."

"She's a great gal. She still misses my dad but—"

"He died?"

Mark nodded. "Yeah, two years ago. Mom took it really hard. She's just now coming out of her funk. This trip has been good for her."

"I'm so sorry. I didn't know."

"Thanks. I really miss him. But—back to our discussion about Mom. I thought maybe the three of us could have lunch together Saturday. Mom's friend's sister is driving over from Vail to spend the day with her, so it'd just be the three of us."

"I'd love it. It'll be so nice to see your mom again."

"Then it's a date." He reached across the table, took both her hands in his, and gazed into her eyes. "I do love being with you, Stormi. I hope you're enjoying being with me—just a little bit?"

"A lotta bit would be more like it," she confessed, his words touching her so deeply she wanted to cry. "I like the new Mark—much, much better than the old one."

"Does that mean you might eventually find it in your heart to forgive me?"

A slight grin tilted at the corners of her mouth. "I'm working on it."

"That's all I ask."

"So, how'd it go with Romeo?" Renee asked as Stormi headed for the little storeroom off to the side of the registration desk to change back into her uniform top. "He's sure giving you a rush. That guy is handsome! Why didn't you tell me he was so good-looking?"

Stormi quickly unbuttoned her blouse, took her arms out of the sleeves, and then pulled on her white shirt. "Looks aren't everything, Renee. Mark is handsome, but it's the man inside who is reaching my heart. He's changed so much that I barely recognize him. He even prays for our meals now."

"He's really getting to you, huh?"

Stormi pulled off her earrings and stuck them in her purse. "I'd be lying if I said no."

"And I'd say you'd be a fool if you let that man get away. It's obvious he's gaga over you."

"I thought he was gaga over me before the whole thing flared up in my face and I got burned. I have to be absolutely sure this time. I can't go through that again."

Andrea stuck her head in the storeroom door. "Stormi, you're needed at the counter. A hotel guest is waiting to be registered."

"I'm ready. I'll take care of it." Stormi pulled on her blazer and moved quickly out the door.

It was nearly nine thirty before they reached The Mexican Hat Dance, and the place was jumping. Eventually, after a twenty-minute wait, they were seated at a small table between two huge cacti. "I like this place," Mark hollered, trying to make his voice heard over the noise of the crowd.

Stormi threw back her head with a laugh. "Between the

happy skiers and the music, it's almost impossible to hear."

He picked up a menu. "What's good?"

"Everything. I like the Juan Carlos."

"What's the Juan Carlos?"

"A huge burrito filled with all kinds of good things. Kinda messy, though."

"Sounds good to me. And we'll need some—" He laughed as he gazed at the menu. "Nasty Nachos? What a name!"

"Awful name, but oh, so good!"

The mariachi band had begun to play, drowning out her sentence.

"What?" Mark shouted, cupping his ear with his hand.

"I said the nachos here are good! So are the burritos."

He nodded. "Gotcha."

The two visited until their order arrived, laughing and shouting at one another so they could be heard.

Mark prayed, then dug into the hot nachos, stringing cheese clear to his mouth, with a little bit of it lingering behind on his chin. "Umm, these are good!"

Muffling a giggle, Stormi reached across the table and, using her fingers, pulled the string of cheese away. But before she could withdraw her hand, Mark grabbed hold of it, his intense gaze locking with hers.

"I can't tell you how much being with you means to me, Stormi. You've changed, too. You're stronger. More independent. More your own person. I like the new you."

"I like the new me, too. Though it was hard at first, I've learned I *can* take care of myself. The best thing I've learned is that I don't have to depend on someone else for my happiness. I'm proud of the fact that I've nearly paid off all my debts instead of declaring bankruptcy and running away from them, even if it has taken working two jobs a day to do it." She flinched and covered her ears as the mariachi band moved closer and struck up another lively tune.

Mark picked up another chip. "I wish I could say that. Unlike you, I ran away from my obligations. Joining the army was my escape, but the best thing I ever did for myself. Uncle Sam turned out to be the taskmaster I needed to add regimentation to my life. Though boot camp nearly killed me, I made it through and actually became friends with my drill sergeant. You knew the *old* me better than anyone else. Don't you think that was pretty amazing?"

She laughed. "I can barely hear you, but if you said what I think you said, then I'd say yes, considering the bad rap those tough drill sergeants get, your completing basic training *was* pretty amazing. It's hard to imagine the Mark Denton I knew taking orders from anyone."

He cupped his ear and shouted back, "It wasn't easy. I hate to think how many times I nearly took a swing at the guy. Glad I didn't. Being cooped up in the brig would have been even worse, not to mention the dishonorable discharge I would have faced."

The two turned their attention to the mariachi band, listening, then applauding along with the restaurant's other patrons as the song ended. The leader, apparently noticing Mark's enthusiastic applause, walked over to their table, his dark eyes sparkling beneath his beaded and sequin-embellished velvet sombrero. "You and your lovely lady have a special song you'd like to hear? Something romantic, maybe?"

Mark reached into his pocket, pulled out his wallet, and handed the man a bill. "Yeah, something romantic would be nice."

Stormi felt a flush rush again to her cheeks as the musical trio began to strum its guitars while circling their table. The song the band played wasn't a familiar one, but from listening to the words as the lead guitarist sang them, it was indeed romantic. *Don't do it! Don't let some sappy love song weaken your resolve,* she told herself. *You've come too far to turn back.*

"I'd better be going," she told him after the song ended. "It's nearly eleven."

"It is, isn't it? Time flies when I'm with you." He motioned for their waiter, presented his Visa card, then signed the tab. "Hard to believe tomorrow is Thursday."

"I know." How well she knew. Thursday. Friday. Saturday. Then he'd be leaving on Sunday. She hated the thought. Despite her original desire to keep herself distanced from him, she found herself dreading his departure.

"The Mexican Hat Dance was a great choice. Lots of ambience and good food, too," he told her when they reached the door to her apartment. "I had a great time."

"I had a great time, too."

He took hold of her hand, then gazed into her eyes. "Am I getting anywhere with you, Stormi? Are you beginning to realize the man who hurt you is gone? The one holding your hand has taken his place? This man would never hurt you."

With his pleading eyes and his handsome face so close to her, she could barely think straight. "You do seem different."

"I *am* different, Stormi. You have to believe me."

She tried to look away, but his seemingly sincere gaze held her captive. "I'm considering accepting your apology."

Letting loose of her hand, he slipped his arms about her waist. "For which I'm very thankful, but accepting my apology isn't enough. The only way I'll ever be free of the guilt is if you forgive me."

"I'm not sure I can do that," she said honestly.

"And I understand that. I would have a hard time forgiving someone who'd treated me like I treated you. I'm being selfish for even asking. But without it, I know I'll be miserable the rest of my life. You wouldn't want that, would you?"

She looked away. She had to break eye contact. "Come on, Mark. Isn't that a bit of an exaggeration? I'm sure you've had plenty of other girlfriends in the past five years. How gullible do you think I am? Surely you don't expect me to believe I have been on your mind all that time? The old Mark would—"

"Forget about that guy. He isn't worth remembering." Using his finger, he lifted her chin. "Look at me, Stormi. Look into my eyes. There hasn't been a day since I accepted Christ as my Savior that I haven't thought of you. God, in His mercy, forgave me when I didn't deserve forgiveness, but I also need your forgiveness. And along with that forgiveness, I'd like to have your trust."

Stormi's brain said, *He's probably the same old scoundrel. Don't listen to him.* But her heart said, *Every person deserves a second chance. Even Mark.*

"I'm trying to forgive you, Mark, but it's so hard. You broke my heart. Broken hearts don't mend easily."

He bent and lightly kissed her forehead. "But you will keep trying, won't you?"

"I want to forgive you. Forgiving you would make my life so much easier."

He kissed her forehead again, then one cheek, then the other before whispering, "I was a fool. Letting you get away was the stupidest thing I've ever done."

She pressed her eyes tightly shut, needing to block out his penetrating gaze. "You didn't *let* me get away, Mark. You shoved me away. Do I have to keep reminding you?"

"You're right, and I am so sorry."

Before she knew what was happening, his lips claimed hers. Though she wanted to push him away, she couldn't. How many times had she dreamed of this moment? Longed to be held in his arms? Feel his lips pressed against hers? When their kiss ended, she found herself speechless and almost too weak to stand.

"I've wanted to do that since the moment I found you."

Be still, my heart. Don't pound like that. Don't wish for another kiss.

"Stormi, aren't you going to say something? Scream at me? Slap me?"

She swallowed hard, then formed her mouth, but the words wouldn't come.

He pressed his cheek against hers. "I think that kiss was sweeter than any kiss you and I ever shared. Was it that way for you?"

All she could do was stand motionless.

"Would you slap me if I kissed you again?"

She gave her head a slight shake.

This time, Mark's lips sought hers slowly, lightly touching at first as his hands splayed across her back, gently drawing her to him. Her breath caught as the softness of his mouth brushed gently over her lips, eventually pressing against them in a full-blown kiss.

"Oh, Mark," she mumbled breathlessly as he pulled away, stopping with his face merely inches from hers. "I'm so confused. Being with you these few days is like being with a stranger."

His forehead pressed against hers. "I used to think *maybe* I was in love with you, but I wasn't sure."

She bristled slightly. "You weren't sure?"

He gave her a gentle smile. "Let me finish. I was going to say, but now—after being with you again—I have an entirely different feeling for you."

"Exactly what does that mean?"

He lifted his shoulders in a slight shrug. "To be honest, I'm not exactly sure what it means. I just know I love being with you and am miserable every minute I'm away from you."

"Don't toy with my emotions, Mark. I had enough of that once, and it nearly killed me. Don't give me pretty words and then disappear on Sunday. I couldn't handle it a second time."

"I'm not toying with your emotions, Stormi. I'd never do

that to you a second time, but I can't allow these new feelings for you to turn into love."

Now she *was* confused. "You can't *let* your feelings turn into love? Why not? Is there a girlfriend, a fiancée, or maybe a wife waiting for you back in Denver?"

Chapter 5

Mark grabbed her arm. "No, nothing like that. I've dated a few women since we parted, but none of them seriously."

Her chin jutting out, Stormi's hands went to her hips. "Then what, Mark? I think I deserve an answer."

"It's kind of hard to explain."

"Give it a try."

He gazed off into space, as if trying to make sure his words came out correctly. "I told you I'm a Christian."

"Yes, you told me, but what does that have to do with love?"

"Stormi, remember when I told you God's Word says all people are sinners?"

She nodded. "I remember."

"It also says Christians shouldn't be yoked together with unbelievers. I've turned my life over to God, given it to Him to do with as He sees fit. I know that life can't be all it should be if the woman I am attracted to, and want to marry, doesn't share my faith."

She gave her head a shake to clear it. "What do you mean— share your faith?"

"Any woman I would become serious with would have to

do what I did. Realize she is a sinner, confess her sins to God, and ask His forgiveness, then turn the control of her life over to Him."

Her eyes narrowed as she considered Mark's words. "That's a pretty tall order. Isn't that asking a lot?"

"We've all sinned, Stormi. Me, my mom, the chaplain I told you about. God asks the same of each of us. You included."

She held up her hands defensively. "Whoa. Stop. I'm not sure I want to hear this. A sinner? I've done a few things I'm not proud of, but I'm not a sinner. Aside from my drinking those few years, I've actually been pretty good all my life."

He took hold of her hand, drew it to him, and kissed her fingertips. "I'm not saying these things to make you mad. Remember I told you Chaplain Ron took his big, old, tattered Bible and showed me where God said *all* men are sinners?"

"But I wasn't a heavy drinker like you."

"Out-of-control drinking is only one of the thousands of sins people commit every day. Chaplain Ron reminded me it was God who had said all of us are sinners, and there was only one way to make things right with Him. I had to acknowledge *I* was a sinner, confess my sins to God, and ask for His forgiveness."

She gave her chin a haughty tilt. "I still find it hard to think of myself as a sinner."

"In addition to all my other sins, I was turning my back on God, refusing to accept Him and His deity." He cupped her chin with his hand and gazed into her eyes, then said in a mere whisper, "You're doing the same thing right now, Stormi."

His words stung as much as if a swarm of bees had attacked

her. "It's late." She turned her key in the lock and pushed open her apartment door. "I have to get to bed."

He grabbed the doorknob and refused to let her close it. "Wait—we haven't decided where we're going to have lunch tomorrow."

"You decide—then meet me at the registration desk at one." With that, she closed the door and slid the dead bolt into position. "How dare he call me a sinner?" she nearly shouted as she leaned her back against the door, her heart racing and causing a discomfort in her chest.

But deep inside, a little voice seemed to say, *If Mark is telling the truth, according to God's Word, all have sinned. That means you, too.*

"You look awful!" Renee moved her hand to Stormi's forehead when she reported for work the next morning.

"Didn't sleep very well. I had—things—on my mind."

"You and that man of yours have a fight?"

"Not exactly. He said a few things that upset me, that's all."

Renee blanched. "That's all? I'd say that's quite a bit for someone who is obviously trying to impress you."

Stormi moved to the computer and punched several keys. "Besides, he's not my boyfriend. He used to be, but not now."

"From the way he looks at you, you could have fooled me. I'd say that man is crazy about you."

"Looks can be deceiving. Could we just not talk about it, please?"

Renee eyed her, then asked, "You gonna have lunch with him again today?"

"Yeah. He'll be showing up here around one. Probably a dumb thing to do, but I agreed to see him again."

"Good, then maybe you can right whatever went wrong."

Stormi accidentally punched the wrong key on the computer, bringing up an error message, adding to her frustration. "Not likely."

The morning seemed to drag by, with guests either asking questions she couldn't answer or forgetting their keys and locking themselves out of their rooms. Finally, one o'clock arrived, but no Mark. Not that she was surprised after the way their evening had ended.

Renee glanced at the clock on the back wall. "Thought you said your man was coming at one."

Stormi harrumphed. "I thought he was."

"There he is!" Renee pointed toward the hotel's revolving door.

Clad in his ski jacket and stocking cap, Mark rushed up to the counter, breathing heavily. "Sorry, I decided to ski this morning, and it took me longer to get down the mountain than I'd anticipated." He gave her a shy grin. "Old age, I guess. Besides, I had an errand to run."

Stormi stared at him. "If you didn't want to have lunch with me, you could have just said so."

"But I do want to have lunch with you. Are you ready?"

"Go on." Renee gave her a little shove. "Don't worry about getting back on time. I'll cover for you."

She thanked Renee, grabbed her coat off the rack, then joined Mark. "Did you decide where you want to have lunch?"

He took hold of her arm and moved her toward the front door. "Yep. My car's out front." Less than five minutes later, they pulled up by The Fireside Inn, a glorified sandwich shop and one of Abe's main competitors. Stormi started to mention it but decided it really wasn't that important.

Once they had been seated, the waiter had brought their orders, and Mark had prayed, he smiled at her across the table. "You still mad at me?"

"Who said I was mad at you?"

"You have to admit our evening ended pretty abruptly. I was afraid my words would upset you, but I had to tell it like it is. With God, it's His way or no way. I've wanted so badly to share my faith with you. I just hope I didn't do it in a bungling way. You're important to me, Stormi. I wanted you to know what God has done for me, in hopes you'd want Him to do the same thing for you. But you have to take the first step."

"By admitting I'm a sinner?"

"Yes. There are no shortcuts."

She lifted her sandwich and nibbled at the edges. "I was awake most of the night, thinking about the things you said. I hate to say it, but it kind of makes sense. I've always thought God had to be real. The idea of things just happening—things like the creation of the world, the birth of a baby, and other miraculous kinds of things just evolving themselves perfectly without anyone being in control—didn't make sense."

"I'm so glad to hear you say that, Stormi. Without believing there is a God, there is no way a person would be interested in what He has to say in His Word. It's His desire that all men. . . and women"—he paused and gave her a wink—"come to Him, but He leaves that choice up to each of us. To love and serve God has to be our decision."

"You make it sound so simple."

"It is simple. Actually, God's plan is simple enough a child can understand it."

His voice was so kind she couldn't help grinning. "Which means I should be able to understand it?"

"Yes. Whether you and I continue our newfound relationship after I leave Keystone this Sunday, or if we part and never see each other again in our lifetime, I want to make sure we share the same faith." He pointed to her barely touched sandwich. "You'd better eat if you want to get back to work on time."

Though they laughed and carried on a pleasant conversation as they finished their lunch, to Stormi, beneath it all were the things Mark had said. She wanted to know God like Mark did. She really did. How many times had she wished she knew the God of heaven and could call upon Him when things were going wrong in her life? But she hadn't even bothered to go to church, not that she had the time, working two jobs like she did.

"I think I'll go to my room and take a nap," Mark said, grinning as they walked back into the hotel lobby. "With two women chattering until all hours of the night, I barely get any sleep."

"You can hear them in the next room?"

He laughed. "I couldn't if they'd let me close the door between us, but they're scaredy-cats and insist I leave it open.

They've heard stories about women's hotel rooms being broken into. I guess I'm their big protector."

She smiled back. "I'm sure it comforts them to know you're there."

"You want to do something different tonight?"

"Like what?"

His brow raised in a teasing manner. "How about letting me surprise you again? I'll pick you up at Abe's. About nine?"

She removed her coat and stepped behind the counter. "Nine is fine."

After Mark walked away, Renee sidled up to her. "Looks like you two are back on track."

Stormi smiled, then gave her a nonchalant shrug. "Who knows?"

Though she wouldn't admit it to anyone, not even Renee, in her heart, she was troubled.

Abe handed Stormi a large sack as she pulled on her coat at the end of her shift. "Take these with you."

She peeked into the bag, then eyed him suspiciously. "There's enough food in here for several people. What am I supposed to do with it?"

He smiled like a Cheshire cat. "Trust me. Just take it with you, okay?"

She glanced at the clock on the wall. It was already a few minutes past nine. Mark was probably waiting in the car, wondering what was taking her so long. Rather than spend time arguing with Abe, she folded the top down on the bag, waved, and hurried out the door.

Mark reached across and pushed open the passenger door when she approached his car. "Hi. Looks like Abe's is pretty crowded tonight. I was afraid you'd have trouble getting away."

She closed the door, then lifted the sack. "I was ready to leave on time, but Abe handed me this sack and told me to take it with me. I have no idea why. But rather than argue with him, I brought it along. I don't know if someone called in an order and then didn't pick it up or what. It even has a thermos of hot coffee in it. I'm not sure what to do with it."

Mark shifted into DRIVE, then gave her a wink. "Maybe we'll run into two hungry people who will appreciate it."

Before fastening her seat belt, she turned and placed the bag on the backseat, alongside the large shopping bag that was already there. "Maybe."

They drove past several of Keystone's best eating places, on through the little village, eventually turning onto a nearly deserted road she hadn't been on before. "Where are we going?"

"You said you'd let me surprise you, didn't you?"

"I guess so." She hunkered down in her seat, not sure what she was getting into. It was a beautiful, clear night with a full moon, which lit up the newly fallen snow, making it glisten like a million brightly shining diamonds set in a sea of white velvet. *The moon hanging in the sky, its light beaming all the way to the earth, partially illuminating the darkness, a new-fallen snow giving much-needed moisture to plants, trees, and all things living. These things could not have been happenstance,* she thought as she gazed out the window. *There has to be a God. The God Mark said had caused a miracle in his life.* How she wished she knew God like he did.

"We're here." Mark pulled into a parking spot, alongside several other cars and pickup trucks, and turned off the engine. He reached into the backseat and pulled up the shopping bag. "Here, I bought you something. You'll be needing it." He opened the bag and took out the prettiest ski jacket she had ever seen and handed it to her. A white one, with a fuzzy white collar, in just her size. "It's going to be cold where we're going," he said with a grin, pointing to a pair of heavy white gloves sticking out of the jacket's pockets. He reached into the backseat again and brought up Abe's sack. "We're going to eat our supper on a sleigh ride!"

Stormi's eyes widened. "That's why Abe insisted on me taking that sack? He knew about this?"

"Yep. I called in our order after I left you this afternoon. Now, we'd better hurry. Slip into your new jacket and put on your gloves. I'll take our supper. It looks like our sleigh is ready and waiting for us."

Stormi had never been on a sleigh ride before, but what a joy it turned out to be! The bells on the horses' bridles tinkled merrily with each step they took, making a sound that she'd remember always. But the best part was being snuggled close to Mark under the weight of the big, heavy quilt the sleigh driver provided for them. The whole thing was like a dream, one she'd never expected to happen.

After they'd been on the trail for a while, Mark opened the

sack and pulled out their sandwiches. "I don't know about you, but I'm hungry."

She nodded. "Me, too. This fresh air gives me an appetite."

He prayed, then handed her one of the wrapped sandwiches. "Your favorite—Abe's famous meatball sandwich and chips."

"You remembered, or was the choice of food Abe's idea?"

He grinned. "I remembered." He removed his sandwich from the bag, then poured them two cups of steaming hot coffee from the thermos. "Um, that smells good."

They enjoyed their carryout meal, laughing, talking, and teasing as they devoured Abe's delicious sandwiches and gazed at the amazing winter scene surrounding them. Finally, as they rounded the last turn, Mark asked cautiously, "Have you thought anymore about what we talked about? You know, about having a personal relationship with God?"

Stormi leaped at the chance to talk about it since she had been awake most of the night, thinking about the things Mark had told her were in the Bible. "Yes, I have. I thought over everything you said, and as much as I hate to admit it, it all makes sense. I *am* a sinner, Mark. I know that now. I guess I've always known it but hadn't wanted to face the fact."

"Does that mean—"

"That I'm ready to confess I'm a sinner and ask for God's forgiveness?" She paused, her heart aching to get to know the God that the Bible said loved her and died for her, to know Him in the same personal way Mark did. "Yes, I am ready. I'm just not exactly sure how to start."

With a look of seriousness, Mark took her hand in his. "If

you mean it, Stormi, all you have to do is repeat after me."

"I do mean it, Mark. I've never been more serious about anything."

"Then bow your head and say what I say." He waited until she bowed her head and then began. "Lord, I come to You confessing that I am a sinner."

Stormi took in a deep breath. "Lord, I come to You confessing that I am a sinner."

"I ask You to forgive my sins and cleanse me from all unrighteousness."

She slowly repeated his words, thinking on each one as she voiced it.

"Because I want to be all You want me to be—"

"Because I want to be all You want me to be—" *And I do mean it, Lord. I want to be worthy of Your love.*

"I give my life over to You."

Though she tried, she couldn't hold back her tears, tears of both repentance and joy. "I give my life over to You."

Mark pulled her into his arms and held her tight. "Right now, the angels in heaven are rejoicing, and so am I. I've wanted so much to be able to lead you to my Lord, Stormi. This is one of the happiest days of my life."

She smiled up at him. "Mine, too."

"God is yours, and you are His now. He's ready to listen to you anytime. He wants to take care of you, provide for you, and He wants your praise. God longs to have the worship of His children."

"I do want to praise Him, Mark. God has given me a peace

I've never known before."

He raised one hand toward the heavens. "Thank You, Lord!"

Their ride ended all too soon. There were so many questions about God and the Bible Stormi wanted to ask him.

"I know you're busy working your two jobs, but you really need to find yourself a church that truly preaches God's Word and begin to attend regularly," Mark told her as they crawled into his car. "It's much easier to grow in Him and understand His Word when you have someone to guide you, not to mention the wonderful experience of fellowshipping with other believers."

"I don't usually work on Sunday mornings. It's the day I clean and do laundry. I can find another time to do those things. I'll go to church. I promise."

He grinned. "Sunday school would be helpful to you, too."

"And I'll make it to Sunday school. I really want to learn about God."

When they reached Stormi's door, Mark gave her a gentle kiss on the cheek and once again told her how happy he was that she'd accepted Christ; then he said good night and left.

As she pulled back the quilt and crawled between the sheets, she smiled. For the first time in her life, she knew for sure, if she bowed her head and prayed, God would hear.

"You ready for another adventure?" Mark asked as Stormi answered the phone on the registration counter the next morning. "I thought we could take the ski lift gondola up to the top of the mountain and grab a quick bowl of hot soup. It's a beautiful day. The sun is shining, and it's warmer than usual."

"Can we do all of that in only an hour?"

"I think so. If the line is too long, we'll have lunch in the hotel."

"I'd love to go. I've never ridden on the gondola."

He huffed. "You're kidding. You never have? Then you're in for a treat. See you at one."

The ride up the mountain was even more spectacular than she'd imagined, with thousands of tall trees cloaked in capes of white, the sky as blue as the blue of Mark's eyes, and mountain-tops staggered behind one another as far as the eye could see. Though she'd been a little apprehensive about climbing into the gondola and swinging from the heavy cable suspended high above the ground, Stormi found herself oohing and aahing as she gazed out the window.

"Our God created this wonderland, Stormi. Isn't He awesome?"

All she could do was nod. Mark had said *our* God. She now shared Mark's faith. What a blessing.

He reached into his backpack and pulled out an elegantly gift-wrapped box. "This is for you."

She shook her head. "You've already fed me, taken me to wonderful places, and given me that gorgeous white jacket and gloves. I can't take another present from you."

"You have to take this one. I insist."

There was something about his voice that made it seem important to him that she accept his gift. She took it from his hands and carefully opened it, being careful not to destroy the shiny red bow. "It's a Bible! Oh, Mark, how thoughtful. I can't thank you enough. I've never had my very own Bible before, other than the secondhand one my cousin gave me when I was in the fourth grade. I love it!"

He gave her a grin of satisfaction. "And you promise you'll read it?"

She pressed it to her heart. "Yes, every day. There's so much I want to know. Thank you for being so thoughtful. I'll cherish it always." All the way to the bottom of the lift, Stormi held the gift to her bosom. Her very own Bible—and Mark had given it to her, which made it that much more special.

"You might want to wear your best dress tonight. I thought we'd go to Champeaux for dinner, if that sounds good to you."

"The French restaurant in the hotel? Our hotel guests seem to love it, but I've never even set foot in the door." Though she didn't really have a best dress, she did have a black sheath. Perhaps she could dress it up with a pair of earrings and a necklace from the gift shop since she wouldn't have time to shop elsewhere.

But as she slipped into her sheath that night, a sadness nearly overwhelmed her. Mark would soon be gone. Like he had been for the past five years, he'd once again be just a memory. But, this time, that memory would be a pleasant one—a sweeter one she'd never forget.

❧

"You, milady, look stunning," he told her as Champeaux's maître d' guided them to their table. "I'm honored that you accepted my invitation."

She gave him a coquettish smile. "Thank you, sir. You're looking rather dashing yourself." She was going to miss the compliments he lavished upon her. No man had ever treated her with the respect and admiration as did this new man Mark had become.

After the waiter had brought their drinks and they'd decided neither of them really cared for appetizers, Mark began to scan his menu. "Oh, I know what I'm having. The Saint Jacques. I love jumbo scallops."

Stormi gazed at her own menu. Names like Tournados of Beef, Roasted Squash Tortellini, and Forest Mushroom Risotto were foreign to her. "I'll have what you're having," she told him, hoping her ignorance of French cuisine wasn't showing.

After their orders were placed, they settled back to enjoy the ambience of the spectacular restaurant and its furnishings and their time together. For one who normally shied away from seafood or fish of any kind, to Stormi's surprise, the scallops were excellent, and she loved the Tuxedo Truffle Whipped Potatoes, as the menu called them.

When they'd eaten their fill, the china and silverware removed from the table, and the bill taken care of, Mark scooted his chair close to hers. She nearly melted from his nearness as her heart pounded with erratic little beats that almost frightened her.

He took hold of her hand, lifted it to his face, and kissed her fingertips. "Stormi, when we were together before, I did have feelings for you. You were special in my life, but I wasn't ready or willing to commit to any woman. You were eager for marriage, a home, and a family. So eager that those were the only things you talked about. It scared me. I wasn't ready for marriage, and I hated the way you smothered me. In fact, I was so dead set against being tied down, I mocked you, said things to hurt you, and sent you away. After you left and I couldn't find you, I had a series of girlfriends, thinking each one would take my mind off you, but they didn't. None of them even compared to you. I'd had the best and hadn't recognized it."

"But you—"

"Hear me out, please. My feelings were pretty mixed up at that time. Looking back, I know now I *did* love you, but I didn't *want* you. Does that make sense?"

She gave her head a shake. "No, it doesn't."

"I was immature, self-centered, egotistical, and a whole lot of other things. All I could think about was *me* and what *I* wanted. What you wanted wasn't important to me. I wanted my freedom to do just what I pleased, and in my eyes, you wanted to take that freedom away. So I, Mr. Macho Man, rebelled. I would rather lose you than give in and marry you."

He chortled. "Consider yourself lucky. As selfish as I was, we would have ended up in divorce court in less than a year. I needed to grow up, sweetheart, and that's exactly what the army and accepting Christ did for me. The day I became a Christian, I started praying that wherever you were, God would watch over you and protect you. But most of all, I prayed I'd find you again so I could apologize and ask your forgiveness. He answered my prayer."

"You actually prayed for me?"

"Hundreds of times."

"Mark, when you apologized, I told you I would accept your apology but I wasn't sure I could forgive you. That's all changed now. God has forgiven *me*. Forgiving *you* is the least I can do."

"I do want your forgiveness, Stormi. I've needed desperately to hear those words, but I want so much more than your forgiveness."

She frowned, not sure what he meant. "More? I don't understand."

Mark's expression took on a tenderness that touched the very inner depths of her heart. Was he going to say he wanted them to keep in touch? That maybe he'd drive up from Denver to spend time with her? She hoped so. She couldn't stand the idea of him walking out of her life a second time, not this new Mark she had come to love with all her heart.

Still holding her hand, he gazed into her eyes for a long moment before answering. "Stormi McNeil, I'm asking you to marry me."

Stormi let out a yelp so loud the other patrons turned to see what had happened. "Marry you? You're asking *me* to marry *you*? Are you serious? Don't joke with me, Mark, please."

Wrapping her in his arms, he drew her close. "I couldn't be more serious, sweetheart. The only thing that has kept me from asking you to marry me sooner was that you hadn't made a decision for Christ. I didn't want my love for you to cause you to make that decision if you weren't ready, or to make your peace with God because that's what I wanted you to do. Your decision to ask God into your life had to be because you sincerely and truthfully wanted Him as your personal Savior, so I had to wait until that happened before I could ask you to become my wife. Even though you thought I'd be gone and out of your life on Sunday and we might never see each other again, you made that decision. I knew then it was real. You weren't faking it."

Stormi thought her heart would burst with love for this man.

"I came so close to proposing to you last night, but I had to do something first."

Overcome by his unexpected proposal, all Stormi could do was gaze at him, her heart bubbling over with more love than it could hold.

"Let's get out of here." He rose quickly and tugged her to her feet. "We need some privacy."

They made their way through the hotel to the parking garage. After they'd settled themselves in his car and he'd started the engine and flipped the switch on the heater, he pulled her into his arms and smothered her face with kisses. His beard tickled her lips and made her laugh.

"I love you, Stormi. I want us to spend the rest of our lives together as husband and wife. With God as my witness, I promise to do everything I can to be the husband you deserve. I want us to have children together, serve God together, and grow old together. Please say you'll marry me."

He was so close she could feel his warm breath on her cheeks, the beat of his heart, and sense that he was as nervous as she was. The moment was surreal. Was it really happening? Gazing up into the face of the only man she'd ever loved, she smiled. "Mark, my beloved, the light of my life, of course I'll marry you. I love you with enough love to last several lifetimes."

Freeing his hand, he reached into his jacket pocket and pulled something out. "I hope that means you love me enough to allow me to slip this ring onto your finger."

Stormi stared at his index finger. On its tip perched the most beautiful engagement ring she'd ever seen. But even if it had been a simple band with no diamonds at all, to her, it would have been exquisite because it symbolized his commitment to her. "I—I love it."

Lovingly, Mark took her left hand and, after kissing her finger, slipped the ring onto it. "You're pledged to me now, my love. There's no backing out."

With that, he pulled her into his arms again, his lips tantalizingly grazing her face, teasing and taunting, until she cried out, "Kiss me!"

And kiss her, he did, with the sweetest, most passionate kiss she could imagine.

Before retiring that night, Stormi knelt beside her bed and thanked the Lord for being so good to her when she was so unworthy and for bringing Mark back to her. The last thing she did before turning off the light was gaze at the lovely, unexpected ring Mark had placed on her finger.

"When I got back to my room last night, I told Mom you accepted my proposal," Mark told Stormi the next morning after he'd talked her into taking an early morning coffee break. "She's excited about having you for a daughter-in-law, and she asked me to give you her love and congratulations." He snapped his fingers. "By the way, don't forget that the three of us are having lunch together today."

"Tell her I'm excited about becoming her daughter-in-law. I always liked your mother. I'm sure we'll find lots to talk about." Stormi was about to burst with happiness. She wanted to jump up and shout to everyone in the coffee shop that she was going to marry the man of her dreams.

He gave her a sheepish grin. "I have an idea, but you might think I'm a little crazy."

She thumped his arm with a playful nudge. "Come on. Tell me. I promise I won't think you're crazy."

"Now that I've found you, sweetheart, I don't want to let you go. I want us to get married right away."

"Right away?" She fairly screamed out the words.

Mark glanced around, giving an embarrassed grin toward those who were staring at them. "Knowing you and your loyalty to your employers, I'm sure you'll want to give them a two-week notice, so I'm wondering if we can be married in two weeks?"

Her mind went into a whir. "Two weeks? I—I don't know." She gazed at him and found him anxiously awaiting her answer. "Two weeks isn't much time. There's so much to do."

"Think about it, Stormi. We can have the wedding right here in the hotel and the reception at Abe's. I know the people you have worked with these past five years have become your closest friends."

"But what about yours and your mom's friends? Won't you want to invite them to our wedding?"

He clasped both her hands in his. "Sweetheart, Keystone is only seventy miles from Denver, and it's a beautiful drive. Believe me, they'll enjoy coming here."

"You really want us to be married here in the hotel?"

"Yes, maybe in the small ballroom. I want us to have a full formal wedding. White gown, tuxedos, flowers, the whole works, but I don't want you worrying about the planning. Since I have to report back to my job on Monday and won't be here to help you, I'll hire a wedding planner to do all the work. When the wedding is over, the two of us can pack the things in your apartment, have the boxes shipped to my place, and take a honeymoon. And when we get back to Denver, we'll find us a house." He sucked in a breath, then gave her hands a squeeze. "See? I've got it all planned out. All you have to do is say yes."

"Whew, you're not kidding. You do have it all planned out." Her eyes rounded. "I still have the wedding gown I purchased when. . ." She let her voice trail off. No sense bringing up old hurts now, not at this, one of the happiest moments of her life.

"Great! That's one thing you won't have to worry about. Say yes, Stormi, please. I love you. I can't wait to make you my bride."

She gazed dreamily into his eyes. "Tell me again, my darling. Say it over and over and over. I love hearing you say you love me."

Mark wrapped his arms around her and pulled her close,

nestling his chin in her hair. "I love you. I love you. I love you. I'll always love you."

"And I love you. There are no adequate words to tell you how much I love you."

"So? Will you do me the honor of becoming my wife in two weeks?"

Lifting her face, she kissed his lips. "Yes! Oh yes!"

"I'm so glad you agreed to marry my son, Stormi, and I love the idea of your wedding being in two weeks." Mrs. Denton gave Stormi's hand a gentle pat as the three enjoyed their lunch in the hotel's Edgewater Café.

"It was Mark's idea. I hope you don't think it's too soon. I'm in love with your son, Mrs. Denton. I promise I'm going to do everything I can to be the wife Mark deserves."

"I'm sure you will. I really liked you when you two were dating, and I was heartsick when you and Mark broke up. But now God has answered my prayers and you're back together. I think having your wedding in two weeks *is* a little fast. . . ." She paused and wrinkled up her nose playfully. "But perfect. That son of mine is dead set on making you his wife as soon as possible, and I tend to agree with him. You two have already lost five years." She smiled sweetly. "I guess Mark told you he led my husband and me to the Lord just before his father died. To be honest, I was afraid the army wouldn't be good for him, but how wrong I was. Joining the army and meeting Chaplain Ron changed my son into the caring, considerate, God-fearing man he is today. I'm so proud of him."

"God's timing is perfect, Mom," Mark added, wedging his way into their conversation. "The biggest mistake Stormi could have made was marrying me when we were together before. But praise God, I'm a changed man. With Him as the head of our home, I'm determined to be the husband God wants me to be."

Mrs. Denton sent Mark a smile of adoration. "I'm sure you will." She turned her attention to Stormi. "Now, I know Mark made arrangements with the hotel staff this morning to hold your wedding here, and he plans to hire a wedding planner, but in addition to calling all our friends and inviting them to your wedding, what can I do to help?"

By the time their lunch had come to an end, Stormi felt more at ease about the many details involved in planning a successful wedding. Since Mrs. Denton had eagerly offered to help with so many of the things Stormi had thought she'd have to do herself, it seemed the wedding was going to come off easily, provided the wedding planner did her part.

Abe joined Stormi and Mark at a table near the kitchen at the end of her shift that night. "So you two are actually gonna tie the knot."

Smiling as if he'd been the top winner in a downhill race, Mark slipped his arm around Stormi and nestled her to his side. "Yep, two weeks from today at two o'clock."

Stormi latched onto her boss's arm. "But I promise I'll drive back up here to fill in when you go to celebrate your parents' anniversary. I'm sure I can stay with Renee."

"Don't you worry your pretty little head about that. I'm sure one of the other employees can fill in. You just concentrate on being a good wife to your husband."

Mark grinned. "I have a feeling Stormi is going to be the best wife a guy could ask for. I know it's asking a lot, but we want to have the reception here."

Abe's eyes widened. "Here? At Abe's? Sure, I'd love to have your reception here. I'll even hang a sign in the window and close the joint for the rest of the day. Make it a private party. The reception will be my wedding gift to the two of you."

Mark gave his head a shake. "No, Abe, I'm paying for the reception. I'm only asking that you allow us to have it here."

Abe playfully banged his fist on the table. "No, I insist. This little gal is the best employee I've ever had. She's like one of the family. I know her parents are gone. Let me pretend I'm her dad for that one day and provide the reception. I'll do it up right, I promise. It'll be my honor."

Though so touched by Abe's generous offer she could barely speak, Stormi finally managed to utter a few words. "If you're going to pretend to be my dad for the reception—would you give me away at my wedding? There's no one else I'd rather have."

For the first time since she'd known him, crusty old Abe misted up. "It'd be my privilege." Wiping at his eyes with the tip of his apron, he rose. "Gotta get back to work. Why don't the two of you have supper here tonight? It's on the house."

Stormi cast a quick glance toward Mark. When he gave her

a nod, she smiled up at her employer. "Thank you, Abe. We'd love to."

Mark grinned. "How about two of those meatball sandwiches and a side order of your famous baked beans?"

Sunday, the day both Stormi and Mark had been dreading, arrived with softly falling snow. After visiting one of the local churches for its morning service and an enjoyable, leisurely lunch at one of the out-of-the-way village cafés, Mark pulled Stormi into his arms and leaned his forehead against hers. "Time for me to go, babe. Mom and her friend are waiting for me."

With a heart so filled with love for this man it ached, she nodded. "I know. This has been the most wonderful week of my life."

"And it's just the beginning. In two weeks, we'll be Mr. and Mrs. Mark Denton." Lifting her face to his, he kissed her once, twice, and then a third time—the third one lingering and lasting. "Push me away, dearest," he murmured into her hair. "I can't leave you."

She wrapped her arms about his neck, clasping her hands at the nape. "And I can't let you go."

He kissed her again, then slowly backed away. "If I didn't have to take Mom and her friend back, I'd be tempted to stay, but I can't. I have to get back to work and wind things up so we can take our honeymoon, but I'll be back next weekend." He sighed. "Two whole weeks—just you and me. It sounds like sheer bliss."

"It sounds like that to me, too." She took several steps backward, then blew him a kiss. "Go, my beloved, before I beg you to stay. My love goes with you."

"I'll call you every day."

"I'll be waiting for your call."

"I love you, Stormi."

"I love you, Mark."

Turning quickly, he hurried down the steps of her apartment and into his car, calling back one more time as he drove away, "I love you, Stormi!"

When his car was no longer in sight, she moved into her bedroom, opened her closet door, and pulled a huge clear plastic bag off the rod. Her wedding gown—the gown she'd bought over five years ago. Carefully removing it from the bag, she lovingly spread it across her bed and gazed at the glistening satin, the delicate lace, the perfect seed pearls and beads that embellished its bodice, and she wanted to cry with happiness. Though at times she'd considered selling that gown, she had never been able to bring herself to part with it.

She fingered the tiny rhinestones scattered over the gown's silky surface, then touched the long, fragile pointed tips at the ends of the sleeves, all the time praising God for not only bringing her and Mark together, but for becoming her God, the God she now worshipped and to whom she had given control of her life.

In two weeks, she would become Mrs. Stormi Denton. How she loved the sound of those words.

Chapter 6

Though she had seen Mark the night before at their wedding rehearsal and had joined him for an early breakfast, Stormi spent the rest of the morning in the room Mark had reserved for her at the hotel, relaxing in the Jacuzzi bath, doing her nails, and fixing her hair, and the myriad of other things brides do before their wedding. At eleven o'clock, a man from the catering staff delivered a light lunch of honeydew and watermelon balls, ordered by Mark who had warned her she needed to eat or she'd be too weak to stand by him and take her vows.

"You look lovely, dear," her future mother-in-law told her as she entered Stormi's room a little before two and stood gazing at Stormi's reflection in the full-length mirror. "I've never seen a more beautiful bride. God looked on my son with favor when He sent you into his life."

"She is beautiful, isn't she?" Renee handed Stormi the handkerchief she was loaning her as the necessary "something borrowed" all brides carried on their wedding day. "I'd say she's a real knockout. I can hardly wait for Mark to see her."

Staci Green, the wedding planner Mark had hired, clapped her hands together. "Time to go, ladies. Mrs. Denton, you go on ahead so the usher can seat you. The flower girl and the ring bearer are already in their places." She smiled as she put her hand on Stormi's arm. "I've already checked. Your handsome groom and his best man are near the altar waiting for you." She nodded toward Renee. "Be sure you keep Stormi's train straightened once you reach the altar. I want this wedding to be perfect. I hate it when the bride's train gets messed up and the maid of honor just leaves it that way. But remember, Stormi, take your time and smile. This is your day. Enjoy it." She moved to the door and flung it wide open. "There's the music. Let's go."

Abe was already in the hallway, waiting for Stormi, and gave her a low, appreciative whistle. She almost didn't recognize him in his black tuxedo, with the little amount of gray hair he had slicked back over his ears. She loved Abe and was so glad he'd agreed to take her father's place. In some ways, he *had* become a father figure to her.

Hanging on tightly to his arm, she watched nervously as the flower girl and then the ring bearer, both relatives of Mark's, made their way through the double doors leading into the ballroom, which had been decorated with a wrought iron arch laden with live greenery, several banks of white lilies in tall vases on either side of the aisle, a lovely carved oak altar, and several tall candelabra, all boasting tall, white candles and hanging trails of dark green ivy.

"You're next," Staci told Renee. "Chin up, smile, and walk slowly."

Renee sent an air kiss toward Stormi, then, lifting her chin as instructed, moved through the doors.

"Hold me up," Stormi told Abe as she clung to his arm for support. "Can you believe it? I'm actually getting married!"

As the strains of "Here Comes the Bride" filled the air, Staci gave Abe a little push. "Okay, you two, it's time. Hold on to her, Abe. We don't want our bride tripping on her gown and falling. Take your time. Don't rush things." Then smiling toward Stormi, she added, "Your groom is waiting for you. Go to him. Pledge your life to him. He loves you."

After breathing a quick prayer to God, Stormi moved toward the man who symbolized everything she could ever want in a husband and the new life the two of them would share.

Mark beamed, a joyous smile blanketing his face as she drew closer. He looked so handsome in his tuxedo. Just the sight of him took her breath away, causing her to utter a gasp. She wanted to run up the aisle and leap into his arms. But, taking her time as Staci had suggested, she slowed down her gait by convincing herself each step was bringing her closer to the love of her life.

By the time she reached him, she was almost to the point of hysteria as joy and feelings of euphoria flooded her being. Having Abe stand between them, separating them, until the pastor asked, "Who gives this woman to this man?" was sheer torture. After responding, Abe kissed her cheek, then placed her hand in Mark's and moved away.

The look of adoration on Mark's face was almost more than she could bear. Though she tried to hold them back, tears of exquisite joy filled her eyes and tumbled down her cheeks as

Mark turned to her and took both her hands in his, as they listened to the soloist sing "Wind Beneath My Wings." In some ways, Mark *was* the wind beneath *her* wings since he was the one who had led her to the Lord, but *God* was the wind beneath *both* their wings now and would always have first place in their home.

Though Stormi was sure she would either forget her vows or mess them up, she didn't. Neither did Mark. Probably because they weren't simply words they had memorized, but because they truly meant each word they said. Their "I dos" had real meaning and would last a lifetime.

When the pastor pronounced them husband and wife, Mark kissed his wife with a long and lingering kiss that made Stormi feel almost giddy. Then, taking her hand in his, the newlyweds moved down the aisle past family and friends toward their new life as Mr. and Mrs. Mark Denton.

"I'll need to change since the reception is being held at Abe's instead of here in the hotel," Stormi told Mark, still holding on to his arm when they finally broke away from those who had lingered after the photographer finished taking pictures.

He gave her a mischievous smile. "Sorry, you'll have to leave that wedding gown on. I've made other plans, and they include your wedding gown. I have another surprise for you."

Her eyes rounded. "Another surprise? What?"

"I'm not sure you'll like it, but it'll be fun."

"You're not sure I'll like it?"

He pulled his handkerchief from his pocket. "I need to blindfold you. I have to take you somewhere."

She backed away. "Oh no, you don't."

His face took on a pouty expression. "Please? For me?"

Stormi rolled her eyes. "What if I trip?"

"I won't let you trip, I promise. I'll be holding on to you every step of the way."

She searched her mind for anything that would require such a ridiculous thing and came up with nothing. "I can trust you, can't I?"

"With your life. I'm your protector now."

She gestured toward his handkerchief. "Okay. I'm game. Tie it on."

Once the blindfold was in place, Mark took her hand and gently began to lead her. Where, she had no idea. They rounded several corners, then walked a good distance down what she assumed to be a hall, then stepped into an elevator. The elevator started, and she could feel it moving upward, but why? Where was he taking her?

When the elevator stopped, Mark led her forward, made another turn, then stopped. "Okay, I'm going to take your blindfold off now."

After Mark carefully tugged it off, Stormi stood gaping at the area around her. Though she'd known that area of the hotel was attached to the ski run and a number of their hotel guests regularly used it to ski down the mountain from their rooms to catch the lifts and gondolas at the bottom, she'd never actually been there. Several of Mark's friends were standing near the doorway leading out onto the slope, still dressed in their tuxedos, and they were all wearing skis! Even Renee had on skis. She eyed them one by one. "I don't get it. What's going on?"

Mark turned loose of her hand, then put on his own boots and skis. "All our friends, business associates, and relatives are waiting for us at the bottom of the mountain, along with the photographer. We're going to ski down to meet them, then take the limo to Abe's for our reception."

Now she really backed away, holding her hands up between them. "*We?* Who is this *we?* Surely you don't mean *me*! I've never skied in my life. Besides, even if I could ski, I couldn't possibly do it with my wedding gown on!"

"No problem, sweetheart. *I'm* going to ski you down. You'll be perfectly safe. I'm an excellent skier."

Her mouth gaped open. "*You're* going to ski me down? Do you think I'm crazy?"

He gestured toward the doorway. "It's absolutely gorgeous outside. The sun is shining. The temperature is in the mid-forties. The perfect day for it. Think of the story you'll have to tell our grandchildren." He reached out his arms. "Come on, Stormi. I'll take it slow and easy. I promise. You wouldn't want to disappoint our friends, would you? They're all waiting for us."

Renee gave her arm a nudge. "Go on, Stormi. I'll take your bouquet down. You trust Mark, don't you?"

Stormi gazed up into Mark's face. She did trust him, and like he said, it would be fun. She reached out her arms to him. "Okay, you win. Ski me down, but don't expect me to enjoy it or open my eyes!"

The look of joy on Mark's face made her decision worthwhile. Swooping her up in his arms, he gestured toward the others who were waiting, ski poles in hand. "Let's go, gang! My wife and I have a reception to attend."

Stormi held her breath as Mark stepped out onto the snow-covered slope and they began to move downhill, the train of her beautiful wedding gown billowing out behind them like a silken white parachute. Despite her resolve, she opened her eyes, taking in the wonder God had created as they whizzed past snow-laden trees sparkling in the warm afternoon sun. To her delight, she felt safe in Mark's arms as he gently wove his way down the hill.

"I love you, Mrs. Denton," he whispered in her ear. "I'll always love you."

"I love you, too." With a grateful heart, Stormi lifted her face heavenward, all fear suddenly gone.

Why should she be afraid? Mark was hers, she was his, and they both were God's.

The Wedding

Planner

Dedication

To my youngest daughter, Dari Lynn Leyba,
whom I also love dearly.
Like me, Dari Lynn is an optimist.
We go through life singing a happy song,
expecting good things to happen.
Even when an obstacle rears its ugly head,
we look at it as a momentary challenge
and start looking for ways around it.
Maybe we're too naive to know when real trouble
is staring us in the face. We look at life as a true blessing.
Dari Lynn is the mother of twelve—nine daughters
and three sons—and she has homeschooled them all!
Her children truly rise up and call her blessed,
as well they should.
She trusts in God, and He has never failed her.
I pray that she will be close to Him always.

Chapter 1

C lint Murphy latched on to a cup of punch from the waiter's tray as the man passed by, then ambled slowly toward one of the few empty chairs in the large fellowship hall. "I guess this was a beautiful wedding, but it sure wasn't to my liking."

He smiled at the pretty lady watching him as he seated himself next to her. Being a gentleman, and realizing she wasn't holding a cup of punch, he lifted his own cup and gave her a grin. "This stuff's pretty good. Can I get you some?"

Returning his smile, she gave her head a slight shake. "No, thank you. I'm fine."

He gestured toward the reception area where the new bride and groom were working their way through the long line of well-wishers. "I wasn't too crazy about the wedding, but the punch tastes great."

The woman eyed him warily. "What exactly didn't you like about the wedding?"

"I liked that it was a morning wedding, but that's about all I liked." He huffed. "It was too formal. Too fancy. Too long."

"Too formal in what way?"

"Too much pomp and circumstance. What woman needs

eight bridesmaids? And what man needs eight groomsmen?"

"Usually, the bride's attendants are her closest friends, and it's a way for her to honor them by inviting them to be near her and share her joy on her special day."

"So the groom has to drum up eight guys as his groomsmen so the bridesmaids will have someone to escort them down the aisle?"

She offered a slight snicker. "I guess you could say that."

He took a quick sip of punch before going on. "And that wedding gown the bride wore. It was kind of pretty, but there's enough fabric in that train thing to provide drapery for a whole house. A waste of good material, if you ask me."

"I don't suppose you liked all the heavy beading and sequins either."

"Oh, I liked those all right, but there was way too many of them. All I could think about was some little gal sittin' in a back room somewhere, sewin' those things on. Must have taken her days. A bit sprinkled here and there would have been better."

The woman smoothed at her skirt, then gazed up at him, her face still wearing the smile. "What did you think of the men's tuxedos?"

Clint wrinkled up his face. "White is for sissies. I'd have liked it better if they'd worn black. And those red pleated things around their waists? I wouldn't be caught dead in one of those things."

Another snicker emitted from her tilted-up lips. "I almost hate to mention the music. I'm sure you have an opinion on that, as well."

"That's another thing. Whatever happened to 'Here Comes the Bride'? I liked that song."

"Nowadays, brides and grooms want their weddings to be more personalized. They want music that has a special meaning to them."

Clint shook his head. "Guess I'm not up with the times since I don't go to many weddings. Most of my friends are already married, my age, or dead."

The lady's brows rose. "Oh?"

"Yeah. I'm only here because the groom's uncle and I go way back. He's the one who invited me."

"I'm sure he appreciates your being here."

Clint took the last swig of punch, then sent a glance toward the couple who were still in the receiving line, shaking hands. "Before today, I'd never even met either the bride or the groom. I sure hope their marriage lasts."

A look of surprise caused her brow to rise again. "Hope their marriage lasts? Why would you make such a negative comment?"

"Statistics show 50 percent of all marriages end in divorce, even the Christian ones." He shrugged. "That means the odds they'll make it aren't too great. It's sad but true."

She leaned back in her chair and sighed. "I hate to admit it, but you're right. Most couples come to the altar with such high hopes. But I guess living together is more difficult than they'd ever imagined. Perhaps it's because couples marry later than people generations earlier. It seems once a woman is out on her own, has her own apartment, car, and a good income, it's more difficult for her to give up her independence. Merging two incomes, two apartments, and two people who have had time to get set in their ways has to be difficult."

"Yeah, I think you're right, and what man doesn't want to be the head of the house? Makes it almost impossible for a man to head up the household when the little gal he marries may be bringing in more money than he is." Clint glanced at the woman's finger. "I don't see a ring. I guess you're not married."

She glanced down at her hand. "No, I'm not, but I'm not one of those divorce statistics you mentioned. I'm a widow. My husband died two years ago. He was only forty-one."

The sad look on her face made Clint feel like a heel for mentioning her lack of a ring. "I'm sorry. I'm sure you miss him."

She blinked hard. "Actually, no. I don't miss him. I am much better off without him. I'm just thankful we never had children for him to treat like he treated me."

Clint found himself speechless, which was a rarity for him.

"I probably shouldn't be saying this since I've made it a policy to keep my problems to myself, but my husband was a cruel man. The best thing he ever did for me was give me the desire to get out on my own and succeed." She sent another glance toward her finger, then, lifting saddened eyes, took on a look of contrition. "Please forget what I said. Normally, I'm a very reserved person. I don't know what got into me. Besides, I'm sure you're not interested in the ramblings of a disgruntled widow."

Not sure how to respond, but feeling somewhat responsible for her emotional outburst, he gave her shoulder an awkward pat. "It's okay. I'm a good listener. I'm just sorry he had such a cruel nature. No man has a right to treat any woman disrespectfully."

She closed her eyes tightly and swallowed several times, as if trying to regain her composure before continuing. "I wish all men felt that way. Maybe if they did, those statistics would change."

"I sure felt that way. I treated my wife like the queen she was and loved every minute of it."

"Was?"

"Sarah is with the Lord now. It's been a few years, but I still miss her." Needing to change the subject before he got all bleary-eyed, Clint stuck out his hand. "I'm Clint Murphy, and you're—?"

The woman pulled a tissue from her purse and dabbed at her eyes. "I'm Tula. Tula O'Brian."

"You're Irish?"

"Oh yes. Irish through and through. O'Brian is my maiden name. I decided to take it back after—well, you know."

He snapped his fingers. "Can you beat that? We're both Irish. I knew there was something special about you."

She dipped her head shyly. "Maybe that's why I've been so open with you. We have a kinship." After placing the strap of her handbag over her shoulder, she rose. "It's been nice meeting you, Mr. Murphy, but I'd better be going. I've bored you enough, and I have work to do."

He stood quickly, giving her a puzzled look. "Work?"

The grin she gave him made him even more puzzled. "Yes, work."

His curiosity got the better of him. "What kind of work do you do?"

Her grin broadened into a full-fledged smile. "I'm a wedding planner. I planned this wedding."

Chapter 2

"Y*ou* planned *this* wedding?"

She smiled proudly. "Sure did. Exactly the way the family wanted it."

Clint screwed up his face, then put his hand briefly over his mouth. "Oh boy. Now I've done it. My wife always told me I was too quick to speak my mind."

She gave him an indifferent wave of her hand. "Don't worry about it. As much as I'd like everyone to be in awe of the lovely weddings I plan, my only real concern is that the bride and groom and their families are satisfied with my work. They're the ones who pay the bill."

Clint pursed his lips and let out a low whistle. "I'm sorry, Ms. O'Brian. If I'd known you were the one—"

"Come on; admit it. If you'd known, you wouldn't have felt one bit differently about the wedding."

"That's true," he countered, regretting his hasty words and wishing he could take them back, "but *if* I'd known, I would have kept my big mouth shut or said things more diplomatically."

She glanced around, then conspiratorially leaned toward him. "Don't tell the family I said so, but I thought their wedding was a little stuffy, too."

He brightened. "Honest? You're not just saying that to make me feel better?"

"No, I'm saying it because that's the way I feel, too. But to be successful as a wedding planner, you have no choice other than to put your own likes and opinions aside and do as you are told by your client."

He shrugged. "Guess that's basically the way it is with all jobs. The boss is the boss."

She nodded and smiled. "Exactly. Speaking of bosses, I'd better go insist the bride and groom take a small break. I'm sure they're getting weary of smiling and shaking hands." She backed away, then gave him a wave as she moved toward the reception line.

Clint felt like a real jerk as he watched her go. Why did he always speak before thinking? Well, he'd probably never see her again anyway. His thoughts went back to the comment she'd made about her husband. She seemed like such a nice person. What could she possibly have done to aggravate that man enough to treat her as badly as she had implied? Of course, he was only hearing *her* side of the story. Maybe there was more to their rocky relationship than she was telling him. But then, it really wasn't any of his business anyway.

"More punch, sir?"

Startled, Clint spun around and looked into the face of the young man clad in a server's uniform. "Punch? Yeah, sure." He took a cup from the tray and shifted it to his other hand. "Thanks. That's good stuff."

He tried to keep his attention focused on the little string

group that had taken its place on the platform and had begun to play chamber music, but his gaze kept roving across the big room to where the wedding planner stood, smiling and talking with the parents of the bride. There was something about her even more than the fact that she was Irish that kept drawing his attention to her. *Come on, Clint,* he told himself, giving his head a shake. *Haven't you told everyone you have no interest in having another woman in your life? Why do you keep looking at that one?*

He turned his head away. *Yeah, that's exactly what I said, and I meant it. But sometimes I get so lonely. I know, by experience, God never made man to live alone. Only problem is—no sane woman would ever want to live with a cantankerous, outspoken old codger like me except my Sarah, and she's gone.*

He nearly snickered aloud as he recalled the dozens of widows and single women who attended his church or lived in the Yampa area and made a regular habit of parading to his ranch, all gussied up, bringing casseroles and baked goods for him to enjoy. They had done everything including flaunting themselves at him, some even proposing marriage, since he'd lost Sarah.

Well, maybe a few sane ones would live with me, but none I'd want to marry. Those women are nice, and though I'm sure they're well-meaning, I am not interested in finding a replacement for my Sarah. She was one in a million.

Despite his self-declared resolve, his gaze kept drifting back to Tula O'Brian.

"Hey, Clint. I've had about all the punch and cake I can

hold. You about ready to go home?"

Clint recognized the voice immediately. It was the groom's uncle who just happened to be his neighbor and the one who had invited him. "I take it that question means you're ready to leave."

The man nodded. "Yep. My legs are getting tired. I'm ready to go home and hit my easy chair."

Clint rose, then placed his empty cup on a nearby tray. "Then let's get out of here." As the two men headed toward the exit, he cast one final glance across the room. But Tula O'Brian was nowhere in sight.

"My daughter's wedding was perfect, Tula. It went just the way I wanted it."

Tula felt a slight burst of pride at the woman's comment. Mrs. Harper had been one of her most difficult clients, an exceedingly strong-willed woman who had overruled nearly all of the bride's and groom's wishes, constantly reminding them that *she* and her husband were the ones paying the bills. Many times during the eight months it had taken to plan the wedding, Tula had considered resigning. Though the bride's parents were truly the ones paying for the wedding, it seemed to her the final decisions, so long as they were reasonable, should have belonged to the bride and groom. After all, it was *their* wedding. But she had to admit the wedding had turned out well.

"I'm going to recommend you to all my friends, Tula," the woman went on, waving her hands in the air dramatically and speaking loudly enough so all those within her range could hear. "You and I made a great team."

Too bad your daughter and the groom weren't a part of that team! Swallowing the words she'd like to say, Tula forced a smile. "Thank you, Mrs. Harper. A good recommendation is always welcome."

As Tula walked away, she took the opportunity to glance toward the area where she and Mr. Murphy had visited earlier, but his chair was empty. She scanned the remaining crowd, but apparently, he had already gone. For some unknown reason, she felt a pang of disappointment.

"You deserve a bonus, Tula."

Whirling around, she came face-to-face with Mr. Harper. "I hope that means you're happy with your daughter's wedding."

He lifted his cup of punch in salute. "Yeah, I'm happy with Sharla's wedding, but what I meant was—you deserve a bonus for putting up with my wife and her pushy ways. I love my wife, but I know how demanding she can be."

Surprised by his words and not sure how she should respond, Tula allowed her face to take on a slight smile but kept her silence.

"I'm afraid I'm somewhat responsible for my wife being difficult to work with. She did without practically everything those first few years we were married. So, when my business took off, I went overboard and spoiled her by giving her anything she'd ever wanted. She might seem arrogant and uppity at times, and wear her social standing like a badge of honor, but I love that woman and will do everything I can to make her happy."

Tula, feeling somewhat better toward Mrs. Harper now that she knew a little about her background and where she had come from, smiled up at Mr. Harper, tactfully choosing her words. "From the sound of things, I'd say you two are lucky to have each other."

He grinned. "Yeah, we are."

She couldn't help thinking of her own marriage. All she'd ever wanted out of life was to love and respect the man she married, and for him to love and respect her. She would have been content living in the tiniest of homes, happily doing without the finer things of life, but that was not to be. Of course, she had no one to blame but herself. She'd been so enamored with the idea of becoming a wife and mother she had married the first man who paid attention to her. Three weeks. That was all the time they had known each another.

She shuddered at the thought. *Known each another? We barely knew each other! He was nothing like I thought he was. Our values and goals were worlds apart. I hated his excessive beer drinking, cigar smoking, and gambling, and I hated his friends who were just like him. I couldn't stand the way he dropped his dirty clothes on the floor, swore at me for nothing at all, and let all our bills go unpaid until the bill collectors threatened to garnishee his paycheck. We had nothing in common! Marrying him was the biggest mistake of my life.*

Someone grabbed her arm. It was Mrs. Harper, and the expression on her face said she was none too happy. "Tula, you have to go calm down my daughter. Sharla has locked herself in the bride's room. She's crying hysterically and won't let me in."

Without hesitation, Tula headed toward the corridor. "What's wrong with her? I just spoke with her a few minutes ago, and she was fine."

Mrs. Harper lifted her hands in despair. "I have no idea. I was helping Sharla take off her gown, and she started screaming at me and ordered me to leave. She actually pushed me out of the room and locked the door!"

"She was changing out of her gown? I told her to let me know when she was ready and I'd help her." Tula always helped the brides with that task. It was part of her job. She'd made it perfectly clear she would be doing it this time, as well. Sharla had actually seemed relieved when she'd told her she'd be the one helping her. Why had she gone ahead without her?

Mrs. Harper shrugged. "Sometimes she acts like the spoiled child she is. Can you believe she was going to put on that awful, short, ruffled lime green thing to wear as her going-away outfit? With those ridiculous canvas wedged shoes? The outfit *I* brought for her to wear is much better."

Tula's eyes narrowed. "The outfit *you* brought for her?"

The woman lifted her head proudly. "Yes. The outfit *I* insisted she wear is much more appropriate. A lovely pink shantung suit with matching dyed linen shoes."

Oh, Mrs. Harper, this is your daughter's wedding day. Couldn't you have let her have her way with this one thing? "But your daughter wanted to wear the lime green dress. She was so excited about it when she showed it to me. It's the kind of thing all the girls her age are wearing."

"I don't care what all the girls are wearing. *My* daughter

is going to dress like a lady." Mrs. Harper grabbed Tula's arm again, dragged her up to the door where the bride had barricaded herself, and loudly pounded on it. "You open this door this minute, Sharla; do you hear me?"

From behind the door, a timid voice responded. "No, Mother. You're not coming in. I want Tula."

Tula pulled away from the woman's grasp. "I'm here, Sharla. Let me in."

"Not if Mother is coming in with you."

Tula gave Mrs. Harper's shoulder a slight nudge, then stepped between her and the door. "I'm sure you don't want to ruin your daughter's wedding day by arguing over something as trivial as a dress when everything else has gone so well."

Mrs. Harper stared at her. "That dress is ugly. Surely you're not suggesting I let her wear it. What will my friends think when they see her enter the limo in that ridiculous little fluff of fabric and those stupid-looking shoes?"

"I'm not suggesting you *let* her wear those things, Mrs. Harper. I'm suggesting you leave that decision up to Sharla. After all, she *is* a married woman now. From now on, she, along with her husband's input, will be making her own decisions." With a consoling pat to the woman's hand, Tula took hold of the doorknob. "Maybe you should go back to your guests and let me take care of this. I'm sure they're all wondering where you are."

"Sweetie, Tula's right. Our daughter *is* a married woman now. It's time we give her some space."

Both women spun around to find Mr. Harper approaching them.

"But *I'm* her mother," the woman said defensively. "She has no right to lock me out like that."

"I know, dear." Mr. Harper gave her a patient smile. "And I'm sure Sharla appreciates all you do for her, but if she wants to wear the dress, why don't we let her? She wore the wedding gown *you* selected. Is what she wears to drive off in the limo really that important?"

To Tula's surprise, when Mr. Harper reached out his hand, Mrs. Harper paused for only a brief moment before taking it and, along with her husband, made her way back to the ballroom, leaving Tula alone in the hall.

"Open the door, Sharla," she said softly, pressing her cheek against it. "Your mother is gone."

"I *am* going to wear the lime green dress," Sharla answered back with a determination in her voice Tula had never heard before. "I don't care what Mother says."

"And you'll look lovely in it. Now, unlock the door so I can help you."

After a slight pause, the door opened.

Chapter 3

Clint hung his suit in the closet, then slid the door closed. It wasn't that he minded dressing up in a suit for the wedding; he didn't. But he much preferred his sport coat with the leather patches on the elbows, and he hated conventional neckties. More to his liking was his hammered-silver and turquoise bolo at the neck of his Western-cut shirt. But, out of respect for the bride and groom and the groom's uncle who had invited him, he'd worn that miserable suit, starched shirt, and the dreadful paisley tie.

He had to smile as he remembered the many times Sarah had kidded him about his affection for Western dressing. "Clint, I know you're a rancher and farmer at heart," she'd say, shaking her finger at him, "but you don't always have to dress like one." How he'd loved that woman. He would have worn one of those sissy white tuxedos to work the ranch if it had made her happy.

Sissy white tuxedo? Those three words instantly brought to mind another woman. One who was very much alive and had the smile of an angel. Tula O'Brian.

Tula. What a beautiful name. He wished he'd been able to spend more time with her. Get to know her better. Maybe, if he were lucky, their paths would cross again sometime. *Not likely.*

I don't go to many weddings, and I doubt she goes to rodeos and cattle sales.

He strode out onto his home's spacious deck, seated himself in one of the redwood chairs, then sat gazing out across his land toward the massive Routt National Forest, taking in its beauty and feeling sorry for himself. *It's a shame for a man to have so much and no one to share it with,* he told himself as his memory darted back to the many wonderful times he'd had growing up on the Murphy Ranch, the land homesteaded by his great-grandfather Milford Murphy.

Leaning his head against the chair's back, he closed his eyes and let the warm rays of the sun kiss his face. Was he going to die a lonely old man? With no one to carry on the Murphy name? That's exactly what he'd thought would happen until, at the age of forty-two, God had answered his prayers and blessed him and Sarah with a son, the most beautiful baby Clint had ever seen. He'd bought that boy his first horse when he was only six and had taught him everything he could about ranching. Little Gage Murphy was the heir apparent of all Clint owned, the sole successor to a long line of Murphys.

But that all changed when God decided to call his son home. Clint rubbed at his eyes at the remembrance. His only child's death had come so quickly, with Clint kneeling beside him in total helplessness. The horse Clint had hoped would carry his son through life had carried him to his death. To this day, Clint was convinced Gage's death was what had caused his beloved wife's heart to fail less than one year later.

"It's nearly one o'clock. What would you like for lunch,

Clint?" his housekeeper asked as she moved out onto the deck, dish towel in hand. "There's ham left over from yesterday. How about a nice ham sandwich and some potato salad?"

"Sounds good, Aggie. Any of that pie left?"

She swatted at his arm. "You know you're not supposed to eat so many sweets."

He grinned at her. "A man my age is entitled to a few vices. Pie's one of mine. Besides, you bake the best apple pie of any woman around."

She rolled her eyes. "Tryin' to make brownie points, are you?"

They both turned as Clint's long, lanky foreman stepped up onto the porch.

"I gotta drive into Yampa and pick up some parts, Boss. Want me to get you anything?"

Clint pondered his question, then shook his head. "No, thanks. I'll be goin' into Steamboat Monday for my annual checkup. If I need anything, I can get it then."

Seeming concerned, Hayes Jenkins bent and put a hand on Clint's shoulder. "You okay, Boss? You seem—strange."

Aggie nodded in agreement. "I was thinking the same thing."

"I'm okay. Just reminiscing about my wife and Gage, and the good times we had."

"I kinda figured you was. How'd the wedding go?"

"Okay, I guess."

Hayes pulled his worn Stetson low on his brow. "Okay then, I'll be goin'. Jake's mending fences up along Moody Creek and won't be back until dark, but a couple of the hands are working in the east barn if you need anything."

Aggie patted Clint's shoulder. "And I'll be in the kitchen, fixing your lunch."

"You two needn't worry about me. I'll be fine. That wedding made me a little nostalgic; that's all. I may saddle up Blue Streak and take a ride later on."

"Great idea. Be good for both of you."

Clint watched until Hayes' pickup disappeared out of sight, then rose and let his gaze wander. As far as he could see and well beyond, the land was his, a crown jewel in Colorado's northern Yampa Valley. Though he had been approached many times to sell it, as long as he had breath and a beating heart, the land would remain his. After all, he was only fifty-seven. If he was anything like his grandpa, he could live there and enjoy it for another thirty years.

It was a beautiful spring day. The kind of day a person wished he could bottle and keep. If he were an artist, he'd paint a picture of it. After stretching his arms first one way and then the other, he ambled to the far end of the massive deck and leaned his elbows on the railing. The day might be magnificent and his ranch spectacular, but what fun was it to enjoy it all alone? The joy of living had gone out of his heart when his son died, and the purpose of living had evaporated the day he'd buried his wife.

"Sorry, God," he said aloud, lifting his arms heavenward. "I just don't get it. What am I supposed to do with the rest of my life? I have nothing to live for any longer. Maybe it's time You called me home, too."

Later that afternoon, still feeling an air of despondency,

Clint saddled up Blue Streak and rode the big stallion over to Watson Creek, one of many streams that meandered through his property. He used to love fishing, using every excuse he could think of to take a day off and fish until his heart was content, but even his love of fishing had vanished. What good was it to catch the big ones when you had no one but ranch hands to show them off to?

"Are we gettin' old, Blue Streak?" he asked the big horse, giving his mane a pat. "Even you seem discontent. Don't pay as much attention to you as I used to, do I, fella? I'm turning into a couch potato. What I need in my life is something to make me want to jump out of bed in the morning, eager to get on with things."

An idea occurred to him as he stroked his friend's shiny neck. "I may be shooting in the dark, but didn't my mom always tell me a person should act on his instincts?"

Tugging on the reins, then turning the big horse back toward home, Clint leaned forward in the saddle and nudged Blue Streak in the sides with his heels. He had plans to make. "Wish me luck, boy. Come Monday, I'm gonna do something really outrageous. Something totally out of character for me. I may get a kick in the pants for what I am about to do, but hey, it won't be the first time I got a kick."

With feelings of euphoria, he lifted his face and sucked in several rapid whiffs of the clear mountain air. The wind in his hair felt good, exhilarating, a feeling he hadn't experienced in a long time. "I can't just sit in my chair and wait to die. I gotta take action. Make things happen. Take chances like I used to. If

I wanted something, I'd go after it. That's exactly what I intend to do now! I gotta make me a plan."

At exactly ten o'clock on Monday morning, Clint left the flower shop in Steamboat Springs and, feeling nearly as nervous as the day he'd proposed to Sarah, walked toward one of Main Street's small businesses.

The jangling of the bell as he pushed the door open was even louder than the jangling of his heart as the woman behind the desk looked up and smiled at him.

Without preamble, he moved quickly forward and thrust the bouquet of apricot roses into her hand.

Her mouth gaping, she looked first at the roses, then up at him with an expression of bewilderment. "Mr. Murphy! What—what are you doing here?"

He doffed his Stetson, then squared his shoulders, determined not to come off sounding like some bumpkin. "I came to bring you the flowers. I hope you like apricot roses."

"I—I love apricot roses. They're my favorites. But—but why did you bring them to me? And how did you find me?"

"Wasn't too hard. I figured Nick, the best florist in town, was bound to know how to reach the best wedding planner in town. And he did!" He glanced around. The place looked like her. All girlie and soft, with candles, lace, ruffles, feathers, and satin everywhere; shelves filled with books; and ivy tucked into every corner. "The minute I said your name, he told me where to find you, so here I am."

"I'm glad to see you again, but. . ." She eyed him suspiciously. "But I still don't know why you're here. Or why you brought me these beautiful roses."

He squared his shoulders and mustered up his courage. "Tula, I'm fifty-seven years old, and I'm lonely. I haven't seen a woman I'd want to be with since I lost my Sarah." He paused and gave her a grin, afraid he was blushing, though he hadn't blushed in years. "That is—until I met you."

Her hand rose to cover her mouth. Then, lowering her hand to the base of her neck, she swallowed hard, and said, "Until you met me? Whatever do you mean?"

He leaned across her desk, his face so close to hers he could see the blue flecks in her eyes and smell the cologne or perfume or whatever she had on that caused that tantalizing fragrance. Or was it the roses? "Yep, until I met you. I know I'm older than you, but I want to marry you, Tula. Will you do me the honor of becoming my wife?"

Chapter 4

Tula nearly choked. Clint's outlandish proposal was the last thing she'd expected when he'd shown up at the door of her little shop.

The man went on without even giving her a chance to respond to his bizarre proposal. "I know you didn't expect me to come waltzing in here, unannounced like this, but I kept thinking about you all weekend. Couldn't get you off my mind. I even talked to Blue Streak about you."

"Who is Blue Streak?" she finally managed to utter coherently.

"My horse," he replied as casually as if he'd been speaking of a lifelong friend. "You'll get to know him when we get married."

Tula struggled to catch her breath. "Is—is this your idea of a joke, Mr. Murphy? Because if it is, I am not laughing. To me, marriage is a sacred thing. Nothing to be laughed at. If I hadn't been so cavalier about marrying my first husband and taken time to get to know him like I should have, my life would have been much different."

Seeing a nearby chair, Clint grabbed it and pulled it up beside her. "I think marriage is sacred, too, Tula. Me and my wife were happily married for many years. I want that kind of marriage again. With you!"

Still holding on to the roses, she noisily scooted her chair across the hardwood floor, putting a few more inches between them. "You don't even know me!"

He reached for her hand, but she pulled it away.

"I *want* to know you. I want us to spend time together, get to know each other real good. How about letting me take you to lunch?"

She glanced at the clock on the wall. "It's only ten fifteen!"

He reached for her hand again. "Okay, we'll go have a cup of coffee and a doughnut now and eat lunch later."

I must be dreaming. This can't be happening. "I—I can't just leave. I have work to do. Besides, what makes you think I'd want to take a break with you or have lunch with you?"

He shrugged. "If you don't, how are you going to get to know me before we get married?"

Tula didn't know whether she should call 9-1-1 and ask them to come and rescue her from this loco man or laugh at the ridiculousness of the situation.

"Don't tell me you haven't thought about me."

"Why would I think about you? I only met you Saturday. You're barely a blip on my memory's radar screen."

"Be honest, Tula. You have thought about me, haven't you? You and I got along real well for strangers. We seem to think alike. Remember? We both thought that wedding was a little stuffy."

She stared at him. "This is insane."

He gave his head a shake. "No, it's not. It's fate. You wouldn't believe the number of women who have been interested in me since I lost Sarah. I could have my pick of nearly any of the widows and single women who live around the Yampa area, but I don't want any of them. Then I met you, and all I can think about is being with you. If it wasn't fate that brought us together, why do I feel this way?"

She had no answers. If she were honest, she'd have to admit he had been on her mind countless times since they'd talked, but consider marriage? No. She was too levelheaded for that. She had no plans to marry anyone, especially someone she barely knew. She'd been down that path before and hated where it had taken her. Whales would be swimming in Kansas lakes before she would trust her intuition about men enough to marry another one.

He glanced around the room. "Looks like you have a good thing going here. You got a nice little shop and office, but if you marry me, you won't have to work."

"Won't *have* to work? I like working," she countered, wondering why she'd even bothered to explain.

Still glancing around, he nodded. "Okay then, you can work. I can live with that, but it's going to be a cold drive in the winter from my place to Steamboat. Thirty-some miles is a long way when the snow is blowing and the air's cold enough to freeze the breath in your nostrils. But I could leave my man Hayes in charge and drive you most days, I guess."

She crossed her arms over her chest and huffed. "I'm perfectly capable of driving myself, thank you."

"I'll make sure you have a nice dependable vehicle. Something heavier than that minivan you drive."

She gaped at him. "How do you know I drive a minivan?"

"Wild guess. You do drive one, don't you?"

She stared at him in amazement. "Yes, but—"

"Not safe enough. I'll get you one of those SUV-type things with a winch on the front. I wouldn't want my wife sliding off the road into a snowdrift with nothing to pull her out."

She stood quickly to her feet, her hands anchoring on her hips. "Mr. Murphy—"

"Clint."

"Clint. I met you Saturday, we shared maybe ten minutes together, and today you've got me married to you and we're discussing the kind of vehicle I'll need to drive from your place in Yampa to my business in Steamboat? Are you some kind of nut or something?"

He rose and faced her, nose to nose. "Nut? Nope. Just a man in love."

She pointed to the door. "Out! Now! Or I'll call the police."

He gave her an incredulous look. "You want me out? How are we going to get acquainted if we don't spend time together?"

She moved quickly to the door and threw it open. "We're not! I'm afraid of you, Clint," she confessed, her heart thumping in her chest. "I've never met anyone like you. For all I know, you may be trying to seduce me for who knows what purpose? There is no way I am leaving my office with you. I want you out of here—now!"

All the fire and thunder he'd had when he'd entered seemed

to go out of him as he turned and walked slowly through the door. "I'm sorry, Tula. Maybe I came on too strong. I—I wouldn't hurt you for anything. I don't know what possessed me to come roaring into your business like I did and expect you to say yes to my proposal, but I loved being with you Saturday. I was hoping you felt the same way about me as I did about you, but I guess I was wrong. Please accept my apology. I won't bother you again."

The hurt look on his face tugged at her heart, but she refused to be someone's victim. "I accept your apology. Now go."

He gestured toward the flowers lying on her desk. "Better get those roses in some water before they wilt."

"I'll do it as soon as I close the door."

"I know you're around flowers all the time, you being a wedding planner, but I'd hoped you'd like them."

"I do like them. Not often someone brings me flowers."

With a look of embarrassment, he twirled the Stetson's brim nervously in his hands. "I'd hoped you'd like me, too."

She chose her words carefully, not wanting to be misunderstood. "I do like you, Clint, but not in the way you suggested."

"So what you're saying is—there's no hope for the two of us?"

"I have no plans to remarry."

"I thought sure you'd be interested in my proposal." Appearing crestfallen, he sucked in a deep breath. "I guess it's time for me to tuck in my tail and run. Sorry to have been such a bother. Good-bye, Tula."

When he stuck out his hand, she took it. It felt warm, strong, secure, and safe, and for a brief moment, she wondered if she were doing the right thing by sending him away. Of course, she was doing the right thing. The man was a lunatic. No sane man would come bursting into a place of business at ten o'clock on a Monday morning with such an off-the-cuff proposal to a woman he'd met only two days ago. "Good—good-bye, Clint."

After closing the door behind him, she parted the lace curtains and watched as he climbed into his truck and sped away. *You can't judge all men by that scoundrel you married,* her heart seemed to say. *If you do, you'll be a lonely old lady, one who perhaps missed the chance of a lifetime when she turned down the unexpected love of a good man.*

Tula gazed at the empty parking stall in front of her building, almost wishing Clint would turn his truck around and come back.

But he didn't.

Clint stopped by the doctor's office and rescheduled his appointment for a week later. He was in no mood to be weighed, prodded, and poked. All he wanted was to get home, try to forget the rejection he'd suffered, and take a nap. He'd put his heart on the line, and Tula had trampled it and crushed it with her words. He'd had such high hopes for the two of them. Maybe he'd bungled everything by coming on too soon and too strong. Yes, that was it. If he'd given her time to get to know him before he'd blurted out his sudden feelings for her, perhaps things would have been different. Hadn't *he* backed away when those women had put their moves on him? Hadn't *he* then run in the opposite direction as fast as he could?

Of course, he'd had no interest in those women and would never accept their advances under any circumstances. Was that the way it was with Tula? Would she never accept him or his proposal after his unorthodox behavior? Was she as repulsed by his advances as much as he had been repulsed by the way those women pursued him? The women who were after him were nice enough, probably would have made good wives, but they just weren't his type. Maybe Tula thought *he* wasn't her type.

Eventually, he arrived back at the ranch. Hayes greeted him with a scowl of concern. "By your hangdog look, I'd say the doc must have given you some bad news."

He snorted. "Didn't see the doc."

Hayes grabbed his arm when Clint tried to brush past him. "I thought that's why you were going into Steamboat."

Clint jerked his arm away and glared at the man. "Do I have to account for every minute of my time? I decided I didn't want to see the doc after all. Now, let it be. I'm gonna take a nap."

Hayes followed him into the house. "Somethin' wrong, Boss? You've been moody ever since you went into town to that wedding Saturday."

Clint continued to glare at him. "You're imagining things. Now leave me alone. Haven't you got work to do?"

"Sure, but—"

Gesturing toward the door, Clint let out a grunt. "Then get at it. That's what I pay you for."

Frowning and clamping his mouth shut, Hayes turned on

his heel and disappeared through the open doorway.

"Guess I owe that man an apology," Clint mumbled under his breath. "He meant no harm. Seems like all I'm doing today is offending people." He moved down the long hall and into his room, lay down on his bed, then pulled the quilt up over him and closed his eyes. "What I need is a good nap."

Tula stared at the vase of apricot roses on her desk, then reached out and touched their velvety softness. Clint was right. She was around flowers all the time, but somehow, these flowers were special. Someone had purchased them just for her. A very nice man she'd treated badly.

With hopes of forgetting about the giver of the roses, she picked up the phone and dialed a client's number. All she got was a busy signal.

She dialed a second one and waited. The answering machine picked up.

She dialed a third one, and no one answered, not even the machine. *Might as well go to lunch. I'm sure not accomplishing anything here.* She grabbed her shoulder bag, locked the front door, walked across the street to the little sandwich shop, and sat down at her favorite table, the one facing the front window. Since she ate alone most days, she liked watching the towns-folk and tourists as they walked back and forth on the sidewalk, laughing and visiting with one another. Their smiles always made her feel happy.

"Hi, Tula. I suppose, as usual, you want the special and iced tea." The waitress poised her pencil over her pad.

Tula nodded. "Hi yourself, Sharon. The special and tea will be fine. I don't suppose you can talk the boss into letting you sit down and eat with me."

Sharon rolled her eyes. "Not likely, but maybe you and I can have dinner Saturday night and go to a movie."

Tula liked Sharon. She was the closest friend she'd made since coming to Steamboat Springs. The two had a lot in common. "I'd like to, Sharon, but I'm meeting with a prospective client that night. Maybe we can do it some evening next week. Call me later with your schedule."

"You got it." The uniformed woman gestured toward the plate glass window. "Hey, wasn't that Clint Murphy I saw rush out of your office a little while ago?"

Her heart pounding at the sound of his name, Tula nodded. "You know him?"

"Sure I know him. Most folks around here do, but I didn't know you knew him."

"I don't know him well." Though her interest was piqued, Tula tried to appear casual. "I only met him two days ago."

"Nice man. One of the best. One of the good guys. Really active in our church. I'd trust that man with my life." She took the menu from Tula's hand and headed toward the kitchen. "I'll be right back with your tea."

Tula watched her go. *Now I really feel bad. After I all but accused the man of being a pervert, I find out that, by Sharon's standards, he's a fine man. I normally give people the benefit of the doubt. Why didn't I do it with him?*

"Cook's behind," Sharon explained as she placed a glass of iced tea in front of Tula. "Be a few more minutes before I can bring your order."

"That's okay, Sharon. I'm in no hurry." Tula took the strap from her shoulder and placed her bag on the empty chair next to her. "Tell me more about Mr. Murphy."

"What do you want to know?"

"Does he have a family?"

The woman shook her head. "No. He lost his only son in a tragic horse accident; then his wife died a year later. He's never remarried, and I doubt he's even dated. A bunch of the unmarried women in our church have tried to get close to him, but he seems to have no interest in them, other than that of a friend." She grinned. "I hope someday the right woman comes along and sweeps him off his feet. That man deserves some happiness. If there wasn't so much difference in our ages, I'd go for him myself. He's a real catch."

"He sounds too good to be true."

The woman snapped her fingers as if she'd had a sudden idea. "Hey, you're single. You ought to go for him. I'll bet the two of you would get along real well."

Tula felt heat rise to her cheeks. "I doubt he'd have any genuine interest in me. We got off to a pretty rocky start."

"Clint's not the kind of person to hold a grudge. You ought to give it another try. I think you'd make a great couple."

"I have a feeling we're each too set in our ways. We're both quite opinionated."

"Believe me, Clint's an understanding man. If he fell in

love with you, he'd treat you like a queen and go out of his way to make you happy." She glanced toward the little window where she picked up orders. "Looks like the cook has your plate ready."

Though Tula always enjoyed the food she ordered at the little sandwich shop, today she barely noticed it. She had too many things on her mind to pay attention to the taste of the special that had been set before her. Could she possibly mend fences with Clint Murphy? And why would she want to? She had her business, and she had become used to living alone. What more did she need? Just the thought of driving from his place in Yampa to her work in Steamboat Springs every day was enough to discourage any relationship she might consider with him.

She laughed aloud, then looked around quickly to see if anyone had noticed. *The man will probably never speak to me again, and I'm worrying about driving in the snow from his house to my business? I must be as crazy as he is!*

When she returned to her office, Tula scanned the phone book and found Clint's listing. She dialed the number, then hurriedly hung up before it rang. She'd had no idea what she was going to say if he answered. All she knew was that she wanted to hear his voice.

She jumped as the phone rang in her hand.

"Is this Tula O'Brian?" a woman asked.

"Yes, this is Tula. How may I help you?"

"My name is Kate Reardon. My daughter is getting married, and we've heard such nice things about you that we want you to plan her wedding."

Tula grabbed her pad and pencil. "I'd love to work with you and your daughter on her wedding, Mrs. Reardon. Can you meet me here in my office on Thursday? I'm free from noon until three that day."

"I was hoping you could come and meet us here at my home. We live in Yampa."

Tula weighed her options. Yampa was not that far. Driving the thirty miles to Yampa would be a refreshing break. "Give me directions, and I'll be there Thursday about one."

"Only if you'll plan to have lunch with us."

Tula laughed. "Lunch would be nice. I'll plan on it."

The woman gave her explicit directions, thanked her, and hung up. Tula stared at the pad. *Yampa? That's where Clint lives. No, he said he lived in the Yampa area. That could be miles from the Reardon residence.* She wondered if they knew one another, not that it mattered.

She glanced at the phone again, feeling relief that he hadn't picked up when she'd dialed his number. *You're a fool, Tula, to think Clint Murphy's proposal was serious. It was probably the man's sick attempt at a joke. Maybe someone had even dared him to do it. You thought you knew your husband, and you didn't. Face it, woman. You're a poor judge of character. Respond to this man's warped sense of humor by being nice to him and letting your guard down, and you may get yourself into a situation even worse than what you had before.*

She'd barely gathered her composure when her door opened and Nick, the owner of the florist shop where she did most of

her business, stepped in with a bouquet of perky yellow daffodils wrapped in yellow, waxy, ruffle-edged paper clutched
tightly in his hand. "It appears you have an admirer, Tula."

"Those are for me?"

He gave her a teasing smile, then handed them to her. "Uh-
huh. Some scruffy, bearded old cowboy in manure-covered
boots, whom I'm sure wasn't the sender, marched into my shop
a few minutes ago, asked me to deliver them to you, handed me
this little envelope to attach to them, paid in cash, and left. You
got a boyfriend you're not telling me about?"

"No, of course not." With a bashful grin, she took the flowers, then pulled a folded note from the envelope. All it said was
I'm sorry. No signature. No name.

"Come on, Tula. Out with it. What's his name?"

She turned the note in his direction so the man could read
it. "The sender didn't sign it."

" 'I'm sorry'? That's it?" He eyed her suspiciously. "Since
you don't seem upset that it wasn't signed, I assume you know
who this is from."

She allowed a smile to tilt her lips. "I have a pretty good
idea."

Nick placed his palms on her desk, then leaned close and
gave her a mischievous wink. "Wanna tell me who it is? Curiosity is killing me."

"Since I'm not 100 percent sure, I'd best keep my guess to
myself. I wouldn't want to incriminate the wrong person."

He gave her a playful smile. "Don't you think a man has a
right to know who his competition is?"

Tula's expression sobered. Nick had been after her for months to have dinner with him, but she'd refused. Not only because he and his wife were separated and considering divorce, but because there just wasn't anything about him that would make her want to date him. Even if he were single, the attraction wasn't there. "Nick, you're a nice man, but I have no interest in a married man. You know that."

He straightened up with a sigh. "Can't blame a guy for trying. Maybe one of these days my wife and I will get that divorce finalized; then I'll ask you out, and you'll say yes."

She gave him a smile, trying to make it kind. "I'm flattered, Nick. Honest I am, but it's not going to happen." Still retaining the smile, she made a shooing motion with her hand. "Thanks for personally delivering the flowers. Now go back to your shop. I'm sure you have things to do, and so do I."

"You're not going to tell me who your secret admirer is?"

"No, I'm not even sure myself."

"The guy must have really wronged you if he said he's sorry. No man likes to admit he's wrong."

She made another shooing motion. "Forget it. I'm not going to tell you, Nick."

He whirled around and headed for the door. "Okay, but I'll be watching out my window. If that guy comes around, I'll know it. Steamboat's not that big. You can't hide something like this, you know. I'm bound to find out."

She picked up a sheet of scrap paper from her desk, wadded it up, and threw it at him. "Out!"

After tossing back his head with a raucous laugh, he moved

out the door, closing it behind him.

Tula sat gazing at the lovely yellow daffodils. They could have come from only one person.

Clint.

On Tuesday morning, Nick delivered a bouquet of pink carnations and baby's breath. "Okay, out with it, Tula. Who is he?"

She took the flowers from his hands and sniffed at their delicate fragrance. "Wasn't there a note?"

He gave his head a shake. "Nope, the same scruffy old cowboy just paid me in cash and said to deliver them."

Tula smiled as she cradled the bouquet in her arms. "Whoever the sender is, he certainly has good taste in flowers. I love carnations."

"You're still not going to tell me?"

"Like I said, I have an idea who sent them, but I don't know for sure."

Nick scratched at his head. "How many men have wronged you enough lately to send flowers as an apology? Seems to me, you'd know exactly who it is."

When she simply smiled and shrugged, Nick moved out the door and headed back to his shop.

Tula placed the carnations in a vase and set it next to the vase of daffodils, grinning to herself as she gazed at their beauty. *Clint, you old softie, is this another one of your tactics to get me to say yes? 'Cause if it is, it just may work. I love flowers!*

When Nick entered Tula's shop on Wednesday morning, bearing a live dark green plant filled with blooming gardenias, whose fragrance instantly filled the room, she met his troubled expression with a look of surprise. Flowers two days in a row was impressive, but three days?

"The phantom strikes again," he said with a shrug as he placed the lovely plant on the corner of her desk. "Does this guy think he's Romeo?"

"Since I don't know for sure who he is, I have no idea what he thinks, but I have to admit I like his style."

Tula couldn't take her gaze from the spectacular plant. She hadn't enjoyed the wonderful fragrant smell of a gardenia since Dick Stiller had bought her a gardenia corsage to wear to their high school prom.

Nick grimaced, then backed into the open doorway. "Looks to me like he's out to win you, Tula. How can I compete with a guy when I don't even know who he is?"

She laughed. "Don't look at me. As long as he doesn't sign his name, all I can do is speculate as to who he is."

"At least your phantom is doing his floral business with me. I can't complain about that!"

As soon as Nick left, Tula pulled her scissors from her desk drawer and carefully cut a large, single gardenia from the plant, then pinned it to her jacket. The aroma was heavenly. *I can't let Clint continue to send all these lovely flowers without at least thanking him, but if I call him, what can I say? Thanks for the flowers— but get lost!*

Thinking perhaps this might be the last day the flowers would arrive, and not exactly sure how the situation would be best handled, she decided to simply do nothing. At least for now.

At ten o'clock Thursday morning, Tula found herself gazing out the window toward Nick's shop, half afraid and half expecting him to open his door and bring her regular morning delivery of flowers, but it didn't happen.

By eleven, she'd given up the idea, deciding, since she hadn't responded, Clint's floral blast of apology had run its course. With her one o'clock appointment in mind, she moved about the shop, gathering up the books and samples she wanted to take to the Reardon home. Not knowing anything about the members of the Reardon family, she had no idea how large or what kind of a wedding they wanted or how much they were prepared to spend, but she did want to be ready with a good selection from which they could choose. Engrossed with her preparations, she barely noticed when the bell on the front door jangled and someone entered.

"Sorry, Tula, we were so busy that this was the first opportunity I had to deliver these."

Tula turned at the sound of Nick's voice and let out a startled, "Oh!" at the sight of the elegant bouquet of lilies of the valley, sweet peas, red and yellow zinnias, blue status, and white roses he held in his hands. "Nick! What a beautiful bouquet. Surely it's not from—"

Nick let out a grunt. "Yep, your secret admirer. Why don't you put the guy out of his misery and accept his apology?"

Tula felt her heart do a leap when she caught sight of a small envelope pinned to the flowers. Snatching it from its place, she hurriedly ripped open the flap and pulled out the tiny card inside.

*For you, I'd even wear a white tuxedo. Don't you think
these flowers would make a terrific wedding bouquet?*

Even knowing Nick was watching, she couldn't help but
smile.

"What'd he say this time? From the looks of that smile,
must be something funny."

"You mean you didn't read it?"

He grinned. "I would have, but the guy always seals the
envelopes before the cowboy brings them in. I even asked the
cowboy who sent them, but he wasn't talking. Come on, Tula,
let me in on your little secret."

Her smile still in place, she motioned toward the door.
"Good-bye, Nick."

He let loose a heavy sigh. "Good-bye, Tula."

At straight-up noon, Tula locked her shop and headed for
the Reardons'. She wanted to allow plenty of time in case she
had trouble finding the place. Though she was sure she'd followed Mrs. Reardon's directions, after driving for nearly an
hour, she found herself hopelessly lost.

Now what? Crossing her arms on the steering wheel she
stared at the rusty, broken-down fence and huge rotted logs
blocking the way ahead of her on the winding road. The over-
night rains had half filled the ditches on either side and caused
the narrow road's surface to become treacherous and slippery.
She sat spellbound watching the water rush down the hill. *If I'd
followed my instincts and hadn't taken that last turn, I'd never be
in this predicament.*

She glanced at her surroundings. Since her cell phone was out of range, maybe she could walk to a nearby house and use their landline to call someone to come after her. But no houses were in sight, only trees. Lots and lots of trees, some towering straight up the mountain on one side and others plummeting down the rocky slope into a canyon below on the other side, and the worst part? There was no place to turn around. She'd have to back out the entire way. She wanted to strangle whoever had removed the DEAD END sign at the last fork. Backing up on that road any time would be difficult, but backing up with the ditch filling rapidly with torrents of water was terrifying and looked nearly impossible.

"Well," she said aloud, realizing she'd give anything to not be facing this challenge alone, "nothing to do but try to back out of here without going over the side." With a shaking hand, she thrust the gearshift into REVERSE, then slowly eased down on the pedal, inching along as carefully as possible. Everything went smoothly until she reached the curve when suddenly a deer leaped out behind her and she instinctively hit the brake. Before she knew what happened, the rear end of her minivan plunged over the side and into the ditch, all four wheels lodging in the rushing water with a jolt, causing the air bag to hurl against her with enough force to knock the wind out of her and leave her dazed.

"Aaghh," she moaned, rubbing at her burning cheeks while trying to see through the gray haze from the exploded air bag that filled the minivan's interior. "My face! It feels like I've been burned." For a moment, she was afraid she was going to vomit.

Her whole body ached.

Straightening in the seat, she rolled down the window and stared out in amazement. The rear of the minivan sat deeply lodged in the ditch with its hood and front bumper tilted upward at an odd angle. After finally regaining the use of her faculties, Tula looked around for ways to escape, but with the depth her car had gone into the ditch and the rapidly swirling murky water that surrounded it, escape seemed impossible. She was alone and utterly helpless, and no one knew where she was. She'd never been as frightened in her entire life. Not even when her husband had found her cowering under an old desk in their basement and had beaten her nearly senseless.

Chapter 5

Are you sure you're doin' the right thing, Boss, sending all those flowers to that little lady?"

Clint glared at Hayes Jenkins. "Not that it's any of your business, but have you got a better idea?"

His foreman pulled off his beat-up Stetson and rubbed at his head. "I don't know the lady, but from what you've said, I reckon she's a real looker. 'Course, *you* don't know her either. That's what worries me. Maybe she's playin' hard to get with you to catch you off guard."

"Off guard?" For some reason, Clint didn't like the sound of that. "What'd you mean by a statement like that?"

"You're well-known in these parts, Clint. Maybe not everyone in Steamboat knows you, but all the folks in this here valley know you. I hate to say this, but you don't think all those women who cart them casseroles and cakes here for you are only attracted to you, do you? Now don't get me wrong, but I'd say most of them are after your money and your land. Even this fine house you built for Sarah. What makes you think this wedding planner of yours don't know about your wealth and isn't trying to become the next Mrs. Clint Murphy so's she can take the place over?"

Clint wanted to smack Hayes upside the head, but he didn't.

He knew the man had only his best interests at heart. "That thought don't hold water. I've already asked her to marry me, and she turned me down flat."

"Now what'd you go and do that for?" Hayes sidled up next to him. "Maybe that's part of her game."

"How? I don't get it."

"Women are connivers. They know how gullible us men are. We like to be sweet-talked, but we like a woman to give us a challenge, not be a pushover. You know, like when we go fishing. If the old fish would just jump on our hook the first time we cast our line in the water, it'd take all the fun out of fishing. We'd say, forget about it and walk away. Maybe that's the game she's playin' with you. She's probably heard about all the women who've been after you and how you've rejected them. She's using a different approach, and being the avid fisherman that you are, you're playin' right into her hand. She's gonna get her hook into you so deep that you can't back away, and before you know it, you and everything you own will belong to her."

Knowing Hayes was the one person who would never let him down, Clint gave him the honor of hearing him out before speaking. "Look, Hayes, this woman and I have never discussed my land or my financial condition. All she knows is that I live in the Yampa Valley on a ranch and I wear Western garb. That's it, so I doubt she's after me or my money."

"But you don't know that for sure, do you?"

He had to admit he didn't. "But if what you're saying is true, why hasn't she at least called to thank me for the flowers I've sent? Seems to me, if she was trying to win me on her terms, she'd take advantage of my apology and call me."

Hayes tapped his brow with his forefinger. "Ah, you said the magic words. *If* she was trying to win you on *her* terms! Tell me honestly, Boss; if this woman had fawned all over you like the others and hadn't presented you with a challenge to win her, would you have been as interested in her?"

Clint shrugged. "I don't know."

Hayes leaned close. "What if you put her to a test?"

"What kind of test?"

"If she shows any interest in you, imply that you're in financial trouble, maybe even about to lose the ranch. See how loyal she'd be to you then. If she really loves you, like Sarah did, she won't even care and would be happy living with you in that small ranch hand's cabin on the back side of the ranch down by Watson Creek."

Clint thoughtfully rubbed at his chin. "I don't know, Hayes; seems kinda extreme to me. A man could lose a woman for pulling a trick like that."

"I hate to say this, Boss, but you've spent more time and money lookin' into a prospective ranch hand's background than you have lookin' into this woman's. How much do you really know about her?"

"I know she was married once but didn't have children. I know her husband's dead, and he certainly wasn't worthy of her."

"Is she the one who told you that?"

"Yeah."

"What makes you think she wouldn't lie to you? Maybe, if

her husband was alive, he'd have a different story to tell. Maybe *she's* the one who caused his death."

"Hayes!"

"Well, maybe she was. Don't you watch any of them movies on TV or listen to the news? She wouldn't be the first one to get rid of a husband."

Clint narrowed his eyes, Hayes's words upsetting him more than he cared to admit. "I'd say that's just about enough, Hayes. I don't want to hear any more of this foolishness. If you want, from now on, I'll get one of the other hands to go into town and place my flower orders."

The man lifted his hand in defeat. "Naw, I'll do it. I've said my piece, and now I'll be still. Just promise me you'll think about what I said. You're a fine man, Clint. I don't want to see you get hurt."

Clint motioned him away, then leaned back in his chair. *Oh, Hayes, I hope you're wrong about Tula. 'Cause I'm crazy about that little filly, and I've gone too far to turn back. I'm not giving her a minute's peace until she says she'll be my wife. I don't want to grow old alone, and she's just the kind of woman I want by my side.*

Tula tried to push the driver's door open, but with the upward position of the front of the minivan, and the weight of the door working against her, it was impossible. After scooting across the console, she tried the passenger door, but it, too, was impossible. The only way out was through the windows. She glanced down at her open-back high heels, then at her linen suit. Why hadn't she worn the black pantsuit and low-heeled sandals she'd considered? They would have been much more appropriate for climbing out of cars and walking down slick rocky roads.

She glanced at her watch. She was already a half hour late to the Reardons'. If only they'd come to find her, but why should they? They had no idea she'd goofed up on their instructions. Besides, she probably wasn't even close to the route they'd told her to take. Even if they did look for her, they'd be looking in the wrong place. No, her only choice was to get out and walk. It was warm out now; in a few hours, though, the sun would be disappearing behind the trees, and the evening could become quite cool. The last thing she wanted was to spend the night there, without anything with which to cover up.

After anchoring the strap of her bag to her shoulder, she rolled down the window. Then balancing herself on her tummy, she backed out feet first, wiggling her way through the opening. She screamed out when her feet hit the cold, swiftly moving water, soaking her shoes and sucking at her legs. Not sure how deep the ditch was, and afraid if she turned loose of the door's frame there was a chance she could be washed downhill even further and maybe drown, Tula struggled to pull herself back inside. In the process, she lost a shoe. Spent, shaken, and weak, fear gripped her heart like a vise and took her breath away. She'd never felt so isolated and alone.

The sun was already moving behind the mountain range. Scared out of her wits at the thought of spending the night, maybe even days, in her minivan with no one finding her, she closed the window, then hunkered down in the seat, shivering from both cold and fright, and wrapped her arms tightly about herself. Why hadn't she kept a blanket, or at least an afghan, in the minivan? There was nothing inside with which to cover up. Was she destined to die there? It appeared the only one who could help her was God, and she hadn't talked to Him in a long time.

She glanced at her watch and then at her purse. All the latter contained was a package of mints. She hadn't had a thing to eat all day. She'd skipped breakfast, knowing she would be having lunch at the Reardons'. How long could one small package of mints last?

Brushing aside her tears, she began to think about her life. She'd known God as a teenager, had accepted Him as her Savior at a little church she'd attended in Fort Collins with her cousin, but then her father told her to forget about God, insisting God was like the Easter Bunny and Santa Claus, merely made-up characters to make people feel good. He'd even threatened her to never speak God's name in their house again. Then after her wedding, she'd discovered she'd married a wife beater. Suffering so many times at her husband's hand, she'd turned to God again. But when the beatings and the abuse continued, she gave up on Him, once again accepting her father's and friends' stories that God was nothing more than a myth. But, looking back, God had been so real the day she'd asked Him to forgive her sins and come into her heart. The person who had counseled her had told her God didn't always answer our prayers the way we wanted Him to, or when we wanted Him to, but He did answer. Maybe her husband's dying was God's way of answering.

"Was that it, God?" she cried out, lifting one hand toward the heavens. "Was that Your answer to my prayer, and I didn't even recognize it?"

But the only response was the sound of the wind whipping its way through the leafy trees.

At her absolute end and feeling totally helpless, Tula glanced down at her bare foot and began to sob. In her frustration, she cried out. "Help! Someone! Anyone! Help! Help! Help! I'm so alone, and I'm afraid! I don't know what to do! HELP!"

Clint gazed into space as Blue Streak ambled along. Nothing could make him feel calmer when faced with trouble or a monumental decision than a ride on the big horse's back. It didn't make any difference where they rode. In fact, many times he just held lightly to the reins and let Blue Streak decide their destination. Today was one of those days.

Try as he might, he couldn't get Hayes's warnings out of his mind. Maybe he *had* fallen for Tula too quickly. Was he so desperate to have a mate that he'd overlooked some negative things about her that would have been obvious if he'd taken time to get to know her? She really hadn't told him much about herself, except that her husband had been a cruel man. Had she told him that to make him feel sorry for her? And what about children? Most married couples wanted children. He and Sarah certainly had. Had Tula wanted children?

Hayes was right. Maybe she did know more about him than he did her. He knew very little about the woman who'd so quickly captured his heart, especially the most important thing. He'd assumed, because she seemed to be such a nice person, that she shared his faith. What if she didn't? That, in itself, could be a major obstacle to the relationship he thought he wanted. Hadn't he always warned the young people in his church that they should never date someone they wouldn't want to marry, especially if that person didn't share the same faith? *Slow down, boy*, he told himself. *There's no hurry. If you think this woman is the right one for you and God agrees with you, it'll work out. Don't be so anxious.*

When Blue Streak shied at a rabbit, Clint was suddenly brought back to reality. He'd been so caught up in his thoughts he hadn't paid a speck of attention to where they were going. He glanced around for familiar landmarks. True, they were still on his land, but this part was a section he hadn't visited in a long time. "Ah, now I know where we are," he said aloud to Blue Streak, noting a familiar clump of aspen that had been struck and damaged by lightning several years earlier. "Maybe we ought to go and check the supplies in the old ranch hand's cabin before we go back." He'd always loved the area around Watson Creek, and though the terrain was more rugged and not as accessible as the land around Moody Creek, it was amazingly beautiful, the touch of God's hand.

He glanced at his watch, then gave Blue Streak a gentle nudge with his heels. "If we're gonna check out the cabin, old boy, we'd better do it now, before Hayes comes lookin' for us."

But before the big horse could respond, a shrill scream split the peaceful silence, and it came from the direction of the old abandoned road. Clint's heart clenched. Nothing about that old road was good. It was filled with holes big enough to swallow up a Volkswagen and ditches so deep a person could drown in them after a big rain. It should have been barricaded and closed years ago.

A second scream pierced the air, causing the birds to scatter as rapidly from the trees as if a gun had been fired.

Lord, please don't let someone be hurt! Clint tightened his grip on the reins, then gave Blue Streak rapid kicks to his sides. "Hurry, boy! Someone's in trouble. We've got to get to them." Without regard for his or Blue Streak's safety, he urged the horse up the rugged terrain, across a slight clearing, then back down into the mass of mature aspen and pine trees that vied with each other for space and light. The branches tore at his face and tugged at his clothes, but he barely noticed. All he could think about was getting to that person as quickly as possible. He'd nearly reached the old abandoned road when a third scream echoed through the forest. This one was accompanied by a woman's loud cry for help. The desperation in her voice terrified him. It'd rained most of the night. If the ditches were full and she—

"Please! Someone! Help me!"

Blue Streak leaped over one fallen log, then another. Clint tugged on the reins, halting the horse before he could leap over the ditch. He stopped and listened, not sure which direction the scream for help had come from. "Hello! Where are you? I'm coming!" he yelled out. "Are you all right?"

"Here! My car is in the ditch! I'm so scared!"

Relieved the woman had been capable of answering him, Clint quickly headed Blue Streak in the direction of her voice. Hoping, praying the woman was only frightened and not hurt. "I see your car. I'm nearly there! Hang on!"

The moment he got close enough to the vehicle to get a good look, he recognized the woman who was frantically waving at him through an open window. It was Tula!

"Hurry, Clint!" she shouted, her face taking on a look of relief once she realized it was him. "I can't get out!"

He leaped off Blue Streak's back, grabbed one end of the rope he always kept looped to the saddle, and hurried toward her. "Tula. Listen to me. Open the door as far as you can, try to brace yourself on the edge of the seat and the armrest, and grab hold of the rope!"

A look of desperation came over her again. "I can't, Clint. I can't push the door open. I've already tried. The water is pressing against it too hard, holding it shut."

He stood thinking, desperately scanning his brain for easy solutions, but there were none. He had to face the severity of her situation. Getting her safely out of there was not going to be easy. "I'll get you out somehow, Tula, but you're going to have to trust me. Can you do that?"

"I'll try."

"Let me think a minute." He scanned the area for anything that might help, but nothing looked promising. Then he remembered the work gloves he kept in the saddlebag. Those would help! He hurried to Blue Streak and pulled out a pair of nearly new leather gloves and a pair worn enough that he should have thrown away.

"Okay." He kept his voice soft. The last thing he needed was for her to be any more frightened than she was already. "After I tie a pair of gloves onto this rope, I'm going to toss it to you. It already has a loop tied in the end. When you get it, I want you to put the gloves on to protect your hands and then slip the loop over your head and under your arms."

It took three tosses, but she was finally able to grab hold of the rope and, with chattering teeth, follow his instructions. "I've got it around me, and I've put the gloves on. Now what do I do?"

"Is there any way you can get up onto the roof?"

She panicked. "The roof? No!"

"Are you sure you can't reach up and grab hold of the luggage rack and pull yourself up?"

"I—I can't. I'm afraid I'll fall."

"Okay, then push yourself as far out the window as you dare. Then, with the loop wrapped around your body and with your keeping a hold on it, I'll pull you out."

Her face took on a look of sheer terror. "I can't, Clint! I'm not that strong. I'm afraid I might fall into the ditch and drown. The water is moving so fast."

Knowing how deep parts of the ditch could be and how rapidly the water was rushing down the hill, he was as afraid as she was, but he could never let her know. Instead, he forced himself to smile. He had to convince her she could count on him to pull her out, or she would never be willing to do what he said. "I won't let you fall, Tula," he assured her, willing his voice to remain calm. "I'll have you out of there in no time."

She began to cry. "I'm afraid, Clint."

"I know you are, sweetheart, but you have to be brave and trust me."

She nervously fingered the rope. "What if it doesn't hold me?"

"It'll hold you, Tula. That rope will hold a three-hundred-pound man with no trouble at all."

"What if you can't hold on and it slips out of your hands?"

"It won't slip out of my hands. I'll be wearing gloves, too. I can't promise you won't get banged up a bit when you hit the side of the ditch, but I will not let you fall. Besides, just to make double sure, I've tied the other end of the rope to Blue Streak. He'll keep the rope taut. You do want to get out of there, don't you?"

Her wavering yes broke his heart. If he were in her position, with a rocky slope on each side and the whirling, agitated water below, he, too, would be afraid.

"I have another problem. I lost my shoe when I tried to climb out the window. It fell into the water."

Clint expelled a long breath of air. Her losing a shoe complicated things. There was no way she could climb up that steep, rocky bank without tearing up her bare foot. "I'm sorry you lost your shoe, Tula, and you'll probably hurt your foot; but you're going to have to jump without it, or I'll never get you out of there." He extended his hand. "Tula, please. Take a big, deep breath; then leap toward me as hard as you can."

She lowered her head. "I can't, Clint. I'm too afraid."

He lifted his hands in frustration. "Then I'll have to come after you."

"You can't! What if you fall into the ditch? The water could wash you away. I can't let you take that chance."

"There's no other choice. I'm coming. Slip the rope back up over your head and turn it loose. I'll need it to tie around my waist."

She gave her head a hard shake. "No, I won't. I don't want you to get hurt because of me."

He moved as close to the road's jagged edge as he dared and gave the rope a tug, but she held on fast. "Then I'll have to try to jump over there without it, but I'd sure prefer to have that end of the rope tied around me."

"No! You can't!" she shouted, flailing her arms wildly. "I–I'll do what you said!"

He could tell she was at the point of hysterics. "Tula, pay attention to me." He squatted down and gave her a smile, which he hoped would help calm her fears. "Do you know what rappelling is?"

"No, I don't think so."

"Sometimes on the news or a TV program, they show people who wrap a rope around their bodies, then lower themselves to the ground by almost bouncing their feet against the wall. Do you know what I mean?"

She nodded. "Yes, I'd just forgotten that's what they called it."

"That's kind of what I want you to do, only in reverse. With that rope looped around your body under your arms, I want you to jump toward the side of the ditch and try to hit it with both feet."

"But I lost my shoe!"

"I know, and though you may injure your foot, it's the best way to get you out. Now listen. The second your feet touch the wall of the ditch, I'll begin pulling you up, but you'll need to give me some help by bracing against the side of the ditch with your feet, then walking up the wall; otherwise, I'll have to drag you. But if you do like I say, it should take some of the pull and pressure off your arms. It's going to hurt; you'll probably end up with some rope burns across your back and under your arms, but I won't let you fall."

"It sounds so scary."

"I know. The only other choice is that I leave you here while I go for help."

"No! You can't leave me, Clint. Please!"

Clint glanced down at the swirling mass of water circling the minivan. It seemed to have risen a bit higher in the short time he'd been standing there. If there'd been a heavy rain higher up the mountain during the night than they'd had here, it would continue to rise. He'd lived on the ranch all his life. He well knew from experience the power and uncertainty of a raging stream. "I'm not going to leave you, Tula. I promise."

He was surprised when she gathered up the slack of the rope and began maneuvering her body into position. "Careful! I know it's going to be hard, maybe even impossible, but you're pretty small. Try to see if you can wiggle around enough in the open window to where you'll be able to seat yourself on the window's ledge with your feet dangling over the side. Just make sure you keep a good hold on the door frame."

"I don't think I can. There's not that much room."

His concern for her safety was growing more desperate with each passing moment. "Try, Tula, try. But make sure you don't let that loop slip off." He reached out both arms. "Trust me. I'll be holding you safely in my arms in no time."

Tula gazed up at Clint's face. He wanted her to trust him? Trusting someone, even someone as nice as Clint, didn't come easy for her. Every man she'd ever trusted had let her down. But there was something in his voice and the way he looked at her, a gentleness, even in their hour of storm, that made her want to trust him. Not just because he was her only hope, the only one who could help her at that moment, but because she knew, deep in her heart, he was worthy of her trust.

Summoning up every ounce of courage within her, she sent him a feeble smile. "I'm coming, Clint!"

Negotiating her body through the narrow opening was even more of a challenge than she'd expected. She tried to stick her head out the window and then get her shoulders and legs through, but that didn't work. So she tried getting her legs through first, then her head and shoulders, but that didn't work either. In frustration, she began to bawl like a baby, with deep sobs racking her body. "I can't do it."

Clint whacked himself upside the head. "What's the matter with me? Why didn't I think of it before? Tula, keep the gloves—but take the rope off and let me pull it back up to me. Then crawl into the backseat and slide the door open. Since the door slides, it won't have the flow of the water working against it and holding it shut like the front doors!"

She hurriedly pulled the loop over her head and released the rope, letting it go free. Then after scooting over the console and into the backseat, she pressed the button on the door handle. Though it was a bit difficult to get started, once the door began to move, it opened fairly easily. "It worked!" she shouted, an amazing relief flooding her body. The sight of Clint's smile added to her joy. "Now what?"

"We're going to do the same thing we planned, but it's going to be a lot easier for you to make your jump now that you have all that space. Take your gloves off so you won't lose them; then I'm going to toss you the rope again. Put it around you the same way I told you before."

Surprisingly, she caught it on the first toss. "Okay, the loop is under my arms, I have the gloves back on, and I'm holding on to the rope."

"Think about the way those people rappelled on TV, only remember you're going up instead of down and I'll be pulling you all the way. Picture it in your mind. The most important thing is that once both your feet have hit the side of the ditch, you'll need to press them against the wall, lean outward, and walk up the wall. I'll be pulling on the rope. It will keep you from falling. Once you're up to where I can reach you, I'll pull you up beside me."

"What if my feet slip?"

"If your feet slip, your body will still be in the loop and I'll pull you out."

He paused; she could tell he wanted to add something else,

and it frightened her. "What, Clint? What else were you going to say?"

He gave a sheepish grin. "I—I was going to say—I'd never let you fall because I love you."

At that moment, she wanted to say she loved him, too, but was it because he was the only person who could save her? Her hero? Or was what she was feeling true love? To her surprise, she *did* trust him. She trusted him with her life. She'd never trusted anyone else like that. But then again, what choice did she have?

He held out his hand. "It's time, Tula. I don't want to frighten you, but the water is rising. We need to get you out of there now."

She blinked hard, her heart pounding so ferociously in her chest she thought she could hear it. "I'm ready." She could tell by the set of his jaw and the way his grip tightened on the rope that he would do everything in his power to save her. But instead of telling her to jump like she expected, he lifted his face toward the sky.

"Lord," he cried out, raising his free hand high, "thank You for leading me to Tula when I hadn't even planned to come to this area today. If ever I've needed You, it's now. Please, God, give me the strength I need to bring Tula safely to my side. And give her the strength and courage for what she is about to do. We're putting ourselves in Your hands."

Tula's heart was deeply touched by his prayer. No one had ever prayed like that for her before, except the pastor who had led her to the Lord. With tear-filled eyes and a heart of trust and gratitude, she gazed up at him. "Thank you, Clint. Your prayer helped me to be brave."

Clint nodded. "God is able, Tula. He'll see us through this."

She watched as he shifted his position, pressed the heels of his boots into the mud and rock on the road, rotated his shoulders, and then leaned toward her. "On the count of three, jump. Are you ready?"

She nodded. "Ready."

"One. Two. Three!"

Chapter 6

Without hesitation, Tula jumped as hard as she could, planting both feet against the ditch's side just as Clint had told her. A piercing stab of pain shot through her bare foot as it hit a rock, but she barely acknowledged it, or even the agony of the rope bearing her weight as it cut into her flesh. Her focus was on planting her feet firmly and leaning back as Clint had said she should.

He let out a grunt. "Good girl! I've got you. Keep leaning back and walk up to me, Tula. You'll make it. It's only a few steps more!"

Though the pain from the rope had become excruciating, she pressed on, moving up the slippery, rocky wall a few inches with each step. When she'd almost reached Clint, he hollered, "Back, Blue Streak. Back!" then bent and grabbed her arm, pulling her to safety.

He didn't have to pull her into his arms like he'd promised he would. She leaped into them, so relieved she began to laugh hysterically. "I made it!" Clint held her so tight she had to gasp for air, but it felt good. Safe. Secure.

He smothered her cheeks with kisses, then lifted his face and praised God for answering his prayer and bringing her safely to his side.

For the first time since she'd set her feet on level ground, pain ripped at her foot, back, under her arms, and across her chest as Clint's hold on her tightened even more. Pain so unbearable she thought she was going to faint.

Clint felt Tula flinch, and he knew why. He'd been sure the rope around her body, bearing her weight, would do severe damage, but his plan had been the only way to get her out. True, he could have gone for help, but that would have taken time—and time was something they hadn't had. If the raging water in the ditch would have continued to rise at the rate it was already, its force would've more than likely pushed Tula and her minivan on downstream and into the creek. That would have been disastrous. No, he couldn't have taken that chance. He'd done the right thing by insisting she place the loop around her and jump. And, praise God, it had worked.

Releasing his hold on her, he lifted her face so her eyes met his. "Good thing you had on both a blouse and that little jacket, or your injuries would have been even worse. I know you're in pain, sweetheart. I'm going to take you to my cabin and get some salve on those rope burns."

Tula glanced from her disabled minivan to Blue Streak, then back to Clint. "On—him?"

He nodded. "The cabin's not far from here. I keep it stocked with first aid supplies. Don't worry. Blue Streak is a gentle horse. Remember, he's the one who kept your rope taut."

Her face contorted with pain as her gaze went back to Blue Streak. "Then I guess I'll have to take my first ride on a horse."

"You've never ridden before?"

"No. First time." She winced as she pointed to her bare foot. "I think I cut my foot on a rock when I jumped. It hurts, and it's really bleeding."

"I'm not surprised. I'll take a look at it when we get to the cabin." Being careful not to add to her pain, Clint gently gathered her up in his arms, then carried her to Blue Streak. She felt almost limp, and it scared him. Once he'd gently deposited her on the ground, he mounted his horse, then reached down and lifted her up behind him as gently as he could by pulling her by her arm. "I know those deep rope burns are terribly painful, but put your arms around my waist and rest your head on my back. You'll feel more comfortable and secure that way. The cabin isn't far. Think you can make it? I don't want you fainting on me." He cupped her hand with his when he felt it slip around his waist. "Good girl."

Though Clint wove Blue Streak in and out among the trees to avoid uneven ground, sometimes, when going either up or down an incline, he could hear a soft moan come from his passenger, and he knew the movement was heightening her pain. Though it only took about ten minutes to reach the cabin, it seemed much longer to Clint. All he wanted was to get her to where he could treat her wounds and fix her a nice cup of hot coffee to soothe her frazzled nerves.

He lowered her to the ground, then dismounted before

carrying her into the cabin. He liked the feel of her in his arms. Though both her hair and her clothing were in disarray, she was beautiful. He loved the trustful way she looked at him with those big blue eyes.

For some unknown reason, Hayes's words about Tula playing a game of seduction with him came rushing into his mind as he turned the knob and pushed the door open.

She gazed up at him. "You own this place?"

He nodded.

"It's nice." She glanced around the interior. "I've always thought it would be nice to live in a little cabin like this."

He motioned toward the sofa. "I'll get the first aid kit; then, as soon as I get your wounds taken care of, I'll make us a pot of coffee."

She groaned, then let out a sigh. "Coffee would be nice." Clint felt terrible as he assessed the damage to her frail body. The way the rope's loop had torn into her flesh, she had to be in absolute misery.

"Have you eaten anything today?"

She trembled. "No. I was heading out to the Reardons' for lunch and a meeting, but I guess I took a wrong turn. That's how I ended up on that old road."

He sat down beside her and opened up the big first aid kit. "There used to be a ROAD CLOSED sign up there where that road veers off the county road, but either it fell down or someone took it. I'll put up another sign as soon as I get a chance. We don't want this same thing happening to someone else."

He pulled the tin of salve from the kit and gazed at it,

holding it awkwardly in his hand. How was he going to get that stuff on her? "I've got an old shirt hanging over there on that hook. It might be easier to apply the salve if you wear that instead of the blouse thing you're wearing." He held his hands up between them. "I didn't mean for *me* to apply it—I thought you could do that yourself. On the parts *you* could reach," he hastily added. "Then I'll help you with the rest—your back." Feeling like a bumbling dork, he grabbed the shirt off the peg and tossed it to her. "I'll step outside while you change and apply the salve."

"You sure you don't mind waiting outside? It may take awhile. I hate to run you out of your own home."

"Naw. I like it outdoors. Spend most of my time outside." Nearly tripping over his feet, he moved outside and closed the door behind him. *She thinks I live in this cabin! From the sound of things, she has no idea I own this whole ranch. That, or she's playing it coy. Maybe I should avoid the truth for a while and see what happens. I sure don't want to saddle myself with a woman who is more interested in what I own than she is in me.*

"You can come in now!" Tula called out sometime later.

He quickly stepped inside and nearly broke out in laughter when he caught sight of her in his oversized shirt.

"I must look a mess." She dipped her head shyly. "I'm sure my mascara is smeared, I haven't put on a speck of lipstick since I got out of bed this morning, and I'll bet my hair is in need of a good combing." She swiveled slightly on the worn leather sofa, then groaned and turned her back toward him. "I hate to ask, but would you mind putting the salve on my back? I could reach all but the very center. That part hurts almost as much as the area under my arms."

He nodded, then sat down beside her. He'd been dreading that job from the moment he realized she couldn't put the salve on alone. He felt like he should apply it with his eyes closed, but that would never work. How would he see where to put it? He dipped two fingertips into the tin, then, as softly as he could, smoothed the salve to the areas she couldn't reach. Her skin felt as soft to his touch as a baby's bottom. He hoped he wasn't hurting her. "Does this stuff burn?"

"Not too much. Actually, it feels kind of soothing. You've never used it?"

"Not on rope burns, but on other stuff." More embarrassed than he'd ever been in his life, he hurried as fast as he could to apply the salve, then snapped the lid back on the tin. "Okay, that should do it. Now, let me check out that foot."

From the look of misery on her face when she turned back around, he could tell she was in more pain than she was admitting, and her teeth were chattering. "There's some Tylenol in the first aid kit. Maybe you should take some. It might ease the pain and soothe your nerves. You've been through a lot."

She nodded. "Maybe I should."

Clint rose, then moved to the small kitchen area and took a bottle of water from the shelf and the Tylenol from the kit. "Here. Take this; then hold out that foot."

When he caught sight of the nasty cut in the sole of her foot, he turned his head away and screwed up his face. How had she walked up the side of that ditch with that awful cut? Fortunately, though it was long, it wasn't too deep, and he had plenty of disinfectant on hand to wash it out. It probably needed stitches, but that would have to wait until she felt ready enough to go back into town. Right now, the best thing to do was clean it up and let her rest. The terrible ordeal she'd been through was enough to upset even the strongest man. It sure upset him!

"You think it needs stitches?"

Clint took the bottle of disinfectant from the kit and held it up so she could see it. "Maybe, but for now, I'm going to pour some of this on it. It may sting a bit, but we sure don't want it to get infected."

She grinned. "I'm tough. I can take it."

He laughed. With no makeup, her hair in disarray, and wearing his tattered shirt, she looked anything but tough. "Hang on. Here it comes."

Though she grimaced, she didn't cry out like he'd expected she would. "You are tough, aren't you?"

"I'm faking it." Her face sobered. "You're my hero, Clint. I don't know what I would have done if you hadn't come along. I—I could have died out there."

He poured more disinfectant onto her wound. "But you didn't. I'm convinced God sent me to you."

She eyed him suspiciously. "You really believe that, don't you?"

"Tula, when I got on Blue Streak's back today, my only purpose was to take a ride to clear my head. I had no intention of going anywhere near that old abandoned road. Like I do quite often, I leaned back in the saddle and let Blue Streak take me wherever he wanted to go. He brought me to you. It's been weeks since I've even been anywhere near that old road." He removed the lid from the salve again and gently began to massage it into the open wound with his fingertips. "I'd say God had a hand in that."

"I wish I had your faith."

"Anyone can have it. All you have to do is ask God for His forgiveness and to take over your life."

She gazed off dreamily. "I did that once, but when people made a mockery of what I'd done and laughed in my face about God being real, I backed away from Him." She gave him a smile he didn't understand. "Until today. Today, I actually called out to God for help."

Clint gave her foot a pat, then pressed the lid back onto the tin. "Looks to me like He heard you. You're back on solid ground. How're the wounds feeling?"

"A little better, thanks to you." She gestured around the cabin. "You're lucky to live such a simple life, Clint. Out here, away from the pressures of the world."

He decided to test the waters. "You wouldn't rather live in a nice big house with a couple of stone fireplaces and a kitchen big enough to cook for an army?"

She frowned. "Why would I want such a big home? But I have to admit, a fireplace would be nice. One like you have here. And a huge kitchen? You'd be surprised what a good meal I could put together right here in your little kitchen."

"It's pretty isolated out here."

She gestured toward one of the windows. "But look at the

view you have. Money couldn't buy a view like that. You and your wife must have loved living out here. What a beautiful, romantic place to live with the one you love. This place has to be filled with memories."

Though Clint smiled outwardly, inwardly he frowned. *Doesn't sound like she knows I'm a wealthy man. Or if she does, she's a great little actress.*

She glanced around the room. "I think I could live in a place like this and never want to leave."

He decided to try another tactic to check her out. "I already asked you to marry me. If you did, you *could* live out here in this cabin. You could decorate it any way you want."

She gave him a smile that melted his heart. "How about that coffee you promised me?"

"Comin' right up." He hurried into the small kitchen, then struck a match and lit the burner on the little propane stove. In no time, he had a teakettle full of water hot enough to make two steaming mugs of instant coffee.

"Sugar? Powdered cream?"

She shook her head as she reached for the mug. "I like it black."

He placed his mug on the end table, then sat down beside her and folded her free hand in his. "Look, Tula. I know you're trying to be brave, and you are. No one could have suffered the injuries that you have and not be in misery from head to toe. But rather than be so brave about it, I wish you'd cry, scream, kick, do something. Anything to relieve your pain."

"I'm a very private person, Clint. I'm used to keeping my

pain and emotions to myself." She cast her eyes downward and nibbled on her lip. "I told you my husband was a cruel man. But what I didn't tell you was that he beat me mercilessly for nothing. The least little thing I did could set him off. Something so simple as his cup of coffee not being hot enough, or me not putting enough salt on his eggs. And the worst thing of all? I let him do it."

Her revelation surprised him. He'd had no idea things had been *that* bad. "But why, Tula? Why would you let him? It was crazy to put up with a man like that. He could have killed you."

"I realize that now. But my dad treated my mom like his own personal punching bag. I guess I assumed married life was supposed to be that way. After she died, I became his target. Then my husband's."

Clint gave his head a sad shake. "You're lucky he's the one who died instead of you."

She lifted tired eyes. "Please don't think badly of me, but after the initial shock of learning he'd died at the scene of the accident, I actually felt a great sense of relief. His death meant his shouting, calling me names, and beatings would stop."

Clint dropped to his knees and knelt in front of her, carefully cradling her bruised hand in his. "I could never feel badly toward you, Tula. I'm just sorry it happened to you."

With her free hand, she rubbed at her temple. "As much as I wanted children, I lived in fear that I would become pregnant. After the kind of childhood I'd had, I couldn't imagine raising a child in that same type of environment."

He ached for her. What kind of a monster would treat a woman like that?

Clint glanced at his watch. He had to get her out of there before it got dark. "Do you think you'll be okay if I leave you for a while? Rather than have you ride behind me on Blue Streak again, I thought I could ride up to the main house and get my pickup. I'll be back before you know it. Then I can drive you to the emergency room at Steamboat, and they can take a look at that foot."

She looked like a scared child. "I—I guess I could stay by myself. What's going to happen to my car?"

"I'll have a wrecker come and pull it out. You'll probably have to replace it, but let's not worry about that now." Turning loose of her hand, he rose. "I'll hurry as fast as I can. Why don't you stretch out on the sofa and take a nap?"

"I doubt I can sleep."

"But you can rest. Hopefully, that Tylenol will kick in before long. I promise I'll be back soon." He backed toward the door. "Your water bottle is on the table. The cupboards are pretty empty, but I did find a box of crackers. I put them by your water."

She nodded. "Thank you, Clint. Please hurry."

He flashed her a smile. "You can count on it."

Tula stared at the closed door. She hated to see Clint go. Without him there, the eerie silence of the cabin was overwhelming. The only sound cutting the air was the beat of her heart.

Though it pained her to move, she swiveled around on the sofa and stretched out, covering up with the homemade afghan she'd found folded on the end table.

As she lay snuggled beneath the intricate pattern of crocheted brown, green, and purple yarn, all sorts of scenarios ran through her head. What if Clint hadn't found her when he did? Would she still be in her minivan, hungry and freezing in the cold night air? Or would the raging waters in the ditch have dislodged her car and carried it downstream and into the creek? She shuddered at the thought.

The only persons who'd known she had driven out that way were the Reardons. If they'd called her office to check on her, they would have gotten the message on her answering machine, which said she was out for the afternoon, and probably thought she'd forgotten their appointment, gotten the days mixed up, or been too busy to come. She doubted they would have even thought of calling the authorities and reporting she hadn't shown up at the appointed time. Though she'd been in Steamboat Springs for over a year, there was really no one who would be checking on her other than her friend Sharon, and she didn't have a car. Tula had been too busy building up the wedding-planning business she'd bought from its former owner to take time to make close friends. It could have been days before someone became concerned about her absence.

Tula stared at the ceiling with its old-fashioned, bare-bulb light fixture. "God, did You really send Clint to find me? Is that why he and Blue Streak rode in that direction?" Still frazzled by her experience, she blinked at her tears. "I really did want You to come into my heart when I was a child. I should never have listened to those people who said You weren't real. Everywhere I look, there is evidence You're real. I want to know You, God, like Clint knows You. I know I've sinned, but I'm asking You to forgive me. I believe in You, God, and I believe in Jesus. Is that really all I have to do to become a Christian? It sounds so simple, too good to be true."

The word *trust* came to her mind. "It's always been hard for me to trust anyone, God. Even You. Every person I've ever trusted let me down." A big smile crossed her face. "Well, not quite everyone. I trusted Clint with my life today, and he didn't let me down. I honestly think that man would have put his own life on the line to come after me if I hadn't put that rope around me like he said and jumped. He told me to trust him—and I did—and here I am, safe and sound. If Clint, a mortal man, wouldn't let me down, I know You won't either. You're God. You can do anything. I now know I can trust You."

As she glanced at the oversized, tattered shirt she still wore, she couldn't help but wonder if Clint had reached his pickup truck yet. Though the cabin was growing dark, it had lights. Surely, Clint had a generator. But even if she could hobble on one foot and find it, she had no idea how to start it. She'd just have to be patient and wait.

Clint pulled on his Stetson, grabbed his flashlight and the quilt he'd brought to wrap Tula in, and leaped out the door as soon as he squealed his truck to a sudden halt in front of the cabin.

He wished he'd started the generator before he'd left, or at least lit the Coleman lantern.

Tula smiled and lifted her arms toward him the minute he rushed through the door and sent the beam of his flashlight in her direction. "Oh, Clint. You're back!"

"It's dark in here." He lit the Coleman lantern, then hurried to her. After tossing the quilt onto the arm of the sofa, he pulled her into the safety of his arms and held her tight, nestling his chin in her hair. "I told you I'd be back."

She lifted her face and gazed at him with those big, blue, innocent eyes that gave him feelings he hadn't experienced since he'd lost Sarah.

"I never doubted you, Clint. Not once. You said I'd have to trust you, and I did."

She was so close, so kissable, he couldn't resist pressing his lips against hers, and he was both pleased and surprised when she didn't turn away. When their kiss ended, he gazed dreamily into her eyes. "I know you don't have feelings for me but—"

She lightly touched his lips with the tip of her finger. "Who says I don't?"

"But when I came to your shop, you sent me away. And you didn't acknowledge the flowers I sent."

"I had to, Clint. Don't you see? I was afraid to get close to you, or any man."

"Because of your husband?"

"Yes, and my father, and just about any man I've ever known, including some of the guys I dated in high school. I've never had a meaningful relationship with a good man. I had no idea what I was missing."

"And you were afraid to trust me, afraid I'd let you down, too, weren't you?"

She nodded. "Yes."

Though he wanted nothing more than to continue to hold her, he couldn't. He needed to get her to the emergency room so they could check out her wounds. "I hope, after today, you know you can trust me, Tula. I would never do anything to hurt you." He wrapped the quilt about her, being careful not to touch the areas on her back where the rope had dug into her flesh, then easily lifted her in his arms. "We'd better be going. We have a long drive ahead of us."

"You actually tied the rope around you, then leaped across the water in the ditch, and Clint pulled you out?" The emergency room doctor put the last piece of tape on Tula's foot, then gave his head a shake. "What an ordeal that must have been for both of you. Your rope burns are pretty deep, but considering the circus act you had to perform to get out of that ditch, I'm surprised you didn't get hurt any worse than you did. Your face will be sore for a few days from the force of the air bag, but with the pain from your other injuries, I doubt you'll notice."

Clint motioned toward Tula's back. "Do you think those rope burns'll heal without scarring?"

"Maybe. Maybe not, but that's a small price to pay for her life. The deep burns under her arms will give her more grief than her back. If you hadn't come along, she—"

Clint glared at the doctor. "But I did come along. That's all that matters."

Tula's face brightened. "Clint thinks God sent him to me."

The doctor let loose a mocking laugh. "God, huh? Well, it makes a good story."

Clint felt his anger rise. "It's no story, Doc. God did send me."

The man shrugged. "I guess it's your right to believe whatever you like." He gestured toward Tula's foot. "You're going to have to stay off of that for a few days. Is there someone who can take care of you?"

"No—"

Clint broke in before she could finish her answer. "Yes. Me. She's coming home with me. I'll take care of her."

Tula frowned at him. "You've done enough already. I'm sure I can find someone to do whatever is necessary. Maybe my friend at the diner."

He took hold of her hand. "Don't argue with me, Tula. It's all settled. You *are* coming home with me."

Tula stared at him in amazement. He was going to take her back to that isolated cabin? She loved the cabin—that wasn't it—but there appeared to be only one bedroom, and she certainly wasn't going to share it with him. Nor did she think it proper for the two of them to be there alone for whatever time it took before she could return to her apartment. Maybe all that *trust* stuff was part of his come-on, a ploy to make her think he was as good as he seemed.

"Can't I just hobble around on crutches?"

Again the doctor shrugged. "If you think you can handle them."

She glanced toward Clint. "See, you won't have to take care of me after all." Though he looked disappointed, he didn't argue with her.

The doctor motioned toward the nurses' station. "The hospital has loaners. I'll have the nurse get you a pair." He sized her up. "What are you? About five-five?"

"Five-six."

Within minutes, the nurse arrived with the crutches. Tula took them, but when she placed them under her arms and they touched the rope burns, she cried out in pain.

Clint grabbed them away from her. "You are *not* going to use crutches. Not with those wounds under your arms. You're coming with me."

The doctor nodded. "He's right. It's obvious you're going to need someone to help you for a few days. I suggest you go with him."

Tula lifted her hands in surrender. "Fine. I'll go with him."

Before she knew what was happening, Clint lifted her up in his arms and headed for his truck.

"Take me to my apartment," she said firmly as he placed her on the seat. "I only said I'd go with you to get out of there."

He closed the door, then rushed around to the driver's side. "Tula, this is ridiculous. You can't take care of yourself. Let me care for you."

"No matter what you think, I'm a lady, and I don't think

it is proper for a lady to share a small, one-bedroom, isolated cabin with a man, no matter how dire the circumstances."

"But—"

She shook a finger in his face. "No buts, Mr. Murphy. If you were half the gentleman I'd thought you were, even though you wanted to help, you wouldn't even consider such a thing."

"But—"

"And furthermore—"

Clint clapped his hand over her mouth. "Tula, listen to me! I don't live in that cabin. I—"

She pushed his hand away. "You took me to a stranger's cabin? Left me there while you went after your truck? You told me you owned it. You lied to me, Clint! What if that person had come back?"

"I didn't lie to you. I do own it."

Narrowing her eyes, she glared at him. "You're telling me one lie to cover up another? And to think I trusted you!"

Clint leaned back against the seat, pulled his Stetson low on his brow, and stared straight ahead. "Are you gonna keep on yappin', or are you gonna let me explain?"

"You mean *listen* to another one of your lies?"

"Nope. I mean listen to the absolute truth. That's what I'm aiming to tell you. But I don't want you interrupting."

What choice did she have? "I'll listen if you promise to take me back to my apartment when you're finished."

He seemed to consider her offer. "Let's put it this way. If, after you've heard me out, you still want to go to your apartment, I'll take you without a word of argument. Okay?"

After giving her chin a haughty tilt, she nodded. "Okay."

Clint turned to face her. "I wasn't lying to you, Tula. I do own that cabin. Occasionally, I stop there and check on things, but my ranch hands are the ones who use the place. I also own a house. A nice house, and I have a housekeeper. Aggie. She lives with me full-time, and I have plenty of bedrooms for the three of us. So you see, you don't have to worry about us being alone, or me not being a gentleman. I'll be caring for you as best I can, but it will be Aggie who will be dressing your wounds and seeing to your personal needs."

Tula didn't know what to say. "Why didn't you tell me about the cabin when you took me there? You could have explained you owned it but didn't live in it. Why the mystery?"

He gave her a shy grin. "You'd be mad if I told you."

"Mad? Why? What would make me mad?"

Clint rubbed at the stubble on his chin while trying to decide how he should word his confession. Well, he'd come clean about the cabin, so he might as well blurt out the rest and get it over with. No sense prolonging the agony.

"It's like this, Tula. When you turned me down, I was afraid you were playing hard to get because you, like most of the other women I've known, were more interested in what I owned than in me. I guess one of the reasons I've never dated another woman since I lost Sarah was because I didn't want a woman to marry me for all the wrong reasons. I didn't want to be anyone's fool." He warily reached for her hand, but she pulled it away. "I figured if you learned to love me when you thought I was only a ranch hand, then I'd know your love was true and you weren't out to marry me for whatever I've accumulated in my life."

Her jaw dropped. "That's what you thought about me?"

"I didn't really *think* it about you, but I was concerned. I haven't really known you that long. In fact, I know very little about you."

Tula folded her hands in her lap and sat quietly, as if thinking over his words. "It seems we're both lacking in the trust department. I had a hard time trusting you, but I never imagined you were having trouble trusting me. I don't know much about you either, Clint."

He raised his right palm toward her. "Honest, Tula. Everything I've told you tonight is true."

A slight smile played at the corners of her mouth. "I believe you, Clint."

"Then you'll go home with me? Let me and Aggie take care of you?"

She reached out and put her hand on his arm. "I'd consider it an honor."

Tula stared out the windshield in amazement when Clint pulled his truck up in front of his home. Even in the semidarkness of the yard lights, she could see how grand it was. "You actually live in this beautiful house?"

"Yep. Lived in it all my life. 'Course it's been added on to and remodeled several times. My great-granddad homesteaded this place. He and my great-grandma lived in that little cabin, where I took you today, for the biggest part of their married life. Then my grandpa built this place, and they moved in with him. My mom and dad lived here, then me and Sarah. Aggie's been with me nearly twenty years now."

Spellbound, Tula stared at the massive structure, the wrap-around porch, and the gigantic bay window. "Oh, Clint. This is lovely. It's like a picture from a magazine. I never imagined—"

A frown creased his brow. "You really didn't, did you? You had no idea I owned this ranch and this fine house."

She shook her head. "No, I didn't. Honest I didn't. I've been so busy getting my business on its feet I haven't had time to get acquainted with many of the Steamboat residents, let alone those living out here in the Yampa area."

He pushed his door open, then grinned at her. "You have no idea how glad I am to hear that. Now you sit right there until I come around and get you."

Tula felt like an invalid. She hated that she had to depend on someone to help her, even a nice man like Clint. She hoped his housekeeper wouldn't be upset with him for bringing her home and causing extra work.

He opened her door and reached out his arms. "Okay, little lady, let's go."

Tula slung the strap of her shoulder bag over her arm, then allowed Clint to lift her out of the truck. He carried her up the steps as easily as he would have a child. It was nice to have a man treating her as if she were important and had value, something she wasn't used to, and it felt good.

Before Clint could reach the door, it swung open as a round-faced, pleasant-looking woman greeted them, smiling and holding out welcoming hands. "You must be Tula."

Tula smiled. "And you're Aggie. Clint told me all about you." She glanced past the woman and into the huge living room. It was all Clint. A floor-to-ceiling stone fireplace, an amazing chandelier made from several pair of antlers, wood plank floors, and comfy leather furniture everywhere. The only feminine touches were the lovely Western-style tapestries hanging on the walls and the oversized silk floral arrangement on the carved oak credenza.

Aggie bobbed her head toward Tula, then toward a hallway. "I've got the blue guest room all ready for you. I wasn't sure what all you'd have with you, so I placed one of Sarah's gowns and a robe on the bed. I even placed Sarah's walker at the foot of the bed. It might help you to get around a little later. We always keep a supply of shampoos, body creams, that sort of thing in the bathrooms; but anything else you need, you just say so, and I'll do my best to get it."

"I'm sorry to be such a bother, but Clint insisted—"

"You're no bother at all. It's nice to have a woman around here again." Aggie gave Clint a playful frown. "I get tired of nothing but a parade of men. Seems since Sarah left us, the only people I ever see around here are Clint and the ranch hands."

Clint rolled his eyes. "As I'm sure you can tell, Tula, I may own this place, but Aggie is the real boss."

Aggie pointed to the hallway. "And this boss says this girl is probably worn out from her ordeal and needs to get some sleep.

You put her on the bed, Clint, and I'll take over from there."

Tula couldn't help uttering a little, "Oh," when he carried her into the blue room. Everything about it was feminine, from the blue and white satin-stripe wallpaper, to the elegant hand-made Dresden Plate quilt on the bed, to the white bedroom suite, tastefully hand painted with pink cabbage roses and blue ribbon streamers. Surely Sarah had decorated this room.

Clint carefully lowered her to the bed, then stood gazing at her. "Anything you need, anything at all, tell either me or Aggie. I want you to be comfortable." He gave her a smile that sent her heart tingling. "I'm sorry this awful day had to happen to you, but I can't tell you how nice it is to have you here. Hopefully, our time together will help us get better acquainted." He bent and kissed her cheek.

Before she could stop it, her hand moved to cup his neck, and she pulled him down to her, resting her forehead against his. "Thank you, Clint. For everything. I owe you."

"The only thing you owe me is a chance to let me prove to you that the two of us belong together." His lips found hers, and he kissed her with the sweetest kiss she could imagine. "Good night, Tula. Pleasant dreams."

By midnight, Tula lay tucked under the blue and white quilt, all safe and snug. The medication the doctor had given her to ease her pain was working even better than she'd hoped, and she felt totally comfortable as she lay in the silence of the room, thinking pleasant thoughts about the man who'd rescued her and brought her to this wonderful place. Was what she felt for him gratitude? Or was it love? The kind of love that made you want to commit the rest of your life to love and cherish a man?

"God," she whispered softly, "You've brought me through so much, and I am grateful beyond words. I meant it when I asked You to come into my heart when I was a child, but I foolishly turned my back on You. Now, I'm asking for Your forgiveness. I want so much to know You like Clint knows You. Take me back, God, please take me back."

About two in the morning, a piercing scream jarred Clint out of a sound sleep.

Chapter 7

Without taking time to grab his robe, Clint rushed into the hallway and toward Tula's room. He found her sitting up in bed, a look of terror on her face. For a moment, she stared at him as if she didn't recognize him.

Aggie rushed into the room and flipped on the light. "What's wrong?"

"I don't know." He sat down beside Tula and pulled her into his arms, cradling her like he would a small child. All color had disappeared from her face, and she was trembling.

She gazed up at him with glassy eyes, then threw her arms around his neck so tightly he could barely breathe. "Oh, Clint! I had a dream. I was in my car and was trying desperately to get the doors open, when a huge wall of water came rushing down the ditch and washed it out into the creek. I screamed and screamed for help, but no one came!"

After brushing a lock of hair from her forehead, he lifted her face and kissed her cheek. "I came, Tula. What you had was only a nightmare. You're right where you belong—safe in my arms." He felt her body relax. "Nothing can harm you now. I'm here to protect you."

Aggie gently tapped Clint on the shoulder. "Should I get

her some hot milk?"

He shook his head. "No, I don't think so. Go back to bed, Aggie. I'll take care of her."

Tula snuggled into Clint's embrace. "I'm sorry. I—I didn't mean to wake everyone, but my dream was so real."

"Shh. I know, but you need to forget about it and try to go back to sleep. You need your rest."

He held her until she drifted back to sleep, then lowered her back onto the pillow as easily as he could. He tenderly kissed her forehead, then padded quietly back to his room. He'd meant what he said when he'd held her in his arms. She was right where she belonged, and he'd do whatever he could to protect her.

To Tula, the next few days were sheer bliss. Though her back and her foot gave her constant pain, she nearly forgot about it as she and Clint laughed and talked their way through the days. If they weren't taking a ride in Clint's old-fashioned buggy or listening to his vast array of Southern gospel music, they were sitting on the porch reading the Bible together, enjoying the view, or giggling like two teenagers over one of the many ice cream sodas Aggie made for them. He was such a fine, honorable man. She wondered how she could have been so wrong about him. The love and respect Clint lavished upon her was a brand-new experience for her, and she found herself loving every minute of it. She'd had no idea a relationship between a man and a woman could be so amazingly wonderful.

On the fourth day, as they were sitting in the buggy under a shade tree watching Blue Streak munch on a new growth of green grass, Clint took Tula's hand in his and gazed into her eyes.

"What? Why are you looking at me that way?"

For a moment, he didn't answer. "I was just thinking how lucky I am to have such a beautiful woman by my side on this glorious day God has made."

She glanced around at the heavily leaf-laden trees and the wildflowers growing in the field, then listened to the birds singing in the trees. "It is a glorious day, isn't it?"

He gave her hand a squeeze. "I love you, Tula."

"I—I love you, too, Clint. I didn't know the meaning of true love until I met you."

He turned loose of her hand, then circled his arms about her, drawing her close. "Do you love me enough to marry me, spend the rest of your life with me?"

She didn't have to search her heart for an answer. She already knew the answer. "Yes, my dearest, I long to spend the rest of my life with you. I do want to become Mrs. Clint Murphy, but that desire has nothing to do with this land, or your beautiful home, or any wealth you may have. While those things are nice and I'm enjoying them now, if you lost everything tomorrow, I'd still want to be your wife. I know God led us together, and I know He'll provide for us."

"You mean that?"

She lifted her face toward heaven. "With God as my witness."

Clint's grin spread from one side of his face to the other.

"When, sweetheart? How soon can we be married? Tomorrow? Next week?"

She threw back her head with a laugh. "Clint, planning a proper wedding takes months. I should know. I'm a wedding planner." She sobered. "Oh, Clint, what about my business?"

He, too, sobered. "You *want* to keep working? You don't have to, you know."

"But I love my wedding-planning business, and I've worked so hard to get it on its feet."

He shrugged. "It's your decision. I'll abide by whatever you decide. But I'll be honest. I sure don't want to move into Steamboat, but if that's what it takes to make you happy, I'll do it."

"We could live here, and I could drive back and forth every day. It's not *that* far."

"This part of Colorado's winters can be long and hard, with icy roads and many inches of snow. You'd have to agree to let me drive you in my truck on bad days."

"If you did that, you'd have to spend the entire day in town or drive home, then come back and get me. I couldn't ask you to do that, Clint. That'd be over 120 miles a day. That's a long way even in good weather."

"You aren't asking me. I'm volunteering. Your happiness and safety are my first priority. I'd be glad to do it. Besides, it'd give me more time with you."

Tula wanted to cry. Though she *did* long to be Clint's wife, was she ready to give up her business? Her independence? Plus, she couldn't expect him to drive her in bad weather. Not only that, driving the roads to and from Steamboat Springs to the ranch in wintertime could be dangerous, even life threatening. She'd never want to go through the experience of being stranded in another bad situation like the one she had been through a few days ago. Why did life have to be so complicated? "Maybe we're not as ready for marriage as we thought," she conceded with a heavy heart.

Clint kissed her, then soothed her troubled brow with his fingertips. "Don't worry, honey. We'll work it out someway. Our love is too precious to let go. God has brought us this far; I'm sure He'll show us the way."

The rest of the morning, Tula puzzled over their situation. Everything had seemed so perfect. Why did her business have to become the one thing that could separate them?

About noon, she phoned the answering machine at her office to pick up any messages that had been recorded since she'd last checked. The first two were from prospective clients, but the third one was from the man who owned the building that housed her business.

"Ms. O'Brian. I've been trying to reach you for days. I wanted to talk to you in person, so I stopped by your business; but you were never there, and the door was locked. I hope there isn't a problem. I don't know if you've heard, but the city is going to do some major changes in the downtown area to facilitate a better flow of the tourist traffic. It's going to be necessary for them to tear down the building your wedding business is in. I know it's going to be a hassle to move your business, but I own several other buildings in town that you might want to take a look at. From what they've told me, you'll have six months to vacate your space. Give me a call, and we'll try to work something out."

Feeling almost paralyzed by the news, Tula stared at the phone. Vacate her space? Relocate to another place? Impossible! Moving would be like starting all over again. Another remodeling; choosing wall coverings, floor coverings; adding adequate shelving, dressing rooms, display space; selecting furniture, all new sales books, special lighting; printing new literature and brochures; and on and on and on. She'd spent the first six months after purchasing her business from the former owner doing those very things, and it had been exhausting and expensive. Did she really want to do it again? Besides, it was going to be quite some time before her wounds healed and her foot was recovered enough for her to put her weight on it.

"What's the matter, Tula? I've never seen you look so distraught."

She glanced up at Clint, the phone still anchored in her hand. "They're going to tear down my building."

"Where your business is?" He hurried to her side. "Who said so?"

She gestured to the phone with her other hand. "The owner left a message on my answering machine. I have to be moved out in six months."

Clint took the phone and placed it in its cradle. "Where would you move to?"

She let out a sigh. "I don't know. My location was perfect."

"Maybe we could find a lot somewhere, and I could build

you your own building. That way, you could make it just like you wanted it."

His words surprised her. She'd expected him to tell her losing the building would be an easy way to close down her business. "You'd do that for me?"

He shrugged. "Of course I would. I want whatever will make you happy."

Using the walker, she moved to the sofa, carefully sat down, then leaned back into its softness and crossed her arms. "Do you have any idea how selfish your words make me feel? You've already volunteered to drive me back and forth in bad weather. And now that I learn my business is going to have to move, you tell me you'll build me my own building, when you could have told me this was the best thing that could have happened and I should just forget about it and close up shop. But you didn't. Instead, you're bending over backward to find ways I can keep it going."

He lowered himself down beside her. "I don't understand. Why would that make you feel selfish?"

"Clint! Don't you get it? You're willing to do anything you can to make me happy, when all I'm doing is trying to hang on to a business that is floundering and has yet to produce much in the way of profit, just because it's the first thing that has been truly mine."

"I understand how important your wedding-planning business is to you, Tula. I would never step in and tell you what to do. It's your business. You have every right to be proud of your accomplishments and try to hang on to it."

Though she tried, she couldn't hold back her tears. "But I *don't* want to hang on to it! I realize that now. I wanted it only so I could prove to myself I could make it on my own, have something that no one could take away from me—and to give me a sense of security. I've proven all that! But the day you sat next to me at that wedding, my life began to change. The love I have for you now, and the love you've shown for me, means more to me than anything. My business is nothing in comparison to it."

"Don't give up your business because that's what you think I want, Tula."

She rested her head on his shoulder. "I'm not, dearest. I'm giving it up because it's what *I* want to do. I have six months. If I can't find a buyer for it by then, I'll have a massive sale and sell everything at cost. What's left will go to Goodwill or the Salvation Army Thrift Store."

"You mean it?"

"Absolutely."

"Are we going to have to wait that long to be married?"

"Probably. Otherwise, I'm not sure I'll have the time to plan our wedding, find a buyer, or get ready to sell everything off."

With the tip of his finger, a grinning Clint lifted her face to his. "I have an idea. Why don't *I* plan our wedding?"

She frowned. "You?"

"Sure. It'll be a surprise. My gift to you."

Tula laughed. "I know you and the groomsmen won't be wearing white tuxedos."

"That, I promise. Come on, Tula, it'll be fun. Let me do this for you. Aggie can help me. You know she won't let me do anything that would embarrass you. We'll have it right here on the ranch."

"Your offer is tempting."

"I'll work on it day and night. If you let me plan it, we could be married in less than a month. Let's say three weeks from today."

She felt her eyes widen. "Three weeks from today? Do you have any idea how much is involved in planning a wedding?"

"No, but I know a great wedding planner. If I get in a bind, I can ask her for help."

She tossed the idea over in her mind. She, too, wanted to be married as soon as possible. "I guess I could give you a checklist—to make sure you didn't overlook anything, but I'd have to have an idea of what you were planning so I could select the right wedding gown." She treated him to a teasing smile. "One without a too-long train. Someone once told me such a too-long train was a waste of good material."

He grinned back. "Whoever said that had a good head on his shoulders. But I want to pick out your gown, too, not just plan the wedding."

She shied away from him, giving him an incredulous look. "Oh no. I draw the line there. This is my wedding, too. I'll pick out my *own* gown."

His grin turned to a look of tenderness. "But you're going to be *my* bride. I want the pleasure of selecting your gown."

"You'll have to order it through me, so I'll know what it looks like. Why not just let me pick it out?"

"That'd take all the fun out of it. I'll just bet Denver or some other cities closer to us have bridal shops with huge selections. I could shop there."

"You don't know my size." She thought she had him stymied.

He pursed his face thoughtfully, then smiled. "Trust me. I'll come up with a way to handle it."

She grabbed hold of his hand and gazed up at him. "Oh, Clint, I do trust you. With my life. With my future. Even my wedding gown. If you want to be the one to decide what I wear on our wedding day, I'll gladly leave it in your hands. The gown I wear is a minor thing. Marrying you and becoming your wife is what's important."

As Clint's lips claimed hers, Tula felt a warm glow of peace and serenity.

She'd made peace with God.

He'd led her to the man she'd love forever.

Their wedding was going to happen.

She'd soon become Mrs. Clint Murphy.

For the next few days, Tula stayed at the ranch, using the walker that had belonged to Sarah and contacting people she thought might be interested in buying her wedding-planning business. She didn't see as much of Clint as she'd have liked since he spent so much of his time sequestered in his office, working on their wedding plans or taking care of his ranch responsibilities. But despite their separate goals, they found time to be together. And though she asked him many questions, he managed to keep his plans a secret.

"My rope burns are healing, and my foot is so much better," she told Clint one evening as they sat on the porch. "It's time I moved back to my apartment."

"I'll miss you, but I know it'll be easier on you to have the things you need close at hand, with all the work you have ahead of you." He gave her a mischievous smile. "I need to borrow you for a few minutes."

She narrowed her eyes suspiciously. "For what?"

"You'll see. Aggie and I have a little project." He rose from the high-backed rocker and handed her the walker. "I've asked Aggie to meet us in your bedroom." He waited until she had risen and had a firm grasp on the walker, then led her down the hall and into the room.

"Why did you need me to come in here?"

Clint gestured toward Aggie. "I picked out a couple of wedding dresses I thought would fit you, and I need you to try them on before I decide which one to buy."

Tula had to laugh. "See, I said you couldn't buy a wedding gown without me seeing it."

Aggie stepped forward. "That's where I come in. Clint is going to blindfold you; then I'll help you on and off with the dresses."

"You two are incorrigible," she said with a giggle, "but lovable. Okay, I'll play along. Where is the blindfold?"

Clint pulled a folded bandanna from his pocket and tied it over her face, covering her eyes. "No peeking, okay?"

She bobbed her head. "How many gowns are there?"

"Only four. Aggie has already hung them in your closet.

I'm going to go out of the room while she puts the first one on you. Let me know when you're ready, and I'll come in and take a look at it."

"Can I feel it, to see if it has lace or beads?"

"No!" he answered firmly. "No touching. I've already warned Aggie to keep an eye on you. Now, get into that first dress so I can see how it looks on you."

"That's some boss you've got, Aggie," Tula told her once she heard the door click shut. "Only Clint could have thought of something like this." She lifted her arms and let Aggie slip the dress over her head. "Is this gown silk? It doesn't feel like silk."

Aggie grabbed her hands. "Remember the rules. No touching."

"You ready yet?" Clint's voice came from behind the door.

Aggie released Tula's hands, then gave the dress a final tug to straighten it. "Ready."

Clint came into the room, but all he said was, "Uh-huh, nice, pretty. Okay, try on the next one." They repeated the process three more times, and each time, he responded with the same words.

Tula lifted her hands in frustration. "Clint! Say more than 'Uh-huh, nice, pretty.' Does that mean you like one of the dresses, or don't you?"

He wrapped his arms tightly about her. "You haven't been peeking, have you?"

"No, of course not. You told me not to."

"Then I guess you won't know if one was better than the others."

"You're kidding, right? When you said you wanted to be the one to pick it out, you never said you weren't going to let me see it before our wedding day. What if I don't like it? Or if it's too short or too long or too—"

"Tula, I would never let you wear a dress that didn't do you justice. To be honest, you looked fantastic in all four of them. Choosing which one I like best is going to be the hard part."

She reached for the bandanna, but he grabbed her hand. "Not until you've taken that gown off. I want everything about this wedding to be a surprise."

She let out a sigh. "Okay, I promised I'd trust you, and I do. I'll wear whatever you want me to, even if it's nothing more than a gunnysack with a rope tied around my middle."

Clint let out another chuckle. "Umm, I hadn't thought of that. Sure would be a lot cheaper. Maybe I could wear that tattered old shirt I loaned you, with my bib overalls. And we could have cider and gingerbread instead of punch and cake."

"Clint! You wouldn't!"

"Sounds good to me. I even know a guy who can play tunes on a jug. Maybe he could learn to play 'Here Comes the Bride.'"

Tula loved Clint's humor. He was so much fun to be around. "If that's the kind of wedding you want, mister, it's okay with me. Go for it."

Clint lifted the bandanna just the tiniest bit and kissed her cheek. "I'd never do that to you." He snickered. "But it is tempting."

She gave him a playful shove. "Get out of here so I can get this gown off. This bandanna is hot."

The minute she'd changed back into her clothes and Clint reentered the room, the bandanna disappeared from her eyes. The first thing that came into sight was his smiling face. "Got one other thing you need to do."

She tilted her head coyly. "Oh, no. Now what?"

"Wear this ring so every man who gets near you will know you're spoken for." He reached for her left hand and slipped a ring onto her third finger. "This ring is only a small token of my love for you, Tula. It took me awhile to find the one I thought worthy of you, but I finally did. I hope you like it."

Stunned by the ring's blinding beauty, she found herself unable to do anything but stare at it. She'd never seen a ring like it.

Clint gazed at her with concern. "If you don't like it, I can take it back and get another one."

Tula felt breathless. Though she was a wedding planner and had seen a number of engagement rings, this one was magnificent. "Oh, Clint, it's not that I don't like it. I love it, but it's a much too expensive ring. The diamonds are huge." She took another look at the stones. "Or are they zirconia?"

He threw back his head with a laugh. "Cubic zirconia? No, they're diamonds, sweetheart. I'd never give you anything but the real thing."

"Although the ring is awesome and I love it, I don't need such big diamonds, Clint. A small solitaire would be just as meaningful to me."

He lifted her hand, then kissed her fingertips one by one. "I expected you'd say something like that, but the engagement ring I wanted for you had to be extraspecial, because you're special. This one is. Please say you'll accept it, Tula. It'd mean a lot to me if you would."

Her face took on a frown. "But it's so expensive."

"Tula, if I couldn't have afforded it, I wouldn't have bought it. When you look at that ring, I don't want you to think about how much it cost. I want you to see it as a symbol of my love and devotion. Nothing else. Okay?"

Though she still felt hesitant about accepting such an expensive ring, she could tell by Clint's words and the look on his face he was determined that she should keep it.

Slowly lifting her gaze to meet his, she nodded. "Clint, despite its value, I gladly accept your ring because it is a gift from you and a symbol of our love."

He lifted her hand, then slightly tilted it to the right, then to the left, admiring it as the light in the room fractured its brilliance. "The beauty of this ring pales in contrast to your beauty, Tula, my dear one. Accept it with my undying love."

Through misty eyes, Tula gazed at the wonderful, godly man before her. In her wildest dreams, she'd never imagined she would ever be marrying a fine, honorable man like Clint. "Only if you accept my undying love for you, dearest. May the Lord give us many wonderful years together."

Tula rose early the next morning, wanting plenty of time to gather up her things and help Aggie prepare and clean up after their breakfast before she and Clint left for Steamboat Springs.

"You really think that woman you contacted is serious about buying your business?"

She nodded as he rolled his truck into the stall in front of her shop and shoved the gearshift into PARK. "I've checked out her credit ratings. She should easily qualify for a loan. It'll sure be a lot simpler if she bought the shop, then moved everything, so I didn't have to go through the process of getting ready for a sale."

Clint hurried around to open her door, then lifted her out of the truck and set her on the ground. "I've been praying God would make this change as easy for you as possible."

"So have I."

He pulled her walker from the backseat, then followed her into the shop. "Tula, are you sure you want to sell this shop? You've worked so hard to make it what it is. You know it's fine with me if you keep it."

She cupped his chin in her hands, taking in its little indentation, the tiny scar at the edge of his eyebrow where a puck had hit him while playing ice hockey as a kid, the slightly receding hairline. How she loved this man. "I *want* to sell it, Clint. I can't imagine working days here in Steamboat, knowing I could be at the ranch with you. We're going to have an amazing life together. I just know we are."

"You don't think I'm too old for you? I'm fifty-seven."

She frowned. "Too old for me? Clint, you're the youngest fifty-seven-year-old man I've ever known, with way more energy and zest for life than any of them. I may be twenty years younger than you, but my greatest fear is that *I'm* going to have trouble keeping up with *you*."

"Just think. I'll be sixty when you're forty. Seventy when you're fifty. Ninety when you're seventy. You may end up taking care of an old man."

She slipped her hand around his neck and drew his face close to hers. "Taking care of you, my love, will be a privilege. I want us to grow old together. I want us to sit out on that deck in our rocking chairs and watch the sunsets and the days go by until we're too old to hobble out there."

He kissed her cheek. "I was hoping you'd feel that way. That's what I want, too." Backing away, he gave her a little swat on her bottom. "I hate to leave you, babe, but I've got a wedding to plan and you've got a shop to sell. I'll pick you up at six and drive you to your apartment."

The next two weeks were a whir of activity as Tula negotiated and signed the sale agreement with the woman she'd hoped would buy her business. Tula also spent some time choosing a new SUV to replace the minivan that had been pushed on downstream and totaled. Though she and Clint spent every evening together, he refused to give her any of the details of the wedding he was planning.

Finally, the big day arrived. With great anticipation, Tula drove her vehicle to the ranch. Clint had warned her to arrive no earlier and no later than noon. She arrived at twelve straight up.

Chapter 8

B ut when she drove up to the big house, the place looked deserted. She'd expected to see all kinds of people running in and out, setting up chairs, putting up an arch covered with flowers, preparing the reception table, but there wasn't a single vehicle parked in front of the house.

Tula entered through the front door and found the place deserted. "Clint? Aggie? Is anyone home?"

Aggie came in from the kitchen, dish towel in hand.

"Where is everyone? I thought this place would be humming with activity. This *is* our wedding day, isn't it?"

Aggie nodded. "Clint said to tell you not to worry, everything is taken care of. You're supposed to put your makeup on, do your hair, and wait for him. He'll bring your dress to you in time for the wedding."

Tula wondered if she'd gone too far when she'd agreed to let him take over the planning. "But where is he? Shouldn't he be getting things ready? It looks as though nothing has been done around here."

Aggie gave a nonchalant shrug, but the smile on her face told Tula the woman knew more than she was about to divulge.

Deciding there was nothing she could do but follow Clint's

instructions, she moved into the blue room and opened her makeup case. But when Clint hadn't arrived a little more than an hour before it was time for the wedding to begin, panic seized her. Wondering if he'd changed his mind about marrying her, she was just about to grab up her things, rush out of his house, and head back to Steamboat Springs, when she heard footsteps on the porch.

The door opened, and Clint, clad in a simple jogging suit, hurried in, garment bag in hand, a huge smile blanketing his face. "Hey, gorgeous. I like your hair pulled up like that. Here's your dress, lovely lady. I hope you like it. You have thirty minutes to put it on and do whatever you have left to do. Meantime, I'm off to take a shower."

After taking the bag from his hand, she grabbed his arm and held it fast. "Oh no, you don't! You have some explaining to do." She gestured around the room. "This is it? A dress, but no decorations? No arch, flowers, white runner on the floor? No guests, no friends to witness our wedding? And what about a preacher? Clint, I trusted you to plan this wedding. Me! A wedding planner. I expected more out of you than this." She lifted her arms in frustration. "And where is Sharon? She's supposed to be my maid of honor. She told me yesterday she'd see me at the wedding. And where is your best man?"

Still smiling, Clint leaned forward and planted a kiss on her lips. "Don't worry about it, sweetie. I've got everything under control. All you need to do is put on the dress I picked out for you, then wait for me while I take a quick shower and get into my own duds."

"But, Clint—"

"Just do it, please. For me?"

Though she had no idea what was going on, or if *anything* was going on, she nodded. "Okay, I'll do it, but—"

He kissed her again, cutting her off midsentence. "No more questions, sweetheart, okay? Time's a wastin'."

"Okay. Whatever you say. I'll be ready in thirty minutes. This house had better be ready for a wedding by then, or I'm leaving!" Still holding on to the bag, she headed off again toward the blue room, slamming the door behind her.

Nearly thirty minutes later, Clint smiled at the closed door on the blue room. Tula might be upset and disappointed in him now, but he hoped she'd soon be singing his praises. "Tula? You ready?" he called out, suddenly wondering if he'd allowed enough time for her to do whatever she had to do to prepare herself for their wedding.

When she didn't answer, he knew he was either in more trouble than he'd anticipated or she'd left. He was about to call out her name again when she opened the door a bare crack and peeked through. "Don't you remember it's bad luck for the groom to see the bride in her gown before she walks down the aisle?"

Afraid she'd slam the door in his face if he moved forward, he stood his ground but craned his neck in her direction. "I don't believe in luck, good or bad. All I can say is, if you don't come out right now, there isn't going to be a wedding."

The crack in the doorway widened. "What do you mean—isn't going to be a wedding?"

He reached out his hand. "Aw, Tula, can't you just trust me?" He held his breath, waiting for her response.

To his surprise, the door opened and she appeared. Her loveliness set his heart singing.

"Clint Murphy, sometimes you can be a frustrating man." Her frown turned into a smile as she did a slow turn. "Oh, Clint, I don't understand any of this, but I love the dress. It's beautiful. The most beautiful gown I've ever seen. I couldn't have chosen one I'd love even more."

Her captivating smile gave him funny feelings in the pit of his stomach. He gazed at her, drinking in the innocence of her sweet face, the delicacy of her pink lips, and the shininess of her silken brown hair. Tula O'Brian was going to be his, all his. The delicious thought was almost beyond belief.

She sauntered toward him in a teasing way, her hands moving to clasp themselves behind his neck when she reached him. "And you look absolutely elegant in that long, black, Western-cut jacket and your silver bolo. No woman has ever had a more handsome groom."

Still stunned by her beauty, Clint found himself speechless to reply.

Tula turned and stared at the large living room. "Where is everyone? You mean they're still not here? You didn't forget to send out the invitations, did you?" She looked crestfallen, as if she were about to cry.

Though it hurt to ignore her questions, he quickly pulled

her into his arms. "Are you ready? Is there anything you want to take with you?"

Still seeming totally confused, she lifted misty eyes. "*Take* with me? Where? Where are we going?"

Turning loose his hold on her, he grabbed her hand, twining his fingers with hers. "To our wedding, sweetheart."

"*To* our wedding? Whatever do you mean? It's not going to be here? You said we'd be married at the ranch!"

"You ask too many questions, my love. Come with me, my darling. This is our wedding day." He pulled her toward the outer door before she had time to protest, then gestured toward the circle drive fronting the steps and waved his arm in a gallant manner. "Your chariot, my dear."

Chapter 9

Tula stood mesmerized. There was Blue Streak, saddled up to Clint's antique buggy, and tied onto both the horse and buggy were huge bouquets of fresh, colorful flowers and white satin streamers. The horse was wearing a straw hat with holes poked through for his ears! She laughed when she saw it. He looked so sweet. There was even a wreath of colorful flowers about his neck.

Though she still didn't know what was in store for her in the way of a wedding, she knew Clint had gone out of his way to make sure their day was going to be special in every way. Even knowing her actions might wrinkle her dress, she threw her arms about his neck and showered his clean-shaven face with kisses. "This was your idea?"

He nodded proudly. "Every bit of this wedding was my idea." After gathering up her train in his arms, he led her carefully down the steps and up into the buggy. Then, after taking the reins and giving them a slight snap, he called out, "Giddyap, Blue Streak! This is our wedding day!"

Tula leaned her head against Clint's strong shoulder. Never had she been so happy. "I love you, Clint," she sighed softly, listening to the *clip-clop* of Blue Streak's hooves as they hit the ground, rejoicing in the knowledge that each step was taking her one step closer to where she would become Mrs. Clint Murphy.

"I love you, too, Tula, my precious Irish bride. God surely graced this undeserving man with a big favor when He sent you into my life."

Snuggling even closer, she gazed up into his face, tanned and weathered from years of working out in the sun. "I'm the one who is undeserving, Clint. Even though I turned my back on God all those years, He was still patient with me. Then, when I'd almost given up on life, He sent you to rescue me. What a wonderful God He is."

The buggy rocked gently to and fro as Blue Streak slowly ambled his way across a field and up a gentle slope, winding his way through trees so thick and tall Tula could barely see their tops, and down rocky trails so steep she had to hold her breath. But she felt no fear. Clint was by her side. When they'd been riding for some time, Tula glanced at Clint's watch. "Clint, it's well after two!"

He gave her a gentle smile. "I didn't exactly tell you the truth when I said I'd set our wedding for two o'clock. The invitations I sent out said two thirty. I wanted us to have plenty of time to get there."

She raised a brow. "Get—where?"

"You'll see."

She rested her head on his shoulder again, her excitement growing with each moment. She grinned inwardly as she remembered something. On one of their afternoon rides, she'd noticed an old schoolhouse. That's where they were going! Clint and his crew had cleaned it up and turned it into a wedding chapel. What a beautiful place for an old-fashioned wedding. But when they reached the fork in the road and the schoolhouse could be seen off in the distance, Clint headed Blue Streak in the opposite direction. Where was he taking her?

They passed through several more clearings, down a few more slopes, and through several more groves of dense trees. Though the area looked slightly familiar, with no distinguishing landmarks and all the turns they'd taken, Tula had no idea where they were.

"Close your eyes and keep them closed until I tell you to open them."

She stared up at him. "Why? There's nothing here but trees!"

"Tula."

She gave her head a slight shake, then closed her eyes. "Okay, they're closed."

"Good. Keep them that way."

She could feel the big horse's gait pick up and the buggy jostle a bit more from side to side. She could hardly wait to see what lay ahead of them. "Clint, how much longer before I can open my eyes? My mascara is going to be ruined."

She felt the buggy come to a stop.

"Now, Tula. Open your eyes!"

The sight before her was almost too much to comprehend. They'd reached the old cabin where he'd taken her the day he'd rescued her. In front of it, on a large area of newly mowed grass, was a lacy white gazebo adorned from top to bottom with fresh, colorful flowers. And gathered around it were dozens of friends, neighbors, business associates, and acquaintances, all dressed in old-timey Western-style clothing. The women were even wearing bonnets, with some holding lacy parasols to filter out the afternoon sun. She glanced down at her own dress. Now she understood why her full-length gown was entirely made of lace, with a high, ruffled neckline, long leg-of-mutton sleeves that came to a point at her fingertips, and a narrow fitted waist. "You did all of this?" she finally uttered, so overcome with emotion it was hard to form the words.

"Do you like it?"

Tula's gaze went from Clint's beaming face to their circle of friends, to the little cabin that had been so special to her, to the beautifully decorated gazebo, then back to Clint again. "Like it? I love it!"

She felt giddy with happiness when his lips sought hers. "And you did all this for me?"

"For you, my love, my dear one, my answer to prayer. You're sure you're not disappointed?"

"Disappointed? Never! Having our wedding here is perfect."

He lifted his hands and gestured widely. "This is where it all began, Tula. It seemed only fitting that we would begin our married life here." He climbed down from the buggy, then reached his arms up to her. "Come, my precious one. It's time for us to be married."

Tula leaned into the strength of his grasp as he lifted her from the buggy and set her feet on the ground. Sharon, dressed in a gown of pink lace, her arm linked through Hayes's arm, hurried out to meet her. "Oh, Tula, you look radiant. I've never seen you this happy."

Tula smiled at her friend. "I've never been this happy."

Hayes reached the huge bouquet of apricot roses he'd been carrying in his free hand toward Clint who took them, then placed them in Tula's hand. "Your wedding bouquet, my love. Apricot roses. Your favorite."

"Oh, Clint, apricot roses. You remembered."

Hayes grabbed Clint's arm. "Come on. You and me have to get to that gazebo thing. As your best man, I guess it's my job to make sure you're in the right place when the music starts."

Clint threw Tula a kiss as he slowly backed away. "See you at the altar."

Tula pretended to catch Clint's kiss in her hand, then mouthed the words, *I love you.*

Sharon busied herself straightening out Tula's long train, then gave her a final once-over. "Clint gave me some things to give to you." She pulled off the pink satin drawstring bag that had been dangling from her wrist and opened it. "He said to tell you that this cameo belonged to his mother, and it is to be your 'something old.'" She pinned it onto the lace at Tula's neck. "This beautifully embroidered handkerchief he bought for you is your 'something new.'" She handed it to Tula, who took it and lovingly tucked it into the cuff of her sleeve. "This bobby pin he borrowed from Aggie. It's your 'something borrowed' item."

Tula's love for Clint grew even more as she beheld each

item. She could hardly wait to see what he'd come up with for her "something blue."

Sharon reached deep into the bag and pulled out a tiny gold ring set with a single blue sapphire stone, the perfect size to fit on Tula's pinky finger. "This is your 'something blue.'" She took hold of Tula's right hand and placed the little ring on her finger, then gave her hand an affectionate squeeze. "May you and Clint have a long and happy life together, Tula. You both deserve it."

Tula's heart was touched by Clint's thoughtfulness, as well as by her friend's loving words.

A darling little girl Tula didn't recognize joined them, looking adorable in a lace dress much like Sharon's. Sharon greeted her, then turned to Tula. "This is Becky. She's going to be your flower girl. Her brother Mike is already with Clint and Hayes. He's going to be the ring bearer. You ready?"

Tula nodded. "Oh yes."

Sharon nodded toward Aggie who was seated at the little organ someone—probably Clint—had placed at the right side of the gazebo and waved her hand. Aggie waved back, then began to pump her feet before placing her fingers on the keys.

Tula gazed at the scene before her. An old-fashioned pump organ? Clint had thought of everything. Everything was perfect.

Sharon took hold of little Becky's shoulder, then sent the child forward after reminding her that her job was to drop the rose petals onto the ground, not leave them in the basket, the same instructions Tula had always given the flower girl at the weddings she'd planned.

When Becky reached the gazebo, Sharon nodded toward Tula. "Wait until I reach the gazebo before you start. And take your time, Tula." She paused long enough to take on a smile and playfully shake her finger in Tula's face. "No running, Tula. I know you're anxious to become Mrs. Murphy, but brides are supposed to walk. I guess you know that, though."

Tula watched as Sharon moved slowly down the aisle that Clint had marked off with small, rectangular bales of hay tied with white satin ribbon. When Sharon reached her designated spot, Clint nodded to Aggie, and the strains of "Here Comes the Bride" filled the summer air.

Her heart overflowed with so much happiness Tula felt she could float all the way to the altar, without her feet even touching the ground.

"It's my time," she said aloud even though no one was close enough to hear her. "Be with us, Lord. Make our marriage what You would have it to be." Then, placing one foot in front of the other, she slowly, as instructed, made her way toward the man she would live with as long as God allotted them breath. *Step, together. Step, together. Step, together.*

When she finally reached Clint, he pulled her into his arms and hugged her tight. Pastor Wainwright, the man who had been Clint's pastor for the past twenty-five years, smiled at them and began the ceremony.

Tula tried to concentrate on every word he was saying, but her thoughts kept drifting to the man at her side. Even when the soloist sang their favorite song, she kept thinking of Clint and his gentle ways.

"Clint and Tula have decided to say their vows in their own words," Pastor Wainwright told those assembled after the soloist had finished her song and he'd given the short message they'd asked him to present. Sharon stepped forward and took Tula's bouquet from her hands.

Clint turned to Tula and grasped both her hands in his, tightly holding on to them as he intently gazed on her face. "I'm not a man of flowery words. I barely passed English when I was in school. But, Tula, my beloved, with God as my witness, I love you and promise I will always take care of you to the best of my ability. I will protect you from any harm that may threaten you. I will be at your side anytime you need me. I want to be your anchor in the storm, your friend, your lover. I promise to treat you like the queen you are. You'll never have need to fear me, my darling. I would never hurt you in any way. I hope you know that. All I ask of you is that you love me and stay with me until death do us part."

His words were sweet and filled with meaning probably only she recognized. She *had* feared her husband, been terrified of him at times, and had suffered often at his hand. But she knew Clint meant every word he said and he'd never raise a hand to her. What a comfort it was that he'd chosen to include those words in his vows. Now it was her turn.

She swallowed hard, wondering if she'd be able to say all the words in her heart without crying. "Clint, my dear one, the one who put his own safety aside and thought only of mine and became my hero, I love you with an everlasting love. Because of you and the unwavering faith in God you have shown me through your exemplary life, *my* faith in God has been renewed. I now know Him and love Him, even as you do. God brought us together. I'm convinced of that, and because of Him, I'm about to become your wife. I love you, Clint Murphy, and I, too, will do everything in my power to be the wife you deserve."

Tula looked around at the crowd. Though she didn't know many of them, and some of the ones she did know she didn't know well, she was sure they were all there because they wanted the best for the two of them. Deciding there was no better time to reveal to Clint something she had been planning to tell him for a long time, she sucked in a big gulp of air, looked deep into his loving eyes, then gave his hand a squeeze. "And," she continued, pausing one more time to reconsider what she was about to say. "And, if it be God's will, my precious Clint, I want to give you the child you've always wanted. Our baby will never replace the son you lost, but he—or she—will be the product of our love and most fortunate to have you as a father."

The look on Clint's face tugged at her heartstrings as tears began to roll down his cheeks. "You mean that? Even as old as I am, you really want us to have a baby?"

Tula cupped his face in the palm of her hand. "Yes, I really mean it. You'll be a wonderful father."

The men began to cheer, and the women began to cry. Even the pastor's eyes teared up.

"I never expected to be a father again." Clint took her hand, lifted it to his lips, and kissed her palm. "You have no idea how happy this makes me, Tula. I've always wanted another child."

She cupped her hand over his. "I know you'd prefer a son, but we'll have to take whatever God wills."

Pastor Wainwright cleared his throat loudly. "Maybe you two could continue this conversation later, after you've said *I do*. Right now, we'd better get on with this wedding."

Clint turned and stared at the people surrounding them, as if he'd just remembered they were there. After offering a sheepish grin, he said, "Sorry, folks. I guess I got carried away there for a bit, but I can't tell you how happy Tula's words have made me."

"Hey, I'm just glad to have been here and heard them!" one of his ranch hands called out loudly, cupping his hands to his mouth. "I think you two will make great parents!"

Hayes jabbed Clint in the arm. "Maybe the kid will call me Uncle Hayes. I've never been an uncle before."

Pastor Wainwright rubbed at his eyes, then cleared his throat again. "I guess I don't have to ask this. Seems redundant actually, but, Clint, do you take this woman to be your lawfully wedded wife? To love and cherish until death you do part?"

Clint scrunched up his face. "Yes, sir, I sure do, and I'm mighty happy about it."

Pastor Wainwright turned to Tula. "Tula, do you take this man to be your lawfully wedded husband? To love and cherish until death you do part?"

Tula gave Clint a mischievous smile. "I sure do. I'm not about to let this wonderful man get away."

The pastor laughed. "Then you'd better place your ring on Tula's hand, Clint. Seems she's mighty anxious to become your wife."

Clint untied the ring from the little satin pillow his ring bearer was holding. Then, taking Tula's hand in his, he slipped it onto her finger alongside the engagement ring he'd given her. "This little ring is but a small token of my love for you, Tula. I hope you'll wear it always."

Tula gazed at her hand. The ring she'd suggested to Clint looked nothing like this one. The one she'd shown him had been a simple gold band. Her engagement ring was already more than she could have ever imagined. She looked up at Clint and whispered, "This is the wrong ring."

He grinned at her. "Did you honestly think I was going to give my bride a simple gold band? I want you to have only the best, my love. Please accept it. I want you to have it."

Again, Clint had touched Tula's heart with his thoughtfulness and his unselfish love for her. She hated to place the simple, unadorned gold band she'd purchased on his hand. It seemed so insignificant compared to the one he'd given her. But she did it anyway and was amazed when he gazed at it as though it was the most beautiful ring he'd ever seen.

"When we close on my business, I'll replace it with one of more value," she whispered so only he could hear.

"No way," he whispered back. "I'm keeping this one."

After taking Tula's hand and placing it in Clint's, Pastor Wainwright bent and kissed Tula's cheek before lifting his hand and spreading his palm over their heads. "You have made your vows to one another and exchanged rings, symbols of your love and dedication to each other. So, by the power vested in me by God, and by the state of Colorado, I now pronounce you husband and wife, Mr. and Mrs. Clint Murphy."

Suddenly from behind the little cabin, hundreds of helium-filled apricot and white balloons rushed their way up into the deep blue of the afternoon sky, heralding the joining of Clint and Tula in marriage.

Tula smiled to herself. She'd planned and executed many weddings, but this one, by far, was the very best.

Clint pulled his wife into his arms and kissed her deeply, passionately, the way Tula hoped he'd kiss her for the rest of their lives.

A Letter to Our Readers

Dear Readers:

In order that we might better contribute to your reading enjoyment, we would appreciate your taking a few minutes to respond to the following questions. When completed, please return to the following: Fiction Editor, Barbour Publishing, Inc., P.O. Box 719, Uhrichsville, OH 44683.

1. Did you enjoy reading *Colorado Weddings* by Joyce Livingston?
   ❏ Very much—I would like to see more books like this.
   ❏ Moderately—I would have enjoyed it more if _____
   _____
   _____

2. What influenced your decision to purchase this book?
   (Check those that apply.)
   ❏ Cover   ❏ Back cover copy   ❏ Title   ❏ Price
   ❏ Friends   ❏ Publicity   ❏ Other

3. Which story was your favorite?
   ❏ *A Winning Match*   ❏ *The Wedding Planner*
   ❏ *Downhill*

4. Please check your age range:
   ❏ Under 18   ❏ 18–24   ❏ 25–34
   ❏ 35–45   ❏ 46–55   ❏ Over 55

5. How many hours per week do you read? _____

Name _____

Occupation _____

Address _____

City_____ State_____ Zip_____

E-mail_____

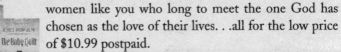
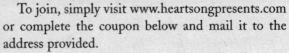